WHERE THE STAIRS DON'T GO

A NOVEL

By

SHAE HUTTO

For my daughter, Lauren, who loves a good story as much as I do.

Where the Stairs Don't Go

Table of Contents

Chapter One: Service

I took the stairs and felt like my childhood took the elevator. - Drew Barrymore

Claire woke slowly. She relished the slow approach of full consciousness like she would a sunrise. Her sense of reality slowly, languorously washed into the world, a tide of awareness encroaching on the beach. Languorously. Claire spun that particular word around in her mind for a minute, savoring the freedom to be lazy that comes with a Saturday morning when you're in High School. She stretched and yawned. Claire had a talent and appreciation for words and prided herself on knowing a lot of difficult ones, including how to spell them. The word pandiculation swam up from her receding subconscious in connection with the stretching and yawning. She would have to look that one up to be sure. She was a fan of new and interesting words.

She was also a fan of Saturday mornings and of birthdays when the birthday was her own. Today was someone else's birthday, however. Well, most likely many millions of peoples' birthdays but more specifically, it was her little brother's birthday. Today marked his ninth annum, which was a fancy Latin way of saying year. Claire had no doubt he was looking forward to today and its attendant festivities quite a bit. That's because he was going to have four of his friends spend the night, a party, a cake and presents. All the usual perquisites of the birthday boy. Perquisites. Yet another example of vocabulary excellence, she reflected as the last vestiges of indulgent indolence receded and left stark reality in its wake.

The immediate reality was that Claire would be stuck helping to ride herd on this bevy of boisterous boys. Yay, she thought, sarcastically. Is sarcasm wasted when you are talking to yourself? Probably. Vaguely, she noted that she should cut out the sarcasm from her inner monologue. Sarcasm and wit should be saved for someone who can appreciate them. So, rule out her brother, Nick, then, she thought to herself with a grin. This was not sarcasm, more like plain old insulting. Which is also wasted when talking to yourself. She sighed, abandoning her inner reflections. Claire mentally resigned herself to a day of domestic servitude and heaved herself out of bed, scattering pillows and stuffed animals wantonly across the floor on her trip across the room to collect clothes.

Nick apparently wasn't up yet. Claire quickly claimed the bathroom for her own and locked the door. She took her time with a hot shower, washing her hair twice just for an excuse to stay in longer. She delayed until Nick banged on the door and clamored to come in. She made sure most of the hot water was used up and with a gleeful inward cackle took her time wringing out her brilliantly red hair, wrapping it up and drying herself off. Nick was yelling outside about needing to pee. She ignored him and dressed herself with the deliberation that such an important task required. Finally, clean and dressed with damp hair wrapped in a towel, she deigned to let the little pest in, making a mental note to not use the word deign in conversation. It sounded too arrogant.

"All yours, Stinky," she said as she brushed past him on the way out. She chose not to notice that the little creep stuck out his tongue at her. Claire refused to stoop to his uncouth level by retaliating. After she dried her hair in her room, she proceeded regally downstairs. Claire had recently learned the word 'flounced' but refused to apply it to someone of her dignity. Proceeded regally would have to do.

"Morning, Sunshine," said her mother from the table in the breakfast nook over a mug of coffee and a piece of toast with jam.

"Good morning, Mother Dear," she replied in her best royalty voice. In a more normal voice for a teenager she asked, "Where's my toast?"

"Sorry, Sweetie," her mom replied. "I didn't know when you were coming down. Dad's still asleep upstairs and I've got to head into the library in a few. Can you make breakfast for yourself and Nick?" She looked up at Claire and smiled. Claire groaned.

"Aw, mom," she complained, royal voice forgotten, "Do I have to?"

"You have to give me a kiss before you start whining, Claire," Mom said in a mock stern voice. "And yes, you have to." Claire dutifully kissed her mother on the cheek and went to the breadbox in search of toast-to-be. There were only three normal slices. Very well, Nick could have the heel if he wanted two pieces.

"Today is Saturday, Mom. Can't you stay home? And in case you forgot, today is also your least favorite child's birthday."

"The library is open on Saturday and this is my week to cover it. I asked to switch but Beth wouldn't do it." Mom frowned slightly. "Your birthday was in October, Claire."

"I know my birthday was in October. What's that got to…. Oh. Ha Ha, Mother. Are you trying to give me an inferiority complex or something?" Her mother snorted to show what she thought the chances of that happening were. Then she stood up to go. Claire's mom picked up her satchel and grabbed the keys to the little green Ford she drove to work.

"Loquacious," challenged Mom.

"Talks a lot," replied Claire and came back with, "Indolent."

"Lazy," said her mom and smiled. "Good one, Sugar Pop." She kissed Claire on the forehead and turned for the door then turned back. "Be nice to Nicky, Claire. It's his birthday. I'll be home before the party with the cake. Love you." And with another quick hug she left Claire alone in the kitchen making toast and trying to think of another good word to challenge her mother with when she got back.

The day progressed about like Claire figured it would. Nick was a brat and whined about getting the heel for toast. He whined because the four trolls he called friends couldn't come over until the party. He whined that his shower wasn't hot enough, and that he couldn't open his presents early. He whined that his favorite Batman t-shirt wasn't clean. So, Dad did some laundry and then made Nick and Claire fold it and put it away. Which Nick whined about, too, and didn't even put on his freshly laundered Batman t-shirt. He said today felt more like a Lightning McQueen day.

Claire did not whine. She accepted her fate with dignity, only making rational arguments about why she shouldn't have to do any of the things that her unreasonable father insisted she do; like clean her room. It wasn't likely any of the cretins coming to the party would see her room anyway. She didn't raise her voice or pout. At least where anyone would notice her… much. Why should she have to put on nicer clothes? Who cared if Nick's friends thought she was a slob? She hardly even slammed her door in protest.

To make matters worse, Mom was late. By the time she burst through the door, cake in hand, all the kids for the party were already there. So was Dad's brother, Uncle Clark and Mom's brother, Uncle Derek. They were in the den sipping Cokes, ignoring the madhouse of nine-year-old boys and trying to be polite to one another. Uncle Clark worked with Dad at the refinery and Uncle Derek was a sometimes artist sometimes blackjack dealer with a ridiculous beard. Uncle Derek came dressed like some sort of hipster in skinny jeans and a tweed sport coat, while Uncle Clark was in his work overalls, since he was heading to the night shift after the party. Predictably, the two uncles didn't see eye to eye when it came to things like politics and philosophy.

Claire had overheard them say things about each other that were unflattering. Hurtful words like 'Bieber wanna-be' and 'communist' vied against slurs like 'Fascist' and 'climate change denier.' She figured that neither uncle idolized either Justin Bieber or Adolf Hitler, but that the communist and climate change denier ones were probably pretty close to on target.

Dad was running her ragged, having her dole out soda and ice cream to screaming psychopathic midgets, and follow them around cleaning up spills and collecting abandoned cups and bowls. When she got a chance, she sneaked away from the hubbub and joined her uncles who were having a stilted conversation about the chance of rain in the coming week. Apparently, they both recognized that short term weather was one of the few safe topics open to both of them that wouldn't likely lead to blatant animosity or attempted murder. She tossed herself into the lazy boy and savored the near silence until unable to resist stirring the pot for her own amusement, Claire threw out the question, "What do you guys think about Bernie Sanders?"

Uncle Derek's face lightened immediately as he smiled involuntarily like a kid who hears Santa Claus is coming. Uncle Clark looked like he wanted to strangle some low-down-no-good so and so who had kicked his dog. Fortunately, before either could put voice to the emotions shining clearly through their countenances, Mom made her promised appearance with a box of delicious cake. And it was delicious, too; even if it was a hideous green color and depicted Teenage Mutant Ninja Turtles inexplicably fighting the Incredible Hulk.

Both uncles stood when Mom came in. Uncle Derek hurried to hug his sister with a joyful, "Deborah, good to see you, let me take that."

Uncle Clark murmured, "Thank God," under his breath. He gave a dutiful brother-in-law hug to Mom and waded into the pool of chaos to find Dad and let him know his reprieve had arrived.

They sang "Happy Birthday," ate cake, and watched the greedy little booger open his presents. They listened to him complain that he didn't have enough Nerf bullets for his new gun, that iTunes gift cards weren't as good as Amazon gift cards and that the Hulk was no match for TMNT and he shouldn't be throwing them around like that on his cake. All to the background music of discord and savage brutality that only a band of fourth grade boys can make. Claire rolled her eyes a lot and enjoyed being seen as the mature one.

Before Claire knew it, both uncles had departed the scene, all the cake was eaten or otherwise destroyed, the dishes were cleared away and bedtime was swiftly approaching. Mom and Dad collapsed on the living room sofa while the herd of terror swept up the stairs for some good natured fights to the death before bed time. Claire plopped down on the love seat and only half pretended she was exhausted. In all honesty, she kinda wanted to take that Nerf gun and chase down and brutalize all the rampaging heathens upstairs.

"I'm beat," exclaimed Mom. "Too bad I can't relax too much. Connie wants me to look over the latest printout of overdue books and see which ones should be written off."

"Can't you do that Monday, Babe?" asked Dad without opening his eyes.

"I could but I'm the only one in on Monday and I've got to rack all the returns myself. Plus, I need to update the new arrivals on the website." With that, she began to rummage in her satchel. Dad grunted in acknowledgement.

"Penury," said Claire into the silence.

"Honey, I don't have time right now, ok? I'm looking for something and I've got work to do."

"Mom," Claire wheedled, "You said-"

"I know, I know, Claire. Fine. It means the quality of being cheap, Greed. Hmm.." she continued to search her satchel, apparently without success. "Avuncular."

This was a word that Claire was unfamiliar with. She had never heard of avuncular. She bit her lip in consternation. There were no context clues to use to guess. As if reading her mind, her mom said, "Clark and Derek were both avuncular this evening." She smirked.

"Was that just an example of how to use it or were they both actually avuncular?"

Dad groaned. "You guys are killing me."

"Oh, you're just jealous that you can't be smart like me and Mom"

Dad opened one eye.

"Uhoh," said Mom, taking her eyes off the uncooperative satchel to watch Dad with obvious interest.

"Avuncular is from the Latin root Avunculus, meaning uncle, which is actually where we get the word uncle. Avuncular literally means 'in the manner of an uncle' or 'having the qualities of an uncle.' So, yes, they were both, by definition, avuncular tonight, Miss Smarty Pants," said Dad with a satisfied grin on his face.

Claire blushed. "Sorry, Dad."

"No biggie, Sweetie," he laughed. "Just remember your mom is too smart to have married a dummy."

"I wonder, sometimes," Mom said as she got up from the couch. Dad tried to swat her playfully on the rear and missed, probably because his eyes were closed again. "But it looks like I'm the dummy tonight. I can't find that printout. Maybe I left it in the car."

"How many overdue library books can there be?" asked Claire and Dad in near unison and then both chuckled.

"Two hundred," guessed Claire.

"Six hundred, fifty-two and a half," guessed Dad.

"A little over four thousand," said Mom. Dad opened his eyes and they both stared at Mom in disbelief. "It's a big library and the list goes back to 1952. That's why I need to get started now. I was planning on highlighting it up tomorrow." She went out to check the car.

"Pontificate," said Claire.

"Oh, good grief," said Dad. "You know I play to win, right? Fine, to hold forth, like a teacher or a priest; to lecture." He paused, thinking. "Antidisestablishmentarianism."

"What? That's not a real word!"

"Is so."

"You must have made it up."

"Nope, it's been around for a couple hundred years. Look it up."

"You're not going to tell me what it means?" asked Claire, irritated.

"Where's the fun in that? Besides, you'll remember it better if I don't."

"Ok, I'll look it up. Uhm.. what was it again?" she asked sheepishly.

"See? You already forgot. Antidisestablishmentarianism," he said slowly, breaking up all the syllables. Claire woke up her iPhone and started trying to spell it while Dad laughed at her. Upstairs, it sounded like many people were being dismembered with chainsaws. Dad cocked a wary eye at the stairs. Mom came back in, clearly in a funk.

"It's not in the car. I must have left it at the library in my hurry to pick up the cake and get back here." Claire and Dad both looked at her expectantly. They both knew she was going to insist on going back to get it. "I guess I'll have to go-"

"Can I come with you?" asked Claire, interrupting. Something exploded upstairs, followed by what sounded like a Boeing 747 crashing into the great pyramid at Giza.

"Sure, leave me here to fend off the cannibals alone, why don't you?" complained Dad as he heaved himself off the couch and marched determinedly towards the stairs, rolling up his shirtsleeves.

"Alright, fine. Come on, but no lollygagging," Mom said to Claire.

Claire was through the door almost before Mom stopped talking. As Mom closed the door behind her, Claire heard what sounded like an army of wild Injuns battling Alpine yodelers using machine guns and riding lawnmowers. Over the din came the strident voice of her father, "CUT THAT OUT!!"

It's odd how you can be alone with someone you love and feel like you're sharing a special moment that would be ruined by speaking aloud. Claire felt that way about the drive to the library with her mother. She was alone in the car with her mother whom she idolized. Her mom was the smartest person she knew and Claire didn't get to spend enough time with her. Here she was getting a big ole slice of Mom's time and not having to share it with her brother or her father. She felt special and was afraid to spoil the moment, but she couldn't resist.

"Lugubrious," she said. Her mom looked at her and grinned.

"Am not," said Mom.

"I wasn't saying you were lugubrious, Mom. Oh. It was a joke. I get it."

"It means sad and melancholy. I think to the point of being humorous. Or it's implied at least," mused her mother. "But I seriously doubt that word will be in a spelling bee. Or a reading team text. Well, not unless you read something by Dickens."

11

"You never know, Mom. I'm prepared. Your turn. Whatcha got?"

"Flatulence."

For the second time that day Claire was stumped. She had never heard of that word. One word by itself. No context clues. Unless it was a double entendre and Mom also meant she had flatulence? If that was the case it had to mean something about being smart or pretty, or something like that. Mom also always smelled really nice, so maybe it meant that.

"Let's see, it's a noun; most likely a quality. Having the quality would make you flatulent. Which means... sophisticated?"

Mom actually laughed out loud and turned red.

"No, that's definitely not it. You'll have to look it up." But as Claire hauled out her phone to do just that, she said, "No, don't look it up. Just forget it. I should never have said that. Forget about it." They pulled into the library parking lot and Mom turned off the car. "I'm serious," she said trying to be stern, but giggling in fits and starts. "Put up your phone, dear."

They got out of the car and Mom used her key to open the lobby door. They went inside and Mom relocked the door behind them. When Claire saw the bathrooms in the lobby, she realized she needed to go.

"Mom, I'm gonna use the restroom real quick. I'll be right up." The first floor was just the lobby, storage and the head librarian's office on one side and a small city museum on the other. The stacks were on the second and third floors. The fourth floor was the microfiche storage and viewing rooms. The fifth floor was all computers. The sixth floor was leased by some investment bank or something equally enigmatic.

"Come find me on the third floor when you're done. Don't get lost," said her mom as she headed for the elevator and Claire quickly ducked into the ladies' room and had to turn on the lights, which was a little bit spooky. After she washed her hands, she tried to look up flatulence but couldn't spell it properly. Finally, she hit the microphone button and just said it out loud. This is what appeared on the screen:

flat·u·lence
noun
noun: **flatulence**

1. the accumulation of gas in the alimentary canal.

    "foods that may cause flatulence"

    (intestinal) gas, wind;
    synonyms: *Informal* farting, tooting;
    formal flatus

"Mom used a word that meant *farting?*" Claire said out loud in the restroom and laughed at the shocked look on her face in the mirror. She was so tickled that it took a couple of minutes to stop laughing. Once she composed herself, Claire left the bathroom, and remembered to turn off the light. She walked down the lobby, her sneakers squeaking on the shiny polished floor, to the elevator and pushed the "up" button. There was no "down" button since the lobby was the lowest floor that the elevator went to. The indicator above the elevator door showed the car was currently on the third floor, which was no surprise, since that's where Mom said she'd be. Then, the light showed the car descending and with a ding, the shiny metal doors swished open.

Claire jumped into the elevator and her finger went to the third floor button but she hesitated. There were six buttons as expected. The top one was labeled (6)-Werkman/Herzog. Below that were (5)-Comp Lab, (4)-Microfiche, (3)-Library, (2)-Library and (1)-Lobby/Museum. But beneath the bottom button was a little metal door with a key hole in it. In the key hole was a tiny key. The door was simply labeled "service." Claire noticed that the little door wasn't latched and when she put her fingernail in the crack and pulled, it swung open. Inside was a button that looked just like the six buttons above but the only label was what looked like an 8, only the button seemed to be turned on its side. That was strange. The building only had six floors, so where did the weird little sideways button send the elevator? After just a second or two of hesitation, Claire pushed the button.

The doors swished shut and the elevator started up. The indicator at the top showed the car going through the second floor, then the third, and so on, when it got to six the indicator light went out, but she could feel it still going up. It kept going up for a little bit and Claire started to get nervous. Was it broken? Where was she? And most importantly, was she going to get in trouble?

With a ding, the elevator stopped ascending and the doors swished open with their usual sound. Outside the door was a normal hallway. Dull grey carpet with golden sideways 8's embroidered in it stretched all the way down the hall. It looked like the hallway went quite a bit farther than it should. The library wasn't that large of a building and the hallway stretched so far, it seemed to Claire it should be sticking out the side of the library and hanging seven (or more?) stories over Williams Avenue. She was pretty sure that there had been nothing sticking out over the road above the library when they drove up a few minutes ago. It also looked like the hallway met another one at the other end, forming a T. Every few feet along the corridor were doors on either side. Plain wooden doors with little plaques next to each one. Because of the angle, Claire couldn't read any of the plaques.

Claire tentatively inched toward the elevator doors, which, either tired of waiting or at the limit of their preprogrammed opening, tried to close. The doors startled Claire and she jumped back, allowing them to meet with a satisfied clunk. She pressed the door open button to the right of the floor buttons, next to the door close and emergency stop buttons. The doors obligingly opened again, once revealing the mysterious corridor. Claire stuck her head out of the elevator and noticed that another corridor, lined on both sides with labeled doors, ran past the elevator in both directions. This hallway also appeared larger than possible. So, the elevator seemed to be situated facing down the crossbar of an enormous H. The doors started to close again and Claire retreated into the elevator car and let them close. With a slightly trembling hand she pressed the 3 button. With no further ado, the elevator started down and after a couple of seconds the indicator came back on, showing her progress past floors six through four and stopping at the selected 'three'. Claire felt a relief at the resumption of normality that closely resembled her experience as a little girl lost in the mall when she finally caught sight of her mother.

She pushed the little metal door on the elevator panel closed and heard it latch with an audible 'click' as the elevator dinged and the doors opened onto the perfectly normal library. When she withdrew her hand from the service door, the little key fell out of the keyhole and plunked onto the carpeted elevator floor. She bent down and picked up the curious little key and saw that it was inscribed with a sideways 8 exactly like the hidden button in the panel and the embroidered carpet in the hallway. When she reached out to put it back, she noticed with a shock that the keyhole itself had vanished.

"Oh, there you are, Babe. I was a little worried," said her Mom who stepped into the elevator next to Claire. Claire quickly pocketed the curious little key without thinking. Mom looked at Claire and Claire knew her face must reflect some of the feelings of shock and confusion because Mom said, "You ok, Claire? You look like you saw a ghost."

"Uh.. yep," she said, her voice sounding forced and strained to her ears. "Everything's fine. A-OK. Okeydokey." The elevator doors closed and Claire flinched just a tad.

"Right," said her Mom, still looking at her strangely. "Are you going to press the button or are we just going to stand here all night?"

"Oh, sorry." Claire pressed the button labeled "lobby/museum" and the elevator started down again. She fought an irrational urge to hum or whistle like a cartoon character trying to act normal. Then she failed to suppress a giggle at the silly mental picture that thought drew in her mind.

"Penny for your thoughts," said her mother.

"Well," she said while thinking quickly, "I was just hoping that since we're cooped up in an elevator, that you weren't *flatulent*." And she laughed out loud.

"Oh, good Lord," said her mother disgustedly. "I should have known better than to use that word. Please, H, don't go using that one in everyday conversation. And if you do, tell people you learned it from your dad, ok?" And Mom laughed too. They laughed together and the key fell out of her mind just like it had fallen out of the keyhole. It stayed in her pocket, forgotten. For the moment.

Chapter Two: Doors

"In the Land of Memory the time is always Now.
In the Kingdom of Ago, the clocks tick... but their hands never move.
There is an Unfound Door
(O lost)
and memory is the key which opens it."
— Stephen King, Song of Susannah

    Like most weekends, Claire's slipped away into oblivion with undue haste and a total lack of regard for the trials and tribulations that Mondays bring. Claire would describe the weekend as unsympathetic. Or perhaps it's time that is unsympathetic. Either way, Claire was forced headlong into a week for which she didn't feel emotionally prepared. Monday was to be the first day in a new system of getting to and from school. Dad was changing shifts at the refinery and wouldn't be able to take them to school in the mornings. Instead, Mom would have to do it and she would have to drop them off a half hour early in order for her to get to work on time. But that wasn't the bad part. Since nobody would be home in the afternoons when school got out, they would have to ride a bus that stopped near the library, then walk there and spend a couple of hours at the library until Mom got off work and could take them home. It was going to stink.

    Claire was also nervous because Wednesday was tryouts for next year's reading team and Thursday was the first Spring spelling bee. Saturday was a track meet, where Claire would be competing in the 800 meter and pole vaulting. She wasn't nervous about that because she had always been able to compete physically without thinking about it much. It was mental competition that got her all twisted up inside. What if she spelled an easy word wrong in front of all those people? She had nightmares about being on stage and not being able to spell a word like "jump" or "cat." Or of getting a word like "asymptotic" or "scurrilously." What if she tried out for the reading team and got all tongue tied or stuttered? It made her hands and armpits all sweaty just thinking about it.

Monday morning arrived like an out of control missile and was about as welcome. When her alarm went off, Claire swam out of a deep slumber, fighting wakefulness like death itself. Bleary eyed and zombielike she stumbled through the motions of getting herself ready for the day. Without noticing what clothes she was putting on, she put on the first pair of jeans her hands touched, which happened to have been draped over her bedpost. Claire wasn't the tidiest freshman in existence. She at least grabbed a clean shirt, even if she did put it on inside out. No shower this morning because she had taken one the night before. Which was fortunate because Nick was in there using all the hot water like an inconsiderate butthead. Claire had to go downstairs to use the bathroom.

Breakfast was oatmeal. Blech. She ignored Mom's morning greetings and began to slurp down mush that tasted vaguely of cinnamon and brown sugar. Mostly it was tasteless. At least she didn't complain about it, which was more than she could say for Nick. When he finally got out of the shower and honored them with his presence, the first words out of his ungrateful little mouth were, "Oatmeal! But I freaking hate oatmeal. I want muffins instead."

"Shut up you little creep," said Claire. "I ate it, so can you."

"Claire Amelia Grant!" said their mother sternly. "Don't you speak to your brother that way. Say you're sorry right now."

"Fine. My most humble apologies, dear brother. Please forgive my lapse of good manners," she said in her most royal voice.

"Whatever," said Nick and added, "Toad," under his breath. But Mom heard him.

"I take it back, she was right. You are a little creep this morning, aren't you? Eat your oatmeal and be silent if you can't say anything nice."

Claire thought he might throw a fit but he stopped himself and ate his oatmeal. Maybe he realized he wouldn't be able to win one this morning. The rest of which proceeded with little to no drama. The ride to school was quiet. Nobody spoke. Claire read on a novel she had started yesterday and Nick played Minecraft on his tablet. Mom didn't turn on the radio because she didn't think morning radio shows were something children should listen to. She was probably right.

When Claire got to school, it was half an hour earlier than she usually got there. Her friends weren't there yet, so she spent the time reading on a bench in front of the school, enjoying the early morning Spring sunshine. When Emma and Danielle showed up, she stowed the book in her bag and they had a very useful and insightful discussion about the fact that Amanda was seeing a Junior on the basketball team. Very philosophical conversation.

The day dragged as if it wanted to get its money's worth for every single agonizing second. Claire accumulated homework at a dizzying rate. Then she almost missed her bus because she forgot and was in the wrong bus line. When she did get on, she was last and the only seat left was next to a rather smelly boy who was busy picking his nose. She sat on the edge of the seat and tried not to breathe much or look at him. Nick was already on the bus in the back. They didn't acknowledge each other's existence. They were the only ones who got off at the stop near the library. They walked the remaining couple of hundred yards, each alone in spite of the close proximity of their sibling.

With a minimum of traded insults, they climbed into the elevator with a middle aged woman in a pants suit. She pushed the sixth floor button, while they pushed the third. They got off the elevator and went and found their mother who was busy typing away on a computer at the librarian's desk.

"You guys go find something to do quietly. You have homework?" They both did.

"Can I do mine in the computer lab?" asked Nick.

"If you promise to actually do your homework and not play on the internet. Here's some quarters if you want a drink from the machine," their mother said distractedly. Nick agreed with a whoop and ran off to the elevator with his battered old Ironman backpack slapping against his back loudly. "And be quiet!" she shouted in a whisper at his quickly receding back.

"I'll do mine in a quiet corner on the second floor," said Claire.

"Alright, Sugar. Come get me if you need anything. Here's a dollar for the soda machine."

Claire stuffed the dollar into her jeans pocket, slung her backpack over her shoulder and walked slowly to the elevator. She wanted to give Nick a chance to leave the floor so she didn't have to share the elevator with him again. It might have been her imagination, but she didn't think he remembered to put on deodorant this morning.

Once in the elevator, she didn't immediately select a button. Claire looked intently at the little metal door marked 'service.' She tried to open it but it was closed and there was no key in it today. She couldn't remember what she had done with the first key. She made a mental note to look for it in her room when she got home. She rode the elevator down to the second floor and was looking for a nice comfy corner to do her homework in when she had an idea.

Claire put her book bag down under a chair in the corner and went to the door marked 'stairs.' She quickly climbed to the third floor landing, then the fourth. She slowed down, both because she was a little out of breath from running up two flights of stairs, and because she didn't want to make a lot of noise passing the floor where her brother was most likely googling Teenage Mutant Ninja Turtle fan fiction. Her thighs were starting to burn by the time she got to the sixth floor landing. She stopped for a couple of seconds to slow her breathing and look around. Through the window in the door to the stairwell she could see a waiting area with uncomfortable looking chairs, a large granite marquee and a receptionist wearing a headset and sitting behind a tall, highly polished wooden desk.

After a minute or so her thighs stopped burning and she went up the next flight of stairs which stopped at a door marked 'roof access.' Claire stared at the door in disbelief. She *knew* there was another story to this building. She had *been* there. Maybe the label on the door was some sort of camouflage. The next level must be so much a secret that the door to it was labeled incorrectly on purpose. It was also probably locked. But it wasn't. The door opened when she pressed the bar with a clank and a whoosh of equalizing air pressure. The bright sunlight, the wind, the smell of hot tar and the sound of traffic told Claire that there was no seventh floor to the Martin Hayward Memorial Library Building.

She let the door clang shut again. Her brain was working overtime trying to make sense of the seeming impossibility of a floor accessible by elevator but that didn't exist otherwise. It was impossible. Unless the elevator had tricked her and had gone down instead of up? It had certainly felt like it was going up… but she was willing to bet her senses could be fooled into thinking she was going up when she was actually going down. To test her theory, she began to run down the stairs, going much more quickly than she had gone up them.

Claire flew down the stairs two at a time until she passed up the door to the lobby and came to a door labeled 'basement' which *was* locked. But it had a little glass window just like the one on the sixth floor. Claire pressed her face against the glass. It was dark on the other side of the door but some light from the stairwell partially illuminated a dusty room full of old chairs and musty boxes of posters and fliers. An old tarp covered something that might have been a piano. The basement bore absolutely no resemblance to the floor with the hallways full of doors. Claire was just as confused as ever. She thought about asking her mother if there was another floor but decided that would be a bad idea. If there was one and she wasn't supposed to know about it, her mother would want to know how she did know about it. If there wasn't, her mom might think she was nuts.

Maybe the extra floor was hidden between the others? No, she would have noticed going up and down the stairs. She decided to go outside and count the windows anyway. Claire went into the lobby and out the front doors and down the steps to the sidewalk where she counted exactly six rows of windows. Maybe she *was* nuts. She wandered desultorily (an excellent word and hard to spell) back into the lobby and up to the vending machine. While fishing for the dollar in her pocket, her fingers brushed something else. At first she thought it was a quarter but quickly realized it was the key from the elevator door. She must have put on the same pants she wore on Saturday!

Abandoning the vending machine, she ran to the elevator but before it opened, a middle aged man in a suit walked up and stood next to her, waiting for the elevator. When they got in, he pressed the button for the sixth floor.

"What about you, miss? Which floor?"

"Oh. Two, please."

She got off at the second floor and went to her book bag, where she sat, trying to watch the indicator inconspicuously. It went to six and stopped. She walked back over and pressed the button again, crossing her fingers that nobody would be in it when it opened. The metal doors slipped open with their customary swish and clunk to reveal a totally empty elevator car. Yes! Claire walked in calmly, trying hard not to appear too eager and pressed the 'door close' button with one hand while simultaneously using her other hand to dig the key out of her jeans. She half expected the key to not fit but it did, sliding smoothly into the keyhole with only a slight clicking resistance. The service door opened and there sat the little sideways 8 button, practically begging to be pressed. She obliged, then closed and locked the service door and pocketed the key. The elevator dutifully started up. By the time the indicator went past six and went dark, she was almost dancing with excitement.

When the doors chimed and opened, the hallway was just as she remembered it. The grey carpet with the golden 8's looked soft and inviting. Tentatively, Claire took a step out into the hallway. The carpet felt thinner and much harder than she had imagined, not soft and welcoming. The lighting was softer than the rest of the library. She looked up and saw not the ubiquitous (awesome word) fluorescent lights of modern buildings, but recessed can lights. A soft zephyr (her vocabulary was on fire today) of cool air caressed her cheek and stirred her hair slightly.

She was so startled by the elevator doors trundling closed that she almost screamed. Claire stopped the doors from closing all the way with her hand and they opened up again. Claire verified that there was indeed a call button by the doors, then let the doors close again. She waited a few seconds and pressed the button. The doors opened. She smiled. Mindful of the time, she ran to the nearest door and examined it.

The door was solid wood and paneled. It had a golden knob with no lock. There was no window or peephole. A wooden plaque covered in brass had some words on it in a language that Claire was unfamiliar with. She didn't even recognize most of the letters. Before she even made a conscious decision, her hand had grasped the golden doorknob. It was smooth and warm and vibrated slightly in her palm like it was a living thing. It turned easily, smoothly, like a well-oiled machine and gave a satisfying click as the latch disengaged and the door swung inward.

Claire fell down in her haste to back away from the door as quickly as humanly possible. Even after falling to the carpet, she kept frantically backpedaling to the opposite wall. She forgot to breathe and her eyes hurt from not blinking. She was shaking and sweating. Framed by the door was not a room you would find in a library. In fact, it was not a room you would find in any building at all because it was not a room. The doorway in the hallway opened on a snow covered landscape of rolling hills. It was overcast and a light snow was falling, but in the background, colorful onion domed buildings rose into an electric blue sky devoid of any clouds. Bright sunlight glinted off ice crystals in the snow. Details leapt out at her. She could see where the clouds ended in the distance and smell a slight tang of wood smoke. A light wind blew a few lazy snowflakes into the hallway where they quickly melted on the carpet, leaving slightly darker grey spots.

Claire fought with herself. She wanted to run back to the elevator as quickly as she could. But she also wanted to walk out into that snowy landscape. But mostly she wanted to close the door because a cold wind was blowing into the hall, making her shiver even more. She steeled herself and stood. She refused to run away. She resolutely crossed the hall, grasped the doorknob and closed the door with a bang and a click. She opened her book bag and took out her phone. No service. Not surprising. She used the phone to take a pic of the plaque with the strange writing. For good measure, she also took out a pen and copied down the writing in her homework notebook.

She moved on to other doors. Some she could read and others she could not. Some of the doors were labeled in weird symbols. She stopped at one labeled "A Castle Meadow," in clearly recognizable English.

When she opened this door, she saw an idyllic green meadow, surrounded on three sides by a forest. There was a gazebo with a bench in the middle of the meadow and in the direction not surrounded by forest, a stone castle rose against the summer sky. Banners waved from the battlements and fluffy white clouds sailed lazily by. Entranced by the beauty, she stepped through the door into the inviting green grass. It was short, as if freshly mown. Claire turned around to look at the door. There was still a door there, but it was a roughly hewn wooden door in a humble stone cottage. Incongruously, she could still see the carpeted hall through it. She reached back and closed the door, then in a moment of panic opened it again. The hallway was still there. She closed it once more and walked over to the bench. Claire looked at her watch to check the time and noticed that it had stopped moving at exactly 4:08. She checked her phone. It too said 4:08 and when she waited what had to be a minute or more, it didn't change.

On impulse, she plopped herself down on the stone bench and crossed her legs and enjoyed the view... which got old after a few minutes. Might as well work on her homework. She dug out her math textbook and got to work. Claire did all her homework: math, reading, history and science before she even thought about the time. When she noticed the sun had worked its way down the sky a very significant amount, she realized she must have been sitting there for a couple of hours. Her mother would be worried sick. Quickly she stuffed all her homework back in her bag and ran for the little cottage.

Claire had a moment of sickening dread when she tried the door and it didn't seem to move, but she was trying to push it when it obviously opened out. Duh. It opened easily when she pulled and revealed the mysterious hallway, which she eagerly stepped into and closed the door behind her. She jogged back to the elevator and pressed the button. The elevator took an agonizing minute to come back to her floor. While she was waiting, she checked her phone again. It said 5:07. So did her watch. She had only been in the meadow for 59 minutes? Impossible. But it was just one more of many impossibilities about the whole situation.

Her mother was not worried sick. In fact, she had not even noticed that Claire had disappeared. When Claire showed up at her desk, she glanced up at her then back down.

"It's almost time to go, Claire. Library's closed and I'm just finishing up. Go get your brother, please and you guys meet me back here in five, ok? Thanks."

"Sure, thing, Mom," Claire heard herself say in a normal voice. She wasn't sure how she was supposed to feel about the situation but mostly what she felt was exhilaration. And impatience. She couldn't wait until tomorrow to open another door.

25

Chapter Three: Elves

"Elvish singing is not a thing to miss, in June under the stars, not if you care for such things."

— *J.R.R. Tolkien, The Hobbit*

Claire had a hard time sleeping that night. It was like the night before Christmas, her birthday and the first day of school all rolled into one. She ended up waking up for good half an hour before her alarm went off. She dressed herself with more care than usual, paying particular attention to her shoes and socks since she might be doing some walking in unknown terrain after school. She also packed some extra gear in her book bag. Sunglasses, a hat, sunscreen, a compass and some other stuff that she thought might come in handy. She made doubly certain that the key was in her pocket, too.

She was also in a much better mood this morning than she was just the day before. Excitement battled impatience all through the day, which seemed to drag by. Concentrating on her schoolwork was getting increasingly difficult and she kept looking at her watch which refused to go faster that a snail's pace. Her imagination kept running away with her when she should have been concentrating. What other interesting and exciting worlds awaited her in the hallway of the floor where the stairs didn't go? Her friends at school noticed her preoccupation and remarked on it, but she laughed it off as nerves about the upcoming reading team tryouts.

The only thing slower than her watch was the school bus. She wanted to yell in frustration every time it hit a red light or slowed down for traffic between the school and the library. Claire ground her teeth and seethed like a tea kettle. Her brother noticed her impatience.

"What's eating you?" he asked.

"Uh, nothing. Just got to pee," she came up with in a hurry.

"Sounds like you could use a good tickling," he teased.

"Try it and I'll beat you until your head looks more like a misshapen potato than it does already," she threatened with her best tough guy voice.

"I'm telling mom you called me a potato head," complained the little whiner.

"Whatever."

The bus finally let them off near the library and they walked the short distance there, with Claire holding herself back from breaking into a run. When they got in, Claire went to the bathroom to justify her impatience on the bus and because she didn't know if there would be any bathrooms where she was going. Best to be safe.

Her mom was busy as usual and after she checked in with her on the third floor, she went to the elevator eagerly. She got it all to herself on the first try and in no time at all she was in the hallway browsing doors like a grocery shopper looking for the cheapest or tastiest deals. Instead of going straight down the hallway like she had last time, Claire immediately turned left out of the elevator. There was no difference between this hallway and the other one that she could see. The first door she came to opened on a desert scene with camels highlighted against a distant dune. Heat blasted out of the door like an oven. She quickly closed it and moved on.

The next door's label was legible and it said "Manderly." This rang a bell but Claire couldn't quite place it. She opened the door and saw a rose garden of a great English country house. For some reason the name Mrs. DeWinter came to mind. Manderly? I dreamed I went to Manderly again last night. Or something similar.

Oh, this was from the book 'Rebecca' by Daphne DeMaurier. Claire had a strong urge to go find Mrs. DeWinter and ask her what her first name was.

"Maybe next time," she said aloud and closed the door. Ok, so this door opened on a world out of a novel. Do they all? Claire made a mental note that the door handle on 'Manderly' door was pewter with intricate ivy patterns carved on it. She moved on. The next door was named 'Cretaceous Period,' which Claire was certain was a time when dinosaurs roamed the Earth, and not a book. Its handle was black and looked like wrought iron. She had no desire to go traipsing through a prehistoric rain forest and get eaten by something with big teeth and claws, so she walked on down the hall.

The next door was silver filigree and the label was in a tall flowing script that she felt like she could almost read, but couldn't. It looked vaguely familiar. She cracked the door open and saw a beautiful forest glade, alive with birds and butterflies flitting about. Forest sounds that were almost musical filled the crystal air. It even smelled like someone's ideal of what a forest should smell like. The scent of exotic flowers and spices mixed with the earthy scent of leaves and loamy earth. Enchanted, she stepped through the door into a world that caressed her senses like a mother does a newborn babe.

She looked behind her and was unsurprised to see the door was set in a huge gnarled tree and from this side looked like living wood. It closed softly, cutting off her view of the carpeted hallway and artificial lighting. Claire walked slowly, savoring how even the most ordinary objects seemed more vivid and *real*. An old rotting log seemed almost magical in its invitation to sit on its mossy flanks. This was as good a place as any to do her homework. Indeed, it was better than any place she could think of. So, she did. Geometry was accompanied by the sounds of small animals playing in the trees and underbrush. The battle of Gettysburg was filled with birdsong. She read about cellular mitosis while enjoying a gentle breeze laden with the smell of jasmine.

It took her a couple of hours and she was a little apprehensive in case her theory that only 59 minutes would elapse should prove false. When she finished, she packed up her books and was about to sling the bag over her shoulder and explore a bit when someone stepped out from behind a tree. The newcomer was as achingly beautiful as the forest she stepped out of. Her hair was an iridescent silver that seemed more like moonlight than a possible shade of hair. Her silvery hair was held back by a fine golden chain that allowed elongated pointy ears to poke through. Even from a distance her eyes where obviously a brightly shining violet. She was dressed in a finely woven green blouse and pants that were almost sheer enough to see through and sparkled with faint highlights of every color of the rainbow and a few that weren't in the rainbow. She carried a bow that looked like it belonged in an art museum, it was so ornately carved and decorated. The woman was slender like a willow and looked to be a few inches shorter than Claire. Claire hadn't heard her approach at all and had absolutely no idea anyone was nearby. How long had this person been watching her?

"Are you a sorceress?" the woman asked. "You have been quite busy with the spells in your codices."

"Spells? Sorceress? I, uh. No. These are school books. Geometry and stuff. For school," she stammered, distantly aware she was repeating herself and sounding like an idiot. She had a vague apprehension of being burned at the stake for witchcraft. "Who are you? Why were you watching me?"

"You are in our forest, student sorceress. I thought it prudent to watch and see what you would do. I am Alidraal." Her face betrayed little emotion. She was obviously alert and watchful but Claire could tell little else about what she might be thinking. "What are you called, child?"

"I guess I'm called Claire, I mean, that's my name. Everyone calls me that."

"Well met, Claire." She moved toward Claire so fluidly that it was more akin to gliding than walking, though her legs and feet very

29

obviously moved. Claire thought she had never seen someone so graceful.

"Can you show me the spells you were working so hard on, Claire?" A little knot of panic rose in Claire. This lady didn't seem to believe her that she was no sorceress. A memory of 'The Wizard of Oz' rose in her mind and she thought about Dorothy being asked if she was a good witch or a bad witch.

"I swear, ma'am, there are no spells in those books. They are just history and math and stuff. See, I'll show you." She opened her book bag again and hauled out her geometry textbook. It flopped open to a page detailing pi with diagrams and how to approximate it. Alidraal looked with interest.

"These words are incomprehensible but I can tell from the pictures that our architects would know what this is. I learned a bit of the relationship that a circle's dimensions have with one another. It is powerful knowledge, but as you say, not magic." She fingered the edge of one of the well-worn pages. "This text is wondrous. Surely it is wrought with sorcery. I have never seen the like, Claire. Your school must be wealthy in the extreme. What school did you say you attend, child?" Claire was tempted to answer with something impressive like MIT or Princeton or even Hogwarts. But she figured that this elfin lady wouldn't know MIT from kindergarten, so why not tell the truth?

"Alex Clancy High School," she said simply. The woman with the bow thought for a few seconds.

"I do not know of this Master Clancy or his High School. Where is this school and what do they teach besides this... geomancy did you call it?

"You wouldn't believe me if I told you, ma'am." The Elf looked at Claire for a few more seconds before harrumphing.

"As you will. But you must come with me. There will be questions. And you must answer them."

"Questions? Why? What did I do? It's not magic, I swear," Claire stammered, her voice cracking. Alidraal's face softened.

"You're not in trouble, child Claire of the High School." But the elders will want to know how you made it past the sentinels. *They* will be in trouble, I'm certain."

"You're not a sentinel?" asked Claire, hoping to change the subject.

Alidraal managed to look amused and insulted at the same time. "Hardly. I came out of Caras Galadhon to hunt. And to think. I hardly expected to find anyone within the second ring of sentries in the forest. You are not very many miles from the Deep Fosse."

"But I didn't come through any sentries. I came through a door. In a tree." Alidraal looked skeptical.

"Show me. The council will want to know of this door."

"Ok, it's this way." And with that, Claire began to make her way back to the tree where the door was. Her progress was marked by the noise of leaves underfoot and brush scraping her clothes. Alidraal, however, made no noise as she slipped like a shadow through the forest in Claire's wake. Claire kept looking back to make sure she was still there. Although Alidraal's clothing was not camouflaged in color, it was still hard to pick her out of the surrounding vegetation. She seemed to have a natural ability to blend into the forest.

After a little while of stumbling through the forest, trying to pick out land marks that looked familiar, she judged her position against the one geographic detail that could be seen above the treetops; a massive smoking peak. A volcanic caldera smoked in the distance but using it as a navigational marker wasn't as easy as Claire thought it would be. There was one horrifying moment when she thought she might be lost but Claire finally came to a landmark that she knew for a fact would lead her directly to her tree. She was quite pleased with herself and turned to Alidraal to let her know they were close. The Elf was not paying attention. She was staring alertly in first one direction, then the other, looking for something.

"What…?" Claire began but broke off abruptly when Alidraal made a chopping gesture with her hand and put an arrow to her bowstring.

"Quiet, child," she whispered. "We are in danger." She raised her bow and aimed it at something Claire couldn't see. "If I loose my arrow, you should run,"

Claire reached in her bag and felt around until her fingers found a cold metal cylinder which she grasped tightly. Slowly, she turned to start back toward the door again but stopped once more when something large and hairy exploded out of the forest. It was lunging directly for Alidraal who immediately let her arrow fly. The arrow hit the huge shaggy beast but not in a vital area and in less than the blink of an eye the massive doglike creature was on Alidraal. It fastened its jaws on the elf's forearm, which was raised to protect the Elf's throat, and bore her to the ground, growling and snarling and shaking its head back and forth, apparently trying to rip off Alidraal's arm.

The snarling and growling abruptly turned to a yelp of pain and a whimpering whine when Claire sprayed it in the face with Bear Spray. It instantly released the Elf's arm and began to paw at its eyes and rub its head in the dirt. Running in circles and tearing up the forest floor, the awful creature was making quite a racket until it finally ran off into the forest. They heard it hit more than one tree as it fled blindly.

Alidraal looked at Claire in astonishment as Claire tucked the can of pain back in her bag. Claire reached down and helped haul Alidraal to her feet. Alidraal's face was red and her eyes were running from getting some of the spray in them.

"Don't rub your eyes. It will only make it worse. When you get home you should wash out your eyes. Maybe with warm milk. The irritation should fade in a while."

"Most potent magic, that," gasped Alidraal and started coughing and gagging. It took a few minutes for her to recover enough to speak again. "What spell did you employ with such effectiveness?"

Claire decided to stop denying the accusations of magic. "Capsaicin."

"You have my thanks, Claire. It isn't often we see direwolves in this area, but they do come around periodically. Obviously. If not for you, I would be in much worse shape." She wrapped her torn blouse sleeve around the bleeding forearm. "Quickly, lead on. And please, keep that spell ready; for my eyes are not clear enough for a good shot."

Obediently, Claire once again started out in the direction of the door. Claire finally came within sight of the massive tree where the door was masquerading as vaguely door-shaped bark. She could just make out the outline of the door, and the knob was just a rough lump in the tree. She smiled in relief and pride in her ability to find her way back to the tree. Alidraal was not smiling, however.

"This is a Mallorn tree, Claire of the High School. It is revered among us. Indeed, we make our homes in their branches in Caras Galadhon. It is perhaps significant that you would lead me to one, but it is no door."

"It is a door, though. Cross my heart."

"Is that an oath at your school? Very well. Cross your heart and show me how it is a door."

"If I open this door, can I leave through it?" asked Claire hopefully. Alidraal thought about it for a depressingly long time, then she walked over to the tree and began to run her hands over it, singing softly. Her voice was beautiful. Claire couldn't understand the words but she could tell the tree was responding to it. It shivered and seemed to lean toward the Elf, almost like it wanted to sing back. The door shimmered slightly but then went back to being just part of the tree. Alidraal didn't appear to have seen the shimmer.

33

"It is a tree. A mighty, majestic, beautiful tree. Not a door. If you can make a door in this tree, your magic is great indeed. I will be very impressed, little Claire. Do it and I will allow you to leave." She smirked. Obviously, she believed Claire would not be able to open a door in what appeared to be a solid tree.

"Pinky swear?" asked Claire, holding out her right pinky.

"I will swear by your pin key, child" and she crooked her pinky finger, obviously not understanding what Claire meant. Then added, "Cross my heart."

"Good enough for me." Claire walked right up to the tree, grasped the knob that was not a knob and turned it. Instantly the door became more door-like and opened to reveal the now familiar and expected hallway. Alidraal gasped in shock and took two steps back, bringing her bow up, arrow nocked, string taught and ready to go. It wasn't pointed at Claire exactly. More like it was pointed midway between her and the door as if to be ready to shoot Claire or anyone who came out of the door. Claire was gratified at the shock on Alidraal's face and she felt a little mischievous. "I showed you mine, Elf. What magic can you show me?"

At first, Alidraal looked downright murderous. Then, relaxing her bow and her face, she surprised Claire.

"What you say is fair. I swore by your pin key. You may go. I owe you a debt of gratitude for the direwolf, as well. Here," she took the golden chain out of her hair, allowing her silver locks to fall onto her shoulders. She tossed the chain to Claire who caught it one-handed. "Hold this and say my name if you have great need and I will hear and come to you if I can. I have showed you mine. Go mighty Claire before I come to my senses."

Claire turned to go but she was touched by Alidraal's gesture and wanted to give something in return.

"Just a sec," she said, reaching into her book bag. She dug around until she found a red plastic ball point pen with 'Alex Clancy High School' on the side. She tossed it to Alidraal who caught it and held it up, examining it. "It's a pen. A writing instrument. Press that button on the end and you can write for days before it runs out of ink."

Alidraal inclined her head gravely, accepting the gift.

Claire stepped through the door in the tree and turned to look back. Alidraal was already gone, leaving nothing but a slight rustling and a lingering odor of pepper. She closed the door.

Claire turned and walked briskly back to where the elevator was… or where she thought it was supposed to be, anyway. There was no sign of the elevator. She must have gotten turned around somehow. She went back to the door with the script on it and made a left instead of a right and went back to where the elevator… wasn't. Ok, no need to panic, Claire, she told herself.

"I'm not panicking!" she insisted out loud, then looked around abashed, as if someone would have seen her talking to herself like some sort of nut job. Maybe if she marked the way she had already come, she could at least know where she had been and not get too lost. She rummaged in her pack and came up with a piece of chalk. A thick blue stick of chalk, the kind you write on sidewalks and driveways with. Claire walked back to where she thought the elevator should be, marking the walls with her blue chalk. She put arrows back toward the door she had come out of at intervals along the wall and at every turn she made.

Suddenly Claire heard a mechanical clanking and whirring sound. It didn't sound exactly like the elevator, but she couldn't think what else it might be. She jogged toward the sound and turned a corner and stopped dead, backpedaling in fright and surprise. Coming toward her at a pretty good clip was some sort of robot. It was like a Roomba on steroids, seeming to clean the carpet as it proceeded. One large red eye sat atop the apparatus's trunk, staring with seeming malevolence. Three robotic arms came out the top and one of these was tipped by a spinning brush, which was busy scouring away her blue chalk marks on the walls. She took one step toward it, thinking she must stop it somehow when she noticed that it was surrounded by several large rats which scurried along in front and behind the Roomba from Hell. They appeared to be smelling the carpet, and licking up dirt and crumbs and who knows what from the floor. Claire had absolutely no desire to get any closer to the rats or the clanking monstrosity.

She turned and ran randomly, taking the first turn she came to blindly. Claire ran until she couldn't hear the clanking whirring robo-devil, then stopped to catch her breath. When she looked up, Claire noticed a familiar looking silver filigreed handle on the nearest door. Sure enough, the plaque read 'Manderly.' She was back in familiar territory. Of course, she didn't understand how she could have gotten so lost in the first place. She hadn't gone all that far or made more than 2 turns, she was sure. Oh well. Better get out of here before the rat parade showed up. She looked around for the elevator. It was around the next corner and she hit the call button gratefully.

Back in the real library that everyone knew only had six floors, it wasn't quite time to go home yet. Once again, only an hour and change had elapsed since she had first checked in with her Mom. Only the expected fifty-nine minutes had passed while in the Elven forest. The rest had elapsed during her search for the elevator. She went to find her brother on the computer floor but he wasn't there. Claire went looking for him and ominously, she found him on the second floor where she was supposedly studying.

The first words out of the little troublemaker's mouth were, "Where were you?"

"Looking for you, Nick. Where were *you?*" Deny, deny, deny, counter-accuse, deny. No idea where she had heard that, but it was good advice when you were discovered doing something illicit. Illicit was a good word. Well, a good word about bad stuff. Whatever.

"I was here, dummy. I've been here for almost an hour, Claire. I went looking for you, too. You were nowhere to be found.

You didn't leave the library did you?" He squinted at her like the truth was really small and stuck to her forehead.

"No, I didn't leave the library," which was technically true. "Where would I go? When I couldn't find you, I did my studying in the computer lab."

"I checked there too, Claire. I'm not stupid, you know. You weren't there. You weren't ANYWHERE!"

"Hey, chillax, Nick. I must have been in the ladies' room when you looked there. No biggie. Stop yelling. I'm here now and it's almost time to go. Get your stuff together and let's go find Mom." He seemed to swallow Claire's equivocations (excellent word), although he kept looking at Claire like the truth would make itself known and visible. Maybe he expected her to sweat the truth? Who knows what the weirdo thought. He had been forestalled for now, but Claire felt certain that she hadn't heard the last of this. She needed an excuse to not be found for an hour every day. Claire would just have to put her prodigious mental abilities to work on it.

Chapter Four: Roger

Wednesday was tryouts for the reading team and Claire was committed. In light of recent developments, she was tempted to come up with an excuse to bow out. Indeed, she had given very little attention to the passages from *Huckleberry Finn* from which she would be reading later. She might end up making a fool out of herself in front of the fifth grade class she was reading to and the teachers who judged. But she decided that it would be really hard to explain if she just up and quit. So she decided to soldier on.

The impending tryouts did manage to take her mind off the hallway full of doors and the myriad (yet another great word brought to you by the mind of Claire Extraordinaire) problems that accompanied them. In light of those difficulties, Claire had added several things to her bulging book bag that she thought might help her cope. Among other things, she had added a small Tupperware container of thumbtacks and a sandwich bag of bread crumbs. And a can of spray paint. She hoped her bag didn't get searched at school because that paint would get her in trouble. Maybe she could claim it was for an art project? Except she wasn't taking art this year. Of course, she would be in even more trouble over Bear Spray... She wanted to bring a hammer from her dad's workshop but thought that was a bad idea. She would have to get it to the library some other way.

As far as her brother went, Claire intended to ask her mother to forbid Nick from bothering her while she worked on her homework. That ought to do the trick for a while, but she knew the sneaky little worm would go looking for her anyway. As long as he didn't tell on her for being not where she said she was. In the grand spirit of Grant procrastination (a word she had just learned this year) she decided to cross that bridge when she came to it.

Unlike the previous two days at school, Wednesday sped by until one o'clock when Mrs. Wallace collected all the students who were trying out for the reading team and escorted them to a big yellow bus for the ride over to the fifth and sixth grade campus for the tryouts. She was really nervous and to distract herself she imagined what kind of worlds awaited her on the top floor of the library. It was her turn in no time flat. She put Alidraal's circlet in her pocket and fingered the fine gold chain with her hand as she read.

She took a deep breath and tried not to stare at any one kid in particular as she began:

Tom told me what his plan was, and I see in a minute it was worth fifteen of mine for style, and would make Jim just as free a man as mine would, and maybe get us all killed besides. So I was satisfied, and said we would waltz in on it…

It was over in no time and she was back with the other volunteers, feeling the sweet relief of a struggle passed. Her armpits started to dry out. She thought she had done really well in spite of being nervous. Having her mind distracted might have helped as did the calming feel of the Elven chain in her pocket.

The rest of the day didn't have a chance to drag by because there wasn't much left. She pretty much got off the bus from tryouts and jumped on the one to the library. On the bus, her brother sat next to her. But it wasn't from brotherly love or some form of altruism. He had something to tell her.

"I think I'm going to study with you today, sis," he said smugly.

"Not," she replied.

"Yeah, I think I might need your help on multiplying fractions."

That manipulative punk. He could multiply fractions just fine. He knew something was up. He could smell it like some sort of animal. A sneaky, wily, booger-eating animal with no manners and B.O.

"I'll be busy preparing for the spelling bee tomorrow. I don't have time for your fractions and I don't want you bothering

39

me. I think Mom will see my point of view." She used her haughty 'I have no time for the likes of you' voice.

They rode the bus for the rest of the trip in silence. Then to mix it up they rode the elevator in near silence. Only punctuating the quiet with pithy observations like "Cretin." And "Dork."

Her mother did not see it entirely her way.

"Help him with his fractions, Claire. It won't take long, then you can study in peace. Nick, after she helps you with your math, you leave her alone, you hear me?"

They both groaned in near unison.

"Yes, ma'am," said Claire, trying to curry favor with politeness. Manners never hurt.

"Fine," said Nick with a distinct lack of couth.

Back in the elevator, she waited for Nick to push the button for the computer lab, but he pushed '2' instead.

"No way, creepizoid. Second floor is mine." She pushed the fifth floor button.

"I'm tired of the computer lab. I think I'll study on 2 with you."

"Whatever."

The elevator went down first and they got off at the second floor. Since he already knew how to multiply fractions, "helping" him didn't take long.

"Ok, scram," she said when they were done with his homework and it was all correct.

"Alright," he said with an angelic look of innocence on his warthog face. And he scrammed all the way to the other side of the aisle, where he could see her plain as day. She got up and walked to the elevator and he did too.

"Mom said leave me alone, buttmunch."

"I'm not bothering you."

"Your very presence bothers me, kiddo."

"Mom didn't say anything about my presence. She just said to let you study in peace."

She was out of ideas. In desperation Claire tried to appear earnest.

"Look, Nick. I really want to be alone. I'm nervous about this spelling bee and I just want some privacy. Please? He didn't look like he believed her but he stepped off the elevator. As the doors closed he motioned with his fingers from his eyes to her and back again. The universal 'I'm watching you...' gesture.

Claire lost no time getting out the key and pushing the hidden button. She thought the anticipation would kill her. This must be what drug addiction felt like.

When she stepped out of the elevator, Claire waited, holding her breath, listening for any sign of the rat parade. She didn't hear anything untoward (yet more vocab goodness) and started down the hallway in search of a promising door. At the first corner, she took out the spray paint and made a mark as high up as she could reach. It was the number '1' to tell her this was the first turn from the elevator. On she went.

Claire saw a door with a knob that looked wicked. It was black like wrought iron, but it was angled and sharp like some sort of medieval weapon. She had never seen a handle like it, in life or in the hallway. She wondered if there was some sort of meaning to be gleaned about a world beyond its door by the handle. The plaque displayed indecipherable angular, angry looking scribbles. Fear battled curiosity and lost. She grasped the handle and opened the door.

Smoke blew into the hallway from cooking fires and blasted battlefield wastes. The door opened on a huge army encampment replete with tents and banners and all manner of martial accoutrements. A volcano that looked vaguely familiar smoked in the distance. Large muscular humanoid warriors with greenish black skin and mouths bulging with wickedly sharp teeth filled the camp to overflowing. They were everywhere, doing what you would expect of monstrous soldiers off-duty. Some were cooking, gambling with dice and cards, sleeping, milling about and fighting with one another. One of them was hooting and shouting while he pointed at Claire with one massive gauntleted fist. He unlimbered a huge axe and was running straight at her and the doorway where she stood scared half to death. She slammed the door as quickly as she could. It was just in time and the door reverberated with a very energetic impact from the other side. Either the Orc-thing or its axe had just slammed into the door but with no visible effects from her side. Claire had a moment of anxiety over whether the door could be broken down from the other side but it passed when there was no further indication of attack on the door. She pulled out her spray paint and painted an X on the door which seemed a pretty clear message that this door was *no bueno.*

Being charged by an Orc soldier made Claire more conscious than ever of not having an effective weapon. Not that anything she could lift would threaten one of those creatures. Except maybe a gun, but she had no experience with guns and would probably present more of a danger to herself than to whatever she wanted to shoot. Guns were out. But she would still like to have a hammer or something similar that maybe she could at least bluff with.

After her little scare, Claire thought about calling it quits for the day, but instead decided to push on. The next door opened on a large circular room with a tile floor and wooden paneling on the walls. There was a black wrought iron staircase hugging the rounded wall, circling up. Cautiously, on the lookout for marauding Orcs, direwolves, manic cleaning robots or parades of rats, she stepped into the room and automatically looked back to see what the door looked like from this side so she could find it again. It was plain wood and was labeled 'Flag Locker.' Across the room, under the winding staircase was another door, similar in size and design but with no label. She crossed to it and opened it, expecting it to be a closet or storage compartment of some sort. It was the exit to the outdoors and she was treated to a view of a rocky seashore with waves crashing and exploding over the granite boulders, sending up clouds of spray and foam. Sunlight shining through the spray cast a rainbow into the sky and painted the rocks with iridescent splendor. Closer to her was a teenage boy. So close in fact that they were both startled and jumped back.

The boy looked to be just a couple of years past her own age. His hair was black and unruly, blown about by the strong sea breeze. His eyes were green and his skin was tanned and wind burnt. He was wearing jeans and a thick cable knit sweater. His work roughened hand was reached out for the door handle she had just opened.

"Oh!" she exclaimed.

"Sorry, miss," he said with an Irish accent, obviously flustered "I didn't know anyone was, that is, I didn't realize. I mean. Who are you?"

She reached out and grasped his outstretched hand and shook it firmly.

"I'm Claire Grant. Nice to meet you."

His hand felt rough in hers. At first it was kind of limp but after a couple of vigorous pumps he started shaking her hand back. A couple more pumps and they released their handshake simultaneously, an unspoken communication that seems bred into the genes of the modern human.

"Roger. Roger Shannon. Likewise, miss. But what are you doing in the lighthouse? And how did you get in? I know the door was locked. Locked it meself."

"Oh, was it? I didn't notice," she said noncommittally.

"Right. Well, might I come in, then?" he asked gesturing towards the doorway she was blocking.

"Oh, of course. Silly me." She backed up to let him through. As he stepped through, his eyes darted to the flag locker.

"What brings you to Inishtrahull Island, Miss Grant?" the black haired young man asked her.

"Is that where I am? Sorry, I'm a bit lost. I was just wandering about and saw the lighthouse and decided to see if anyone was home."

"Just wandering about? Are you off your nut? It's an island, miss. Did you come over on a boat? Who did you come with?"

"Oh, well. Yes, I came over on a boat, of course. With my mom and dad. They're around here somewhere, I'm sure."

Roger looked at her with a smirk that silently screamed that he knew she was lying through her teeth.

"I suppose that makes more sense than having just stepped out of the flag locker," he said smoothly, watching Claire's face for the look of surprise which she was too slow to stop. With a grin of triumph Roger stepped over to the flag locker and flung it open, exclaiming, "Aha!"

They both stared with dismay at the array of multicolored flags arranged in little cubbyholes in the closet called the flag locker. Claire gave a screech of horror and rushed to the door and stood by Roger's side, searching the flag locker with her eyes for any hint of the hallway which was very much not there. Roger watched her just as intently.

"So you did come through this door?" he asked.

"Yes, but where did it go?" she all but wailed.

"It disappeared two years ago." He said resignedly. Claire turned to look at Roger in shock.

"You know about the hallway, Roger?" she asked, trying to reestablish her calm and think rationally. This was a mystery and logic would see her through it, she was sure.

"That'll be true enough. I came through it three years ago. This island is at the tippy top north point of Ireland. It was inhabited until a few years ago; now it's just the lighthouse keeper and me that lives here."

"So the hallway just vanished? I didn't know they could do that."

"I didn't either. They never had before. Of course I'd never stayed as long in one as I did here. They were always there waiting to take me back to 1989 with only 59 minutes having elapsed no matter how much time I stayed in one. I could always ride the lift back to the hotel in Waterford."

"1989?"

"Year of our Lord. Here, it's 1938. It was 1935 when I came here. I opened the door to make sure it was still there most every day. It wasn't there one year to the day that I came through. I couldn't figure how to make it come back. When I saw you, I knew." He closed the door. "Here, you try."

With a shaking hand, Claire reached out and turned the handle. The door opened and instead of neatly folded and arranged flags, they saw the grey carpeted hallway where no hallway should be. Claire looked over at Roger who was shaking. A tear ran down his cheek.

"Oh, Lord," he whispered. "I can go home. But I've grown three years older. My own mum won't know me."

"Roger. Listen. This door doesn't go to 1989 and the elevator doesn't go to a hotel. It opens in 2016 in a library in America."

"No, it can't be." With that he shouldered past Claire into the hallway. She followed him, closing the door behind her. He jogged down the corridor and turned left hastily, searching for something. She ran to keep up with him, her book bag banging against her hip. Roger made a couple more turns and stopped, turning to look in direction, looking bewildered. Claire stopped by him.

"We'll get lost, Roger. Come back with me and I'll show you the elevator." Meekly he turned to her and nodded. He looked white as a ghost and she was afraid he might pass out. She led him back the way they had come until they found a spray painted mark indicating the way back to the elevator. When they got close, they stopped when they heard the whirring and humming coming from the next corner.

"The weird boxy thing," Roger muttered.

"The rat parade," said Claire. Roger nodded. She peeked around the corner. The Roomba/death bot was near to screaming with frustration as it tried to scrub the spray paint off the wall on the corner. The mark was high enough up that the robot couldn't reach it easily. What it could reach didn't seem to be responding to the scrubbing brush. It beeped and booped in frustration and emitted high pitch whistles like a steam engine. Several large rats prowled the nearby area, sniffing the carpet. Claire was a little worried they could track her like a bloodhound, but they didn't seem to stray very far from the robostrosity.

"Maybe we can just walk past it," suggested Roger.

"Maybe. You first," Claire countered then watched in shock as Roger nodded and walked around the corner. She peeked around the corner as he casually sauntered by, ignoring the robot and the rats. At first all appeared to be well with this novel strategy, but then the robot stopped its frantic cleaning attempts and the rats all picked up their noses off the carpet. As one, the whole ensemble turned to watch Roger.

"Uhoh," breathed Claire, frantically digging in her book bag.

Roger couldn't take it anymore and made a dash for the elevator button at about the same moment the robot let out a strident screech and the nearest rat latched onto Roger's pant leg. Claire ran around the corner and kicked the first rat she came to high into the air as she pulled out the Tupperware container of bread crumbs and scattered them in an explosion of stale rye particles. The robot's screech became a wail of anguish as it started trying to vacuum the crumbs up and the rats began running around frantically eating them.

Roger had pressed the button and it was with great relief that they piled into the now open elevator.

Claire considered for a moment which button to press. Not three where her mother would most likely be. Nor five where her brother would be, but then again he might be on two waiting for her. She decided on the lobby and pressed for one.

Roger shrugged noncommittally. "This lift is not the same one I rode," he said.

They stepped out into the lobby. Roger looked around and shrugged again. Claire wished for a minute she had taken him to the computer lab. That would have astonished him for sure. They walked to the lobby doors and she pushed them open so they could walk out and sit on the steps.

"This is not 1989," said Roger. "I don't recognize any of these cars." Claire resisted the urge to tell him that she had told him so. She sat quietly by his side and tried to imagine how he would feel, knowing that although he had escaped the lighthouse island, he was still displaced, not just in geography but also in time. He couldn't go home. Roger had aged three years but twenty-seven had passed. How would he explain that? They sat for a while, lost in their own thoughts and then Claire realized what time it was. Although she had only spent a few minutes in the lighthouse world, 59 minutes had passed. Her mom would be looking for her soon. She explained this to Roger.

"I don't know what I'm going to do. All I can think of is going back to the lighthouse," he said listlessly.

"If you do, I can come and visit. Or I could open the door for you and you could come explore the hallway with me." Roger seemed to brighten at the idea.

"That beats trying to find a place in your world. It would be so strange to me, I'm sure. And we can keep looking for the lift back to my world," Roger said hopefully.

"Ok," Claire replied. "Let's get back to the elevator and see if we can find our way back to your lighthouse. Tomorrow, bring a hammer or something with you."

"A hammer?"

"Never know when it might be needed. For, you know, rats and stuff."

"Ok… a hammer for rats. I'll try." With that, they turned back to the library doors and in a jiff were back in the elevator. Claire pulled out her little key. Roger pulled a large black iron key out of his pocket. It looked like something out of an old movie.

"This is the key I used."

"Cool. Hang on to it. You might get a chance to use it still."

When they re-emerged into the hallway, the robot and its rat entourage were not visible, but they could hear the mechanical lamentations of the cleaning 'bot somewhere nearby. They wasted no time and jogged back to where the lighthouse door was. Roger grasped the handle but it wouldn't open for him.

"Here, let me try," said Claire. It opened easily under her hand. Roger looked into the lighthouse mournfully. "It must only work for someone from the world the elevator leads to," she mused aloud.

"I'll see you tomorrow. Same time as today. And if for some reason I don't show, don't panic. Just keep coming back every day."

"Sure and I'll do it," said Roger in his lilting accent. He stuck out his hand and she shook it firmly.

"Til tomorrow then," she said. He nodded and strode through the door. Claire closed it behind him and raced for the elevator.

_____

"Who was the boy?" was the first thing Nick said to her when she was back in the library.

"What boy?"

"I watched the elevator indicator lights. When they went out, I knew you had gotten in. Then they went down to the lobby. I took the stairs down and saw you sitting with some boy on the steps."

"Oh. Just a boy I met in the library."

"I've never seen him."

"Whatever."

47

Nick didn't say anything else about it, but Claire knew that this was just one more log on the fire. Eventually, the obnoxious little stink was going to do something. She put it out of her mind, since she had to do her homework all the way home and after they ate dinner.

When nobody was paying attention, she searched her mom's bathroom drawers until she found a heavy antique sterling silver hairbrush that she knew was in there somewhere. Claire remembered being swatted on the butt with it as a misbehaving younger child and knew that as a weapon, it had heft and potential. When she found it, she put it in her mom's car under the rear seat for easy retrieval later.

Chapter Five: Vanishing Act

Mrs. Hogwallup done R-U-N-N-O-F-T. – Washington Hogwallup, "O, Brother Where art Thou?"

Claire hardly noticed when she set a record for freshman girls' pole vault at Alex Clancy High on Thursday during PE. Likewise, she sailed through the rest of the school day on autopilot, hardly noticing anything. She couldn't wait to see Roger that afternoon. At least that was the case until one of her friends, Amanda, asked her if she wanted to practice for the spelling bee with her. The spelling bee was today after school! Oh, no. Roger was going to be waiting for her in the lighthouse. How was she going to explain standing him up on the very first time they were supposed to meet? She considered feigning (great word) sickness in order to get out of the bee, but that would just get her taken home. She couldn't very well just skip it. Nothing for it but to go ahead. She would see Roger tomorrow.

She was so distracted she misspelled 'adroit' by adding a 'gh' before the 't.' Amanda looked annoyed.

"Are you on drugs or something, Claire?" she asked rhetorically.

"What? Oh. Not unless you count my allergy medicine." She grinned sheepishly. "Sorry, was just distracted."

"Well, get *un*-distracted, Claire. Or you're gonna bite it on the first round."

"Wouldn't that be a good thing from your point of view, 'Manda?"

Amanda laughed. "Nope. I need you to stay in till the end, because I know I can beat you. You're like on another planet or something. What's his name?"

"Who's name?"

"The boy you're crushing on, doofus." There *was* a boy, but Claire was definitely not crushing on him. She had no romantic feelings toward Roger at all. She was briefly tempted to tell Amanda about Roger. Of course, that wouldn't work unless she left out all of the story of how they met which wouldn't make much sense. And she couldn't tell her the truth. Amanda would never believe Claire. Claire might even end up with a reputation for being a nutjob. Or worse, she might have to explain her crazy story to an adult. She had been tempted for a while to spill the beans to her mom, but couldn't bring herself to do it. It was such a huge secret that she longed to tell someone. Now was not the time, however.

"Whatever. I'm just thinking about the track meet."

"Yeah, I heard you broke the old record of twelve feet by an inch today. Good for you. Now spell clairvoyant."

Claire got 'clairvoyant' right and was gratified when Amanda missed 'mischievous.' Afterwards, time started moving more normally and Claire stopped sleepwalking through class, since she didn't have anything to look forward to. When the bell rang and she went to the auditorium for the spelling bee, butterflies started fluttering about in her stomach. She controlled her breathing and maintained her calm. I've got this, she thought.

And so she did until the sixth round when she bombed 'herpetology.' Fortunately, Amanda cratered on 'malign' the round before, so she wouldn't be tormenting Claire over it. Over all, Claire took fourth place, which wasn't bad. A guy named Ramon won it when he spelled 'misogyny' correctly. Oh, well, she had given it her best. You can't win them all. She could do better next time, yadda

yadda yadda. Her dad was in the audience and said all those things to her in the car on the way home.

The next day when she finally got to the lighthouse, Roger hugged her in excitement, his face a radiant beacon of joy that would have outshone the lighthouse itself.

"When you didn't show yesterday, I was certain I would never see you again, Claire," he admitted. He understood when she explained about the spelling bee and insisted there was nothing to forgive. He did make fun of her for missing such an easy word.

"Oh, yeah? You spell it, Einstein."

"Well, that's not the point is it? I'm not in a competition, now am I?" he evaded.

"Yeah, that's what I thought. You don't even know what herpetology is, do you?"

"It's a disease, isn't it?"

Claire rolled her eyes. "No, silly. It's the study of reptiles and amphibians."

"Well, there ya go, lass," he said, expanding his Irish accent to comical proportions. "The Emerald Isle is no so big on reptiles and such, don't ya know? We dunna have nary a snake on the place. We dunna have the need for a word like that."

Claire laughed heartily at that. He had a point. Not a lot of herpetology going on in Ireland.

Roger wanted to get into the hallway and start opening doors right away, but she explained that she didn't have the time today. Her hour was already spent because she had come into the lighthouse. Roger was crestfallen, but accepted it graciously. She insisted that he show her around the lighthouse and the island. While they took in the stunning view from the top of the lighthouse, she did her homework. Roger helped by making funny faces and throwing pebbles at her from time to time. Funny how it amused

51

her. If her toad faced brother had done such a thing she would have thrown him down the stairs. Her homework didn't take very long and they were off to see the rest of the island.

He showed her the abandoned house that he had made his home. It was nice enough, if a bit rough. No indoor plumbing. There was a well and an outhouse. That must make going to the bathroom in the middle of the winter unpleasant, she thought. When she asked him about it, he confirmed that it was a grim undertaking. There was a garden that he kept up and a couple of feral cats as well as some sheep on the island. In his original time, the island was a designated wildlife refuge, but not yet.

Claire asked Roger why he spent a year in such a bleak and inhospitable place. Roger explained that his great grandfather had lived on the Island and used to tell Roger stories about how wild and beautiful the island was. It was obvious he longed to go back but never got the chance. When Roger discovered the door that led to the island, he used it as a private refuge, knowing that he could spend as much time there as he wanted and only an hour would go by in his home world. He became entranced by the sleepy beauty of the place and eventually grew complacent as he spent time fixing up his cottage. If he had known he could be trapped here, he never would have stayed.

Roger explained that he couldn't introduce her to the lighthouse keeper, for obvious reasons, but pointed out his well-maintained cottage from a nearby ridge. He and the keeper got on well and the older man shared his provisions with Roger willingly, believing him to be a homeless runaway. Between the sharing, his garden and fishing, Roger lived fairly well. It was no life of luxury, but then there were no hard demands on his time either. He was growing weary of it and looked forward to exploring more doors.

Over the next few weeks they did explore more doors. Claire couldn't meet Roger every day, but between after-school activities and weekends, they were able to spend quite a bit of time exploring the many worlds available through the doors in the corridor. Some were places in her world, doors to other times and places. Others were literally doors into other worlds, some she could recognize from works of fiction, most she could not. She came to realize that the hallway was, for all intents, infinite. There was no more limit to the doors than there was to human imagination. Claire was unsurprised when Roger explained the sideways eights were actually the symbol for infinity known as a Moebius Strip. Claire and Roger's exploration was limited more by the difficulty in finding their way back to the elevator and the lighthouse door than by the physical dimensions of the fantastic extra floor. Even that was ameliorated (more vocab goodness) by the fact that the doors didn't keep their exact positions. They… drifted, for lack of a better term.

At first, this realization frightened Claire because she expected to eventually not be able to find the lighthouse door again. But she soon realized that the more she opened the lighthouse door the closer it drifted to the elevator. Soon enough, it was the first door she saw when she stepped out of the elevator doors. They also became quite adept at evading the rat parade. They developed a way of luring it away from the area they wanted. They would make a mess close to a spot where two corridors crossed and blow an airhorn, then retreat around the corner and wait for the robot and its furry entourage to find the mess. Then they just ran around the corner. They used this method several times to good effect. Claire also had her brush, just in case. Every day she would put it behind a row of books on nuclear physics in the library and retrieve it the next day and stow it in her book bag.

She came to realize that a lot of the worlds were dangerous. Some were just weird. There were doors that were both. Once they opened a door that was labeled "Marty." The door handle was a strange pattern, almost like a reptile's skin. Inside was a darkened bedroom. When they stepped through the door, a boy in the bed sat up. He didn't act surprised at all to see them. He did seem a bit alarmed, but for their safety, not his.

"Quickly!" he hissed urgently. "Get onto the bed before he gets you." Claire was going to ask before who got her, but Roger leaped onto the bed extremely quickly.

"Just jump, Claire," he said as he sailed through the air. Her curiosity abandoned in the face of his urgent compliance, Claire also jumped onto the bed as fast as she could.

"Safer to just do it and ask why later," explained Roger. Claire nodded in agreement.

"Are you Marty?" she asked once they were comfortably situated on a large bed, surrounded on three sides by bedroom floor.

"Nope, I'm Bob," said the boy in pajamas with whom they shared the spacious bed covered in a bedspread with a choo choo train motif. "Marty's under the bed," he continued ominously.

"And *why* is Marty under the bed, then?" asked Roger.

"Because that's where he sleeps," replied Bob.

"And it's Marty that we should be afraid of?" asked Claire.

"Nah, no need to fear him. He's easy to manage," said Bob matter-of-factly. "Here, watch." Bob reached under the covers and brought out a can of beans, a can opener and a string. He opened the can of beans and suspended it from the string. Bob then lowered the can of beans over the side of the bed until it was just above the floor, then let it tap the floor rhythmically a couple of times. With a violent eruption of explosive force, a massive alligator burst from under the bed and grabbed the can of beans. The alligator had a patch over one eye socket and was dressed in a torn and ragged lady's housecoat which, under its many discolorations of mud and what appeared to be blood, looked to be pink. Its tail looked like it had tire tracks on it and its face was covered in burn scars. Almost as quickly as he had appeared, Marty vanished back from whence he had come. Splashing and sloshing sounds came from under the bed.

Roger and Claire were both stunned. The expanse of empty floor between them and the closet door through which they had come took on much more sinister proportions. What had been an innocuous distance of soft carpet became more akin to a minefield. It looked like a mile. Claire didn't think she could raise the courage to ever step off this bed. Bob laughed with delight.

"Silly ole 'gator," said Bob, still snickering.

"Uhm, Bob," said Roger, tentatively. "Does Marty eat other things, you know, besides beans? Like maybe people?"

"Heck yeah! People are Marty's favorite food. He once ate five ladies at one of my mother's bridge parties. He ate a mailman… and the principal of my school. And our cat. And the janitor." He seemed most upset about the cat.

"Right," said Roger.

"So. How do you get out of your room, Bob?" asked Claire.

"Oh, that's easy. I usually throw something off the bed into the far corner, then make a dash for the door."

"Ok, that makes sense, I guess," said Claire. "And he never figures that out?"

"Yeah, he has. If he's thinking, he won't fall for it. But that's easy to figure out, cuz he won't go for the bait and you can hear him laughing under the bed at his own cleverness." This whole situation was starting to freak Claire out. There was something extremely wrong with Bob. And his bed. There shouldn't be nearly enough room under this bed for such a huge reptile. And why had nobody called animal control to deal with the ravenous cross dressing alligator under a little boy's bed? And why on earth did Marty have a name?

"Bob, we need to get back to the door to your closet," said Roger, seemingly reading Claire's thoughts. "How do you think we could manage that?"

"I dunno. There's not enough time for both of you to get through that door even if he falls for the bait," whispered Bob.

"Why are we whispering?" asked Claire

Bob looked at Claire like she was maybe a little slow in the head. "So Marty doesn't hear us, of course," he whispered back.

"Of course… You realize that alligators can't understand speech, right?" said Claire. Bob cocked an eyebrow at her as if to say, "Oh really?" From under the bed came the unmistakable sound of Marty snickering. It was a dry, throaty sound and it sent chills up Claire's spine. "Never mind."

"I'll distract him for you," whispered Bob as he leaned in towards Roger and Claire. "I'll throw the bait out and he won't go for it. Then I'll drop this shoe. When he attacks it, thinking it's me, I'll jump out of bed and run out of the room. Hopefully, he'll chase me like usual. After he leaves, you two head for the closet, ok?"

This plan seemed insane to Claire. But then, the whole situation seemed crazy. Bob didn't seem too concerned about being chased by a ten-foot long alligator that could inexplicably fit under a six-foot bed. So they agreed.

Bob produced an old chewed up rubber ball and a half disintegrated shoe covered in reptilian saliva. This was an old tried and true procedure by the looks of it. As soon as he tossed the ball into the corner, Bob dropped the shoe off the end of the bed. When the ball bounced, Marty came halfway out from under the bed like he was going for it, but immediately turned and grabbed the shoe in his mouth. Fearless and cackling madly, Bob jumped onto Marty's head and used it as a springboard to leap through the door out of the room. Fast as lightning, Marty blasted out the door after him. They saw Marty hit a tripwire just outside the door and tumble out of sight down some stairs. Sounds that could only be described as cartoonish grunts of pain and what might have been bad words echoed up the stairs.

Claire sat and stared, speechless. Roger grabbed her by the arm and half dragged her off the bed.

"Come on!" he yelled. Claire recovered her wits enough to run and they both dashed for the closet door. Once it was closed behind them, they collapsed in the hallway, scared half to death. Then they started laughing. It started slow but as the tension drained away, the situation seemed more and more hilarious. Soon they were paralyzed in fits of hysterical laughter. Once they were able to calm down, Claire said simply, "I never want to go to the zoo again."

"What? I thought you wanted to be a herpetologist?" said Roger. She hit him, then they laughed some more.

They began to accumulate interesting gadgets and trinkets from different worlds. These, for the most part, they would store in Roger's lighthouse world. They found that Roger could enter worlds as many times as he liked and the 59 minutes would not pass on the outside, so if they found something they wanted to store or conversely if they needed something they had already saved, he would go into the lighthouse world and deposit or retrieve whatever they needed while Claire waited outside in the corridor. He could go in or out of any world as often as he wanted, but Claire always had to open the door.

Some things they collected they would keep with them. Claire found a magical wand that blasted ice crystals from its tip with quite a lot of power. She kept this item in her book bag. Roger found a pair of sun glasses that let him see in the dark which he kept on all the time now. They made some friends. They made some people angry. They found worlds they liked to visit often and even stay for weeks. And they found doors to avoid at all costs.

Claire and Roger had just returned from a week-long stay on a tropical island overrun with unicorns. Claire had a tan she was worried would be noticed. Her anxiety was increased when she returned to the library and her brother immediately confronted her.

"Where do you go when you get in that elevator?" Nick asked belligerently.

Claire was shocked. "What? What do you mean? I went to the third floor."

"We're on the third floor."

"Exactly. This is where I went."

"When you get in the elevator alone, it goes up to the sixth floor, then it vanishes. It also disappears right before you show up again. And in between you are nowhere to be found. I've searched for you repeatedly. Even in the girls' room, so don't try that. Tell me where you go."

"That's crazy, Nick," said Claire, trying to stay calm and sound logical. "It's an elevator, it only goes where the buttons tell it to. It can't disappear. I bet the indicator light goes out whenever it's not being used."

"Nope. It only goes out when you get into it," Nick insisted angrily, then switched to pleading. "Take me with you, Claire. Please?"

"What? No! I mean, there's nowhere to go." Claire had slipped with that one. From the look on his face, Nick knew it, too. She got him to drop it, but she had the feeling that he had something up his sleeve.

The next day, she and Roger visited a desert bazaar where she purchased a spell to change the color of her eyes at will. She used a variety of gold and silver coins they had picked up here and there. Most coinages would work to some degree in the bazaar, even US pennies and silver dollars. She was eager to see if the spell would work in her own world. It took her several hours to master using the strange, powerful words and the finger motions. But when she did, she was able to turn her eyes a brilliant purple. They were a much more aggressive shade than the softly violet eyes of Alidraal. Claire's eyes were more like an amethyst in the sun. Roger applauded.

"Really compliments your hair, Claire."

Claire was doubtful. Her hair was a violent shade of red. After her history class learned about Erik the Red last year, she had to endure being called Clairic the Red for a month or two. She didn't see how purple eyes would go with red hair. She would definitely be able to see if they stayed purple when she got back, and if she could change them in their world. It was one of the few times she rushed a bit getting back. Roger seemed a bit irritated by her eagerness to abandon him. She felt a little bad about it. He seemed to cheer up a bit when she hugged him bye.

As soon as she got back to the library, she rushed to the bathroom to look in the mirror. Her eyes were still purple! That was awesome. She ran through the spell to change them back, but it didn't work. Claire took a deep calming breath and tried again. Nothing. Maybe she had gotten it wrong? She dug the parchment with the spell out of her pocket and made sure she was doing it right. She practiced for a few minutes and tried again. Nope. Oh, crap. She ran out of the bathroom and to the elevator, hoping the spell would work in the corridor.

When Claire got in the elevator, she noticed the little access door that her key fit was open already. She must have forgotten to close it when she was in such a hurry to get to a mirror. To make matters worse, the elevator stopped on the third floor and her mother of all people got in! Claire avoided looking at her mother's face. Maybe she wouldn't notice that Claire's eyes were purple.

"Oh, there you are, Sweetie. Have you seen Nick? I can't find him anywhere."

"Nope, haven't seen him. Did you try the computer lab?" she said with her head averted.

"Well, duh," answered her mom. "Of course I tried the computer lab. He's not there. What in the Sam Hill...? Oh. Nice contacts, Claire. When did you get those?" Her mother had clearly noticed Claire's purple eyes. She obviously didn't approve but was going out of her way to be a tolerant, understanding parent who didn't force her own preferences on her children. Claire was touched by her leniency. It made her feel bad for lying about her eyes, but there wasn't any option, really. What was she going to do, tell her mother she used sorcery to turn her eyes purple and couldn't seem to turn them back?

"Oh, I ordered them online. From a doctor's office. Totally safe." Please don't ask what website. Please Please Please...

"Well, they are a bit startling, but how you spend your allowance is your business, I suppose. But you're not going to sleep in them. That's just not healthy."

"Ok."

"The one day I get off a bit early and Nick vanishes," muttered her mother. At the word vanish, a horrible suspicion entered Claire's thoughts. She hoped there was no link between Nick's absence and the open service panel in the elevator. "We'll have to split up and search. I wish the library had a PA system. You take the fifth floor computer lab and work your way down. I'll take the lobby and work up. You use the elevator and I'll take the stairs. Be sure and check the bathrooms." They rode the elevator down to the lobby and her mom got off. "If you find him, meet me here in the lobby."

Claire immediately went back to the corridor and worked the spell on her eyes, hoping it worked. She didn't have a mirror and the elevator doors weren't shiny enough to see her reflection. But what she did see was a red crayon mark on the wall leading off to the left. Someone had been in the corridor besides her or Roger. She would bet dollars to doughnuts it was her brother. She started running down the corridor, following the red crayon mark and shouting Nick's name. Claire came to a stop when she saw the cleaning robot and its rodent accompaniment up ahead, diligently scrubbing off the red crayon mark. Great. Her brother was lost in an infinite array of worlds and a robot was scrubbing off his map home.

Chapter Six: The Hunt Begins

"You take people, you put them on a journey, you give them peril, you find out who they really are."

— Joss Whedon

Claire was faced with several choices, all of which looked like bad options. If she started looking for Nick, then her mother would have two missing children and no answers. It would take her an hour for each door she went through looking for Nick. Plus, the hour to go get Roger to help her. She might be gone for days if Nick didn't find his own way out. If she went back to tell her mother, she might not be believed. That would be as good as abandoning Nick. Even if Mom did believe her, there was a good chance she wouldn't allow Claire to go back into the corridors to search. Even worse, she might insist on accompanying Claire. Even in such a dire situation, Claire couldn't bear the thought of exposing her secret to the eyes of parental authority. Or exposing her mother to Orcs or alligators.

Another choice was where to begin her search. And whether to spend an hour to get Roger. Each door they went through in search of Nick that he wasn't in, was another hour for him to get in trouble... or killed. Claire was trying very hard not to freak out, but it was difficult when she thought about her baby brother in some of the horrible situations possible in this corridor. Her rising panic was making good decisions difficult. She took a deep breath and counted to ten. First things first. That robot had to be stopped from erasing any more of the crayon line Nick had drawn. It was a matter of protecting her family and she felt her blood boiling in response to the challenge.

Claire stormed around the corner of the hallway, intent on destruction and mayhem. In her hands were a massive silver hairbrush and what looked like a stick coated in frost. She strode purposefully toward the rat parade, her boots making muffled thuds on the carpet that she made no attempt to hide.

"Hey, you, vacuum cleaner!" she shouted. The cleaning bot and its attendants stopped their scurrying activity and looked at her. The 'bot bleeped in anger and the rats started toward her, their beady eyes glinting in the soft light, whiskers twitching. "Your services are no longer needed. Go back to your closet!" she yelled. More angry beeping. Without slowing her pace, she aimed the stick at the robot and loosed a bolt of speeding ice at the whirring little trashcan. With a bloop of dismay, it tried to dodge to the side, but was far too slow. Her icy missile struck it a glancing blow that sent it spinning across the hall, screeching electronically. A couple of the rats ran back to assist it. The rest kept coming and it wasn't very long before they got too close and she was able to hit one with a well-aimed blow from her silver brush that was really more luck than skill. The silver brush connected with the hairy rodent with a sickening crunch that felt to Claire like hitting a balloon filled with jelly and popsicle sticks.

That unfortunate rat slid down the far wall bonelessly, leaving a bloody smudge. The rest of them stopped and began to back up. Farther down the hall, the robot was retreating slowly, sparks flying from an icy hole in its carapace. She kept advancing as they retreated and soon enough she was standing even with where the crayon mark stopped mid-wall. Claire looked around. She didn't recognize any of the nearby doors except for one, and none of them had marks on them that might indicate Nick had chosen it to go through. Quickly, she wrote down the names on the plaques and the color of the door handles. She also pulled out the spray paint and pained a huge 'X' on the wall where the crayon mark ended. That would have to do.

Time to go tell Mom. She returned to the elevator. As she was pressing the call button, a possibility occurred to her. Why not text her mother an explanation? Or better yet, she could call her and try to explain that she thought she might know where Nick was and that she would be gone a while looking for him. That way, she could keep the details secret. Then she would go get Roger. She climbed in to the elevator and went down to the sixth floor. Once the elevator indicator came on, she got three bars on her cell. With a trembling finger she dialed her mom and braced herself for a very difficult conversation.

"Claire!" Her mom answered. "Thank goodness. I was getting worried. You found him?"

"Not exactly, Mom. But I think I might know where to look for him."

"What do you mean? If you know where he is, go get him. I'm ready to go home."

"It's not that simple, Mom." Silence. "It may take a while to find him."

"You're not making any sense, Claire," her mom answered, a note of hysteria evident in her tone. "If he's in the library, how long could it take to get him?"

"That's just it. He's not exactly in the library. He's… somewhere else."

"What? Where did he go? What are you talking about? Come down to the lobby, and explain this to me."

"Sorry, Mom. I can't. I'm wasting time trying to explain it to you. You'll just have to trust me. I have to go get him."

"Ohmygod. What do you mean? Is he in trouble? Where are you?" her mom was definitely panicking now.

"I may be gone a while, Mom. Hours. Maybe even days. It's my fault. I'm sorry." Claire was starting to tear up. She sniffled. "I love you, Mom." She hit the end button on her phone and the elevator button in the service panel at the same time. Her mom immediately tried to call her back, but before she could even reject the call the elevator left the sixth floor on its way to the mysterious hallway and the call dropped. Claire pocketed the now nearly useless phone, then to keep the battery from dying, she turned it off.

When she stepped out into the corridor for the third time that day, Claire sat against the wall and cried for several minutes. Worry for her brother and her mother gnawed at her. She felt guilty. She had left the panel open. What if she had just told her mother about the elevator? Or even just admitted it to Nick and taken him with her? He might still be here and ok. She had screwed this up royally. Heck, she even felt bad about the rat she had probably killed. Finally, Claire was able to grab hold of herself and get a grip. Slowly, her sniffles ran out. Claire dried her eyes and stood up. First, she had to get Roger. With renewed purpose, she grabbed the lighthouse door handle.

It wasn't yet dark on Inishtrahull Island, but it was close. An oil lamp burned on a hook by the exit door and another one at the bottom of the staircase. Outside, she could see a beam of light sweeping the wind-whipped ocean from the top of the lighthouse. Sporadic drops of cold rain were being pushed about by a blustery, gusty wind from the north. She ran as fast as she could go without risking a fall until she was winded. By that time Claire was close to the little cottage Roger was living in. She could see a light in the window. Good, he was home. Without bothering to knock, Claire opened the door and barged into Roger's little kitchen... Where he was seated eating dinner with an older man.

The lighthouse keeper stared in shock at an oddly dressed young woman on what he thought was an uninhabited island; his spoonful of soup frozen halfway to his mouth. Roger also stared in shock at Claire, but for entirely different reasons. How was he going to explain an obviously American girl who knew him barging in on dinner on the northernmost island in Ireland? For much the same reason, Claire was stunned into immobility in the doorway. Roger broke the awkward tableau.

"Er… Claire! Good to see you. I didn't realize you were arriving today! Danny, this is Claire. Claire, Danny, the lighthouse keeper here on Inishtrahull Island."

Danny stood, putting his spoon back in the bowl. "How do ya do, ma'am?"

"Just fine, and you?" answered Claire who was obviously not fine but near tears again.

"Tolerable well, I suppose. Who brought you over on such a blustery evening, if you don't mind me asking?" asked Danny.

"I came on a helicopter," answered Claire and immediately regretted it when she saw Roger vigorously shaking his head. He mouthed the words 'Not invented yet.' Oops.

"A what?" asked Danny.

"It's a special kind of boat. With motors."

"Yes, of course," said Danny skeptically. "What will they think of next? Still, tis a right nasty evening to be on the sea. At least you look dry, miss."

"I am, thank you, sir."

"Please, have a seat, Claire," said Danny. "And some soup. "Roger, where are your manners this evening?" He pulled a rickety looking chair from the corner and pushed it up to the even more rickety table.

"I'm sorry. I'd love to," said Claire. "But there's no time to lose. I've got to get going."

"Going? Going where? Nonsense. Not on a night like this," said the lighthouse keeper. His back was to Claire and Roger while he was searching for another bowl in the cupboard. Claire took the opportunity to mouth to Roger silently.

"Nick is missing."

Roger looked puzzled and mouthed back, "What?"

"My brother, Nick, is MISSING"

"Oh," Roger said aloud, as a look of understanding appeared on his face. "Sorry, Danny. Claire and I need to take care of something." Roger was already moving toward Claire and the door. Danny turned back toward them, bowl in hand and his look of puzzlement back on his face.

Once outside, they moved away from the door and felt confident the strident wind would keep them from being overheard.

"Your brother Nick is missing?" asked Roger.

"That's what I said, Roger! He's missing!"

"Ok. Isn't that the job for the police?"

"What? No! He's missing in the corridor! He got in when I left the panel open in the elevator. Now he's gone through one of the doors and hasn't come back. We have to find him!"

"How do you know he's in the corridors?"

Claire explained about finding the panel door open in the elevator and the red crayon marks on the walls and finally about her crazed attack on the rat parade. Roger looked impressed. Then she explained about the phone call to her mom. Roger looked perplexed until she remembered he was from the eighties and showed him her iPhone. Then he looked awed.

"Ok," said Roger, overcoming his awe of Claire's temper and her technological gadgets. "What's the plan?"

"I don't know," wailed Claire. "I was hoping you could help me come up with one." Roger thought for a minute.

"Alright. First we need to get our entire stash of supplies and some food, too. Come inside and as soon as we can get rid of

Danny, we'll pack everything we need and head for the lighthouse. Pretend you're tired or sick or something and need to go to bed."

"Uhm. Won't he think it's a bit inappropriate if I sleep in the cottage alone with you?"

"I'll tell him you're my cousin."

"We can try it I suppose. Why was he looking at me all weird? Do you think it's the way I dress?"

Roger snorted. "Let's see. An American girl turns up on a remote uninhabited island in Ireland in a storm, dressed like someone from another time… with purple eyes. I can't think of any reason that would be odd. Can you?" he asked sarcastically.

"They're still purple? Arg. I'm going to get my money back from that cheat."

They went back in and Claire apologized to Danny and said she didn't feel well and needed to lie down. Danny was solicitous and wanted to know if he could help. They assured him she just needed to sleep. Danny allowed how that was a good idea and he needed to get back to his cottage before the rain began in earnest. It wasn't long before he made his retreat into the gathering gloom and left Roger and Claire alone. They wasted no time in packing all the interesting and valuable odds and ends they had collected over the past few weeks. It filled their pockets to the brim as well as Claire's book bag and Roger's old denim backpack. Roger then ransacked his cabin for food. There wasn't much. They would just have to depend on the availability of food to purchase along the way. Claire was optimistic that the search wouldn't take all that long, but Roger seemed convinced this was going to take a while. He seemed excited by the prospect of a prolonged adventure. Claire tried not to be offended by his enthusiasm.

Before they set out, Roger convinced Claire to sit down and eat some soup. It was a traditional Irish vegetable soup with celery, carrots, leeks and other delectable veggies. It was also hot and filled her stomach nicely. She realized she had not eaten anything in hours;

since the bazaar where she and Roger shared some fried pastries with powdered sugar. That was ages ago. Claire had two bowls of delicious vegetable soup while she and Roger discussed their immediate plan of action.

"Should we go to the bazaar and get more supplies or start opening the doors near where the crayon ended, do you think?" asked Roger.

"I think we need to go straight to the doors. I don't want to waste any time. He could be anywhere," she managed around a mouthful of vegetables.

"Did you notice what doors were nearest the mark? In case they move or the robo-maid comes back and scrubs off the mark?"

"I noticed the closest one was the Halloween world. I forget about the others nearby but I wrote down the names on the plaques. I spray painted an 'X' on the Halloween door, so hopefully it can't move much." Long ago, they had noticed the tendency of doors to move less if they were marked visibly. Perhaps that was the reason for the robot and rats; to keep the doors fluid by erasing marks that limited their mobility. She pulled out the short list of names she had made after her victory at the battle of the rats. Roger looked it over and mentioned one that he recognized.

"It's a castle straight out of a fairy tale. Wicked witch, handsome prince, you name it. Horrid place," said Roger, his nose wrinkled in distaste.

"We'll hit Halloween first. I'd hate to have the headless horseman get ahold of him. Or one of those creepy scarecrows with pumpkins for heads," said Claire, wiping soup off of her chin.

"Right. All Hallows Eve it is, then," agreed Roger as he put Claire's bowl in the sink. "Let's get started, shall we?" He hefted his backpack and a walking stick with the head of a dragon he traded for in some world or other.

They made sure Danny wasn't lurking about, which of course he wasn't, then made their way hastily to the lighthouse. Well, as hastily as they possibly could in the rising wind and spitting rain and the darkness punctuated by periodic lightning from just offshore. It was going to be a big storm on the island very shortly. Claire had a sudden irrational fear the door wouldn't open or it would open onto the flag locker, but felt silly when it revealed the grey corridor. Silly but relieved nonetheless. Compared to the building fury of the wind and rain from where they had just come, the unnatural quiet of the corridor felt oppressive and even more artificial than usual. Claire's ears buzzed with the sudden lack of stimuli. Great word, stimuli. Their movements sounded correspondingly inordinately loud to their ears in the quiet. Gradually, they adjusted to the eerie hallway, just as they always did. Although, Claire thought it would be a relief to get into a world that seemed less hostile than the hallway did just then.

It didn't take them long to locate the crayon mark on the wall and follow it to a door with a silver handle carved with vines, pumpkins and what looked like little bats. Bits and pieces of the robo-maid littered the carpet and hadn't been cleaned up. That was a good sign. A thin trail of some viscous liquid led off down the hall. There was a dead rat crumpled on the floor. Roger nudged the stiffening rat body with the toe of his tough leather boots. Claire shivered in revulsion at the way the rat rocked back and forth at Roger's touch. It didn't seem like she was even the same person who had done that. At least until she thought about her brother in trouble and felt her anger again, like a great leviathan rising from the darkness of the deep. Its immensity was both reassuring and troubling at the same time.

"Good job, Claire," said Roger enthusiastically and held up his hand for a high five. Claire dutifully high fived him, and tried to smile. She managed an anemic grin. Resolutely, she put the dead rat out of her mind. She grasped her wand and steeled herself for battle. Her brother could be suffering right on the other side of this door. She tried to find the battle spirit that had consumed her earlier in the hallway. Claire could feel the will to fight answering her call. It felt good to be filled with righteous anger. She felt powerful and recognized the need to keep that feeling from consuming her. Anger was bad if it led to recklessness. Claire was ready. She was resolute. Good word.

"Ready?" she asked. Roger put on his see-in-the-dark sunglasses and grasped a crossbow they had found abandoned at the site of some horrible medieval war.

"Ready," he replied, nodding his head. He looked slightly ridiculous in sunglasses indoors. But kinda cool, too. Like the Terminator. Sheesh. Claire hoped they didn't find a door with one of James Cameron's cybernetic organisms in it.

Claire grasped the silver handle and opened the door, ready for immediate attack. The door opened to reveal a moonlit night in an autumn cornfield. Dry husks rattled softly in the pleasant breeze. An owl hooted. In the distance a wolf, or a werewolf, howled hauntingly. Roger led the way and Claire closed the door behind them. She could clearly see bats flitting through the moonlit night, devouring bugs. She looked back at the door and found it was set in a burned frame of a house sitting in a clearing in an over-ripe cornfield. That should be easy to find, she thought. For a few minutes they tried moving quietly but soon gave it up as a bad job. The dry corn stalks were just too noisy and they had a fair way to go to get to the little town they knew was up ahead. The area was populated by all manner of weird creatures, from seemingly normal 18th century era townsfolk mixed with curiously modern people to harmless friendly ghosts to vicious murderous werewolves. Fortunately, the werewolves were fairly rare. Unfortunately, it seemed to always be a full moon here, so the few werewolves that lurked about were always a dangerous menace. And they were annoying, what with their incessant howling and all.

After what seemed forever, but obviously wasn't, Claire and Roger emerged from the dry crackly cornfield and found themselves on a hard-packed dirt road. A hand carved wooden sign welcomed them to The Hollow. Other than the sign, there was no indication of any town. Sitting by the sign was a Dalmatian which stood up and started wagging its tail enthusiastically when he saw Roger and Claire. He walked toward them but stopped just out of range as if afraid they might try to kick him. When they showed no hostility he sat down again and raised one paw.

"Hey, boy. That's a good dog," said Roger in that playful voice people use when they want dogs to know they're friendly. "You wanna shake, boy? Put 'er there, pardner," this last delivered in a dreadful John Wayne impersonation. Roger reached out and grasped the dog's paw. The black and white dog seemed delighted. When Roger released his paw the dog gave a short enthusiastic 'woof' and moved closer to Claire and started sniffing her book bag.

Claire patted the friendly dog's head. "You must be hungry," she said and started digging in her bag while the dog looked on expectantly. She pulled out a peach and held it out to the dog who looked at her with grave disappointment. Roger burst out laughing.

"Dogs aren't generally big eaters of peaches, Claire," he said. He pulled a hunk of beef jerky out of his backpack. "Awful stuff. Danny makes it, but it's barely edible. Like eating a football." The dog apparently disagreed because he made short work of the jerky and stood there wagging his tail, plainly hoping for more. "Sorry, buddy. That's all I can spare for now." The dog didn't seem offended. He licked Roger's hand.

"I wonder who he belongs to," mused Claire.

"No telling. He's not wearing a collar," answered Roger. "I don't remember seeing him when we came here last time."

"Me neither." Claire shrugged. "Let's keep going. Tempus Fugit."

"Tempus whatsit?"

"It's Latin. Means time is fleeting. Or time flies."

71

"Righto. How do you say red haired purple eyed she-devil in Latin?"

"I think that's 'Claire,'" she said and stuck out her tongue. Roger laughed. They started down the road to the Hollow. Their new canine friend followed closely, tail wagging.

Chapter Seven: Weenie

"What counts is not necessarily the size of the dog in the fight; it's the size of the fight in the dog."

—*Dwight D. Eisenhower*

The road to the Hollow was predictably dark and spooky. It was narrow and meandered through trees whose overhanging branches reached low enough to brush Claire's and Roger's heads. After walking face first into a ginormous spider web, Claire now walked with one hand out in front of her. Roots seemed to grab boots when nobody was looking. Roger had already sprawled head first into the dirt once. It seemed the very world itself wanted to oppress them and they did indeed feel oppressed. Only the dog seemed unaffected by the persistently hostile environment, or maybe he was just hoping for another handout. Either way, his tail never stopped wagging.

"How much farther is this Hollow, anyway?" asked Claire. The one time they had visited this particular world, they had not gone this far. They went back after encountering a roving band of scarecrows who were less than friendly. They had also sighted what looked like a man on a horse with no head and that might have had more to do with the decision to turn back than the scarecrows.

"How should I know?" responded Roger.

"I thought you had been here before," said Claire. "I mean besides the time we came together." He shook his head. "Well, crap," said Claire. "This could go on for days." No sooner had she said that, the trees thinned out as they walked over a gentle hill. A settlement was plainly visible in the silvery light.

"Or not," said Roger, grinning. Claire found herself grinning back despite her anxiety over her brother and the ominous surroundings.

The first building they came to in the town was a rundown shack with a fenced corral next to it. One skeletal black horse stood dejectedly in the gloom. A sign out front proclaimed 'Nags for Rent.' "I think shank's mare will do just fine," muttered Roger.

Next up was a saloon of some sort. Its sign said 'Happy Jack's' and it depicted a scarecrow with a jack-o-lantern for a head dancing in the wind. Minor chord piano music wafted out of the dimly lit interior.

"Good a place to start as any," said Claire. Roger nodded. The dog wagged its tail. The threesome left the dirt road and picked their way through the gloomy entrance walk to the front door and pushed through the rickety old batwing doors. The inside was a little better lighted than the outside and afforded them an interesting view. A massive Steinway grand piano stood in the corner, a forlorn dirge being tortuously wrenched from its yellowed keys by what looked like an extra from a zombie movie. In other words, a zombie. The bar was tended by a mummy wrapped in many layers of bandages which he was using to desultorily swab the interior of an ancient chipped glass. Claire made a mental note to have nothing to drink while in this establishment. An obvious and cliché vampire in his tux and cape sipped a thick red drink through a straw and chatted up a grotesque murder victim sporting an axe through her head. Mary Shelley's Frankenstein monster danced slowly, clumsily and laboriously in the middle of the dusty room, his feet completely out of time with the ghoulish music. But his moaning along was on pitch. A skeleton sat at a table in the corner. It was unclear if this skeleton was a customer or just the remains of a customer.

Claire and Roger made their way to the bar and sat down. Nobody paid them any attention. The dog made a beeline for the skeleton and after a preparatory sniff, grasped a femur in his jaws and wrenched it free. The skeleton made no complaint and the dog began to contentedly gnaw his new toy. The bartender didn't seem interested in helping them; continuing to slowly wipe the inside of that glass, smearing dirt around evenly inside it.

"Oi!" said Roger loudly. The mummy turned burning red eyes in his direction but said nothing.

"Excuse me, sir," began Claire, but the mummy cut her off brusquely.

"Beat it kid," he said in a New York accent slightly muffled by the bandages over his mouth. "You bother me."

Claire was stunned. She wouldn't have been all that surprised to be *attacked* by a mummy, because that's what mummies do. But rudeness seemed shocking because it was more personal than an arbitrary murder attempt. She didn't know how to react. Part of her wanted to be non-confrontational and leave. Her other inclinations were to burst into tears or to set the rude mummy on fire. Neither would be all that productive toward her goal of finding Nick. She swallowed both her tears and her indignation, well, not literally. Boy, was that kid going to owe her when she found him. Roger was clearly about to do something rash. She put up a hand to forestall him.

"Hey, I just want to know if you've seen my brother," she told the bartending undead monster.

"I said scram, meatsicle." He put down his forever being cleaned but never clean glass and walked toward them. The mummy's red eyes glowed menacingly from the dark recesses created by his thick bandaging. When he got to them he reached out one hand ominously and began an awful moaning sound. This sound abruptly turned to a surprised and pained gasp when Roger reached over the bar and grabbed a handful of the mummy's bandages under his chin and slammed his head onto the bar. So fast Claire didn't even see him do it, Roger had a lighter out and lit. He held it next to the extremely dry mummy's wrapped face.

"That was rude, sir," said Roger in a calm, polite tone of voice, the word 'sir' coming out in a prolonged rumbling purr. "All we want is a little cooperation. And maybe some information. Nothing to drink, thanks." Claire belatedly remembered the Irish reputation for fighting, especially in bars.

The mummy's eyes were glued to the waving flame inches from his face. Claire could hear him trying to blow it out, but the bandages covered his mouth and kept his efforts from being effective. All he managed was a little cloud of dust. Everyone had stopped what they were doing and were watching the interaction at the bar intently. Even the piano torturing zombie stared at them. Claire couldn't tell if it was from curiosity or hunger.

Claire dug her phone out and pulled up a pic of Nick. "Let's try again, shall we?" She showed the phone to the mummy, whose glowing red eyes flickered to it and back to the fire. "Have you seen this boy?" asked Claire, trying to match Roger's relaxed demeanor.

"No. I ain't seen him," spat the mummy bartender. And added a half screamed, "I swear!" when the flame came an inch closer to turning him into a torch.

"I see. Do you have any idea where we might look for him around here?"

"How should I know? Go look in the toilet for all I care…" This time when the flame came closer, it was close enough that one of the straggling strands caught fire and curled up into blackened ash. "HEY! Ok! You could go ask the witch!"

"Thank you," said Claire. "You wouldn't mind if we asked around your establishment to see if any of your, uh, patrons might have seen my brother?"

"Help yourself."

"How kind. Thank you." She nodded to Roger who released the mummy's head. It leapt backwards and nearly fell over in its haste to get away from the lighter. Roger flicked it into life a couple of times just to watch the mummy flinch; which it did. Claire heard the bartender mutter something about Happy Jack not being happy about this. She would worry about that later. They would probably be out of this world long before Happy Jack (whoever that was) would learn of their threatening the bar-mummy.

Claire made her way over to the Frankenstein monster now standing in the middle of the room, swaying in time with music that was no longer playing. He towered over Claire. She held the phone up so he could see.

"This is my brother, Nick. We're looking for him. Have you seen him?"

The green behemoth made no response. Rather than press the issue, Claire moved on. She went over to the zombie at the gargantuan Steinway, being careful not to get too close lest she become a snack.

"Seen my brother?" she asked the zombie, showing him the pic.

"Can't say that I have, miss. Of course, I wasn't looking for him either," said the zombie in a surprisingly articulate voice. Claire was startled, but hid it under a smile.

"Any idea where I could look for him?"

"You could look anywhere, I expect. But the odds are poor that you'll find him looking somewhere he's not." The zombie gave a horrid grin, bloody drool running out of his mangled mouth.

"Very logical, sir," said Claire trying to be patient. "Where would you say my odds are best?"

"Not a clue. But as the barman said, you could try the witch. She might know more than I."

"Thank you. Where might I find the witch, then?"

"Here and there. There and here. About. And Out." The zombie chuckled and abruptly went back to playing the piano. Claire recognized *Camptown Races* played in the wrong key and with strangely syncopated timing.

Claire hesitated to approach the vampire and his date, but Roger showed no reticence (another delectable delight of a word). He walked up to the pair with a spring in his step.

"Hey, guys," he interrupted the slick vamp in mid-sentence. "I was wondering, could you help out my friend, Claire? We're looking for her brother. You see a little boy by any chance?" Claire walked over and displayed the pic. Axe-to-head-lady looked at the phone.

"No, Sugar. Nobody like that's been in here."

The vampire licked his lips suggestively. "I haven't been so lucky. Yet." He laughed in a predictably bone chilling way. Claire shivered despite his corny act.

"Any idea where we can find this witch everyone is on about?" asked Roger.

"Who knows. Now if you'll excuse us, we're having a conversation," said the vampire dismissively. Claire shrugged. As they were walking out, the dog came trotting up behind them, bone in mouth.

"Excuse me," said a voice from the other side of the room. They turned to find the skeleton standing on one leg. "Might I have my leg back, if your pal is done chewing it to splinters?"

"Oh, sorry," said Claire. She took the bone from the dog who surrendered it reluctantly and she walked over to the skeleton and handed it to him.

"Thanks, young lady," said the skeleton. "And you might find the witch in the park, feeding the bats."

"Oh, thank you!" she said enthusiastically.

"My pleasure."

"Come on, Roger. Let's see if we can find the park," she said as they exited Happy Jack's. The dog looked up at her quizzically and turned his head to the side and gave a short woof. "Maybe the pooch knows something about the park." The dog barked again as if to affirm that he did indeed know about the park.

"Or maybe Timmy fell down the well," suggested Roger, snidely. Claire elbowed him in the ribs. She knelt down to the dog's level.

"You're a smart boy, aren't you?" Claire asked the dog. He wagged his tail. "You know where the witch in the park is, don't you, boy?" He woofed. "Can you show us to the park?"

"The water is cold in the well and Timmy doesn't have a jacket, you say?" asked Roger under his breath.

The dog trotted out to the road and turned to look at them and woofed again.

"Either he can show us to the park or he's pissed at your stupid jokes and is leading us to our certain demise," Claire said to Roger.

"Fair enough. My money is on demise. Let's go find out." They followed the dog at a brisk walk. He ranged ahead and would stop and look back at them impatiently, his tail slowing and speeding back up when they got close to catching up. If they were dawdling too much he would woof at them. They followed him a fair way down the main road, such as it was, past dilapidated buildings and houses, overgrown lots and yards and the ruins of abandoned, collapsed or burned structures. It was very depressing and more than a little spooky. Claire kept looking back over her shoulder expecting at any moment to see an angry mob of Halloween spooks lead by Happy Jack carrying a pitchfork and screaming for their blood. Instead she kept seeing a dark empty street through the middle of a dreary moonlit town. Sporadic howls continued to tear through the night.

Eventually, the dog turned down a side street and then made another turn, then another. Claire hadn't realized how large this run-down town was. Occasionally, they would pass some weird spook out for a moonlight stroll, but mostly the town was deserted. As they moved farther from the main road, the houses became larger and more grandiose. Now the houses were more than one story, and although they still looked creepy and unkempt, they didn't look like they were about to fall down at any moment. Lights were seen inside as whatever occupants there were went about their spooky creepy lives. Or deaths, undeaths? Whatever they were doing.

The dog came to a stop at a wrought iron gate. Through the fence they could see tombstones overgrown with weeds standing crooked in the moonlight.

"Maybe the dog isn't so bright after all," said Claire. "This is a cemetery, not a park… oh. Yes. I see. Got it."

"Took you long enough," said Roger.

"Woof," agreed the Dalmatian.

The gate wasn't locked. It opened with a horribly loud screech that sounded like nails on a chalkboard. Claire flinched.

"Could use some oil, I'd say," said Roger loudly.

"Shhh," cautioned Claire. "Let's not get the attention of the neighbors." Roger rolled his eyes.

A thick knee-deep mist rolled and swirled around everything in the park, making picking their way through it difficult because it hid things that could grab feet or bark shins. It was slow going. Claire was constantly worried about falling into an open grave concealed by the mists. They didn't immediately see anyone in the 'park' but as they walked a little farther down the main path they saw a darkened shape on a bench near a massive mausoleum. As they approached, they saw whoever it was throw something into the air. Suddenly the space just over their heads was filled with the swish of leathery wings as scores of bats descended upon whatever the person had tossed up. Busily ducking to avoid being hit by swooping bats, Claire and Roger made their way closer to what proved to be a horribly ugly old woman dressed all in black and sporting a crooked peaked hat. Hairy warts adorned her huge twisted schnoz. This was a very obvious Halloween style witch.

Claire began to screech excitedly when one bat got lodged in her voluminous hair which had frizzed out a bit in the humidity. Joining in the excitement, the dog began barking and running in circles. Roger calmly grabbed the flying rodent out of Claire's coiffure and threw it into the air, along with some painfully extracted hair. Claire clutched her chest and tried to fight down the panic associated with a bat caught in one's hair. Her heart hammered in her ears, fast and loud. The witch cackled with amusement.

"Ooo, that's funny. Here, let's do it again!" the witch exclaimed and threw a handful of small buzzing insects up in the air again. Claire dropped to the ground like a soldier expecting a mortar attack. Roger stood still in his special glasses, coolly watching all the bats flit about, devouring the released insects. The dog leapt in the air, vainly attempting to grab one of the bats. "AGAIN," shouted the witch reaching into her bag of flies.

"I think not," said Roger and he reached over and snatched the bag from the witch's grasp. He folded it closed and tucked it into a jacket pocket. The roiling mass of airborne mammals receded a bit. Claire cautiously stood back up. The dog stopped his attempt to grab a light snack and settled onto his haunches.

"Oh, poo," said the witch, pouting. "You would spoil an old woman's fun, eh?"

"ABSO-FREAKING-LUTELY!" shouted Claire. "You old, you old…"

"Witch?" offered the witch.

"Bat?" suggested Roger with a grin.

"Harridan!" finished Claire triumphantly. The witch frowned. So did Roger. Probably neither of them knew what a harridan was. "Look it up," she told them.

Roger cleared his throat. "Sorry to bother you, ma'am," he began, "but we were told you might have seen a young boy named Nick."

"You were, were you? Well, you were told wrong. I haven't seen any kids but you two fun spoilers." Another howl echoed through the night air. It seemed closer than the others. The dog raised an ear and whined.

"They didn't actually say she had seen Nick, Roger," said Claire. "They just said we might want to ask the witch for help finding him." She turned to the witch. "Please, ma'am. I'm looking for my little brother and I'm worried about him. Can you help us find him?"

"That's a different story," said the witch contemplatively. "I do indeed have certain talents and abilities that might be helpful. For instance, I can work wonders with a crystal ball…"

"Great," said Claire enthusiastically. "Let's go have a look in your crystal ball!" The witch didn't move.

"I said I could work wonders with a crystal ball. I didn't say I would." Claire's enthusiasm turned to lead in her stomach. That heavy ball in her midsection kindled to fire which threatened to burn out of control.

"Now look here, you spiteful old-," she began vehemently but stopped when Roger grabbed her by the arm and dragged her behind him.

"What she means to say, madam, is surely if we were to reimburse you for your troubles, you could see your way to help us out. If only you would name your price," Roger said smoothly, the iron in his voice overlaid with velvet.

"A crystal ball," said the witch.

"Right, you would use your crystal ball. What's your price?"

"No, that is my price. A crystal ball. I can't help you because I don't have one at the moment. Mine met with an unfortunate end a while back and I find myself sorely feeling the lack. Anyway, you get me a crystal ball of decent quality and I will do what I can to help you find your brother."

"Oh, for the love of Pete," muttered Claire. An exceptionally loud and drawn out howl reverberated through the graveyard. It echoed off tombstones and crypts and whatnot, making it hard to determine which direction it came from but it was clearly close; in the cemetery itself. The dog growled softly and its hackles raised on the back of its neck.

"I think we should be going," said Roger. "If we find a crystal ball, where can we find you?"

"1313 Elm Street. I'll be eagerly awaiting your return," she said sarcastically with a snide snicker.

Roger and Claire turned back the way they had come, but stopped dead in their tracks because approaching down the path to the gate were two large, slavering, growling werewolves. Roger and Claire quickly reversed direction.

"Is there a back way out…?" Roger tried to ask the old witch but couldn't because she turned into green mist and evaporated with a cackle. "Great," he said. "Let's go see if there's another gate out of here, quickly."

"There is," said a scarecrow with the head of a laughing jack-o-lantern that looked remarkably like the one on the Happy Jack's sign. "But I'm afraid it'll do you no good." He was holding a pitch fork, much as Claire had imagined. Two more scarecrows but with normal stuffed and painted heads were immediately behind Jack. They weren't obviously armed, but neither Roger nor Claire wanted anything to do with the trio of scarecrows advancing out of the mist.

Claire pulled out her silver hairbrush and her wand. Roger cocked his crossbow and with a vicious snapping 'clang' it broke in half, the flying pieces coming perilously close to Roger's face. Undaunted, with one hand Roger pulled out his lighter and then tossed the broken crossbow into the mist. Jack laughed.

"Such a little fire isn't going to scare me, boy," said Jack mockingly. They were still approaching and the werewolves were drawing closer from the opposite direction. Claire, Roger and the dog were trapped. There was no way they could beat werewolves on a footrace through a cemetery with half its obstacles hidden under a blanket of mist. Roger turned to face Jack and his cohorts, Claire and the dog turned to face the two werewolves. Claire tried to summon the earlier rage that helped her deal with the rat parade but it was drowning under a sea of fear. She could see the slobber dripping from their jowls and bits of meat stuck in their yellow, jagged teeth.

Claire was trying hard not to drop her book bag and weapons and run screaming into the night like her instincts were howling that she should. She felt Roger tense against her back as he prepared to do something; something violent, she suspected. The peace before the storm was shattered as the dog launched himself like a black and white spotted missile at the throat of the closest werewolf, snarling and snapping with surprising viciousness. The two of them rolled off the path and into the mist, temporarily lost to sight. Instantly, the other werewolf leapt at Claire, his jaws opened to tear out her throat. Without conscious thought, she swung the heavy silver brush at his face as hard as her pole vaulting arms would let her. Behind her, Roger threw a handful of flies into the faces of the advancing scarecrows who were immediately mobbed by a frenzy of feeding bats. And the fight was on.

Fortunately for Claire, the hairbrush was solid sterling silver and silver does unpleasant things to werewolves. For instance, break their faces; which is exactly what the brush did to Claire's opponent. The heavy thud as it struck home was several orders of magnitude more solid than the impact on the rat in the hallway. She felt bones break like glass as the silver brush turned the werewolf's jaw into a useless bag of broken teeth. Its trajectory changed as it tried to dodge, and it rolled off to the side with an earsplitting howl of pain. Blood flew in a ragged fan from its destroyed mouth as it shook its horrid shaggy head in an attempt to clear it. Although the brush and the force behind it knocked the werewolf off target, as he cratered to the side, his hind quarters struck Claire in the hip, sending her sprawling. She ignored the pain and sprang back to her feet with the speed and agility only a young athlete can produce. Claire took another swing at it with her brush but missed as the werewolf jumped back just in time, gagging and choking on its own blood. Behind her there was a bright flash and a wave of heat as Roger held a can of hair spray up to the lighter and blasted a blinding javelin of fire into the faces of the oncoming scarecrows. There were yells of fright and pain and a WOOSH as the dry straw ignited.

Claire took several more wild swings at the werewolf who obviously couldn't bite her and didn't want to fight anymore. It kept dodging and was looking for an opening to get past her. She could hear Roger continuing to spray fire around and angry shouts as the remaining scarecrows attempted to get at him without turning into their own funeral pyres. Claire reached into her bag, trying to get her ice wand but came up with the bear spray instead. She shrugged mentally, aimed the can at the wolf and ruined his day for sure. The howling and whining lycanthrope backpedaled, turned around and ran headlong into a mausoleum, knocking himself cold. The other werewolf came limping out of the crypt, the dog firmly latched onto its hind leg.

"RUN," screamed Roger as he kicked a flaming scarecrow in the stomach, knocking it to the ground to flail grotesquely as it burned. Happy Jack launched a pitchfork at Roger as the scarecrow fell, and the pitchfork hit him a glancing blow across his forehead leaving a wicked gash and clanged against the stone bench. Claire didn't need to be told twice. She took off back toward the gate as fast as her legs would carry her, ignoring the pain in her side. She could hear the thudding footfalls of Roger hot on her heels. The werewolf with the broken face declined to follow them, mainly because it was unconscious; likewise, the flaming scarecrows didn't give chase but chose to stay in the cemetery and smolder. The one remaining werewolf couldn't dislodge the dog from his haunch and thus had a major speed disadvantage. Claire and Roger didn't slow down despite the lack of obvious pursuit but kept up a prodigious pace until a painful stitch in her side forced Claire to slow to a shambling jog.

Roger didn't show much reluctance to slow down but came to a similarly ungainly trot next to her, huffing and puffing and mopping bloody sweat out of his eyes.

"I'm so out of shape," he moaned.

"Tell me about it. Holy crap, that was intense. I hope the dog is ok."

"Why? Where'd he go?" Apparently, Roger hadn't seen the dog's heroics.

"He's still back there, fighting that werewolf. Maybe we should go back and help him," said Claire halfheartedly. Despite her guilt, she didn't think she could willingly go back and face another snarling slobbering werewolf. It was a miracle they weren't dead. She stopped anyway and was on the verge of turning around, when the dog ran out of the mist, barking madly. When it got to them it stopped and turned, growling at the mist he had just run out of.

"Oh, crap," said Claire.

"Yeah, my sentiments exactly," said Roger. The dog just kept growling. His muzzle was covered in blood and more blood streaked his flanks and dripped from his teeth. Half of one of his ears was torn off, leaving a ragged ruin on that side of his head. Claire wasn't sure how much of the gore was the dog's but he had apparently given as good as he got because the werewolf had an obvious limp and was bleeding from several gaping wounds on his haunches and flanks. He didn't seem in any hurry to charge the trio but advanced slowly and cautiously, leaving a trail of bloody slobber behind him on the road.

"Don't run," said Roger. "Just keep backing slowly."

"Don't worry, Roger," she answered. "I couldn't run if I wanted to. I'm winded."

"We'll make for that house over there," said Roger, indicating an abandoned structure crouched amid weeds and junk, brooding in the silvery light. Claire nodded and they turned off the road, still backing slowly and only looking down or behind them for brief seconds, hoping one of them didn't trip and fall. Surely, that would inspire the werewolf to a more active approach and that would be the end. The dog seemed to understand what they were doing and stood in the doorway growling and snarling while they ducked inside. Once in, the dog followed them and Roger closed and latched the door.

"Quick, we have to find a rear exit," said Claire. "But be quiet."

They split up, the dog following Claire. She was walking through a kitchen covered in mold and smelling strongly of rot when she heard Roger give a yell.

"It's in the back yard, go out the front!"

They wasted no time in getting back to the front door and out onto the porch. Roger was right behind them and so was the werewolf which hit the door at a run from inside the house as Roger pushed the door closed. When the werewolf opened the door, he was hit in the eyes with twin sprays, one of flaming hairspray and one of bear spray. He slammed the door closed with an anguished yelp. Claire laughed despite herself. Roger didn't. Instead he kept the spray going until he had the dry wood of the doorframe burning, then he set fire to the dead grass in the yard and threw the empty can through the window. The house went up like the pile of dry timbers it was. It seemed like mere seconds before the house was burning merrily. Howls came from inside, sounding desperate and panicky.

"Now we go," he said. Once again, they began to run as fast as they could, now past Happy Jack's, then the hostelry. In town, behind them they could hear some sort of siren. The Hollow had a fire brigade? It was mildly amusing to picture skeletons and ghosts trying to fight a fire but they didn't have time or breath to actually make any jokes about it. It wasn't until they were to the sign reading 'The Hollow' that they allowed themselves to slow down again. When they did, they could barely breathe. They stood panting and gasping, chests heaving and aching. Even the dog was winded. But they waited too long. It was only a minute or two before they heard a depressingly close howl from the road behind them. Seconds later they caught the scent of charred hair on the breeze and the dog started growling again.

"This guy doesn't give up, does he?" asked Claire rhetorically. Roger just groaned in agreement and started stumbling through the corn field in the direction of the door. Claire and the dog followed. They made a lot of noise crashing through the field and if the werewolf couldn't smell them, there was no way it could fail to hear them unless it was deaf. In fact, she could hear the werewolf breaking its own way through the corn, making even more noise than they were.

At first it was following them, but oddly it caught up with them and was making a trail parallel to theirs far enough away that they couldn't see it or the corn it disturbed. It wasn't until the werewolf got ahead of them that they realized it knew where they were headed and was going to be waiting for them when they arrived.

Roger emerged from the corn into the clearing by the burned house first, quickly followed by Claire and the dog. Standing in front of the burned shell of a house was the bleeding werewolf, with tendrils of acrid smoke rising from his battered pelt in several places.

"Maybe I could offer it some peaches," joked Claire.

"I'd rather you hit it with that brush," said Roger, between ragged breaths.

"Woof," agreed the dog.

"Let's fan out," said Claire, not taking her eyes off the werewolf as she dug in her bag and pulled out her handy dandy werewolf bashing hair brush. She edged off to the left with her brush gleaming in the eerie light. Roger went to the right, pulling an extendable steel baton from his backpack with a wicked snick snick sound. The dog kept to the center and held the werewolf's attention with his constant low key growling and bared teeth. The werewolf tried to watch them all, but couldn't and kept his attention focused mainly on the dog who he knew from practical experience could cause him pain and anguish. Maybe Claire imagined it, but the werewolf was starting to look a little bit nervous as it realized that it might have bitten off more than it could chew.

Roger's baton gave him a significant reach advantage on the werewolf and he stepped in closer. "En garde, mate," he said and swung at the werewolf's head. The werewolf ducked the blow and lunged at Roger as the baton swished over his ears. Roger dodged in turn and the werewolf's lunge exposed his flank to the dog who latched his teeth onto the werewolf's exposed neck. It turned frantically, clawing at the dog, trying to dislodge it from his neck, and his face ran square into a silver hair brush that was advancing quickly to meet it and they connected with a very audible 'thonk.'

This time, the reverberation from the solid contact made Claire's arm and hand tingle painfully. She felt like she had whacked a tree with a lead pipe. She fumbled the brush and dropped in onto the packed dirt. Fortunately, the lights were quickly dimming in the werewolf's eyes and Roger helped it along with a brutal blow to the back of the head with the steel baton. The werewolf's eyes rolled up in his head and he collapsed in the dirt.

"Quick, let's get outa here, Claire," said Roger. The dog backed off a bit and started licking his bleeding side where the werewolf's claws had raked him.

"I've got an idea," said Claire. "What happens to a werewolf when it's not full moon anymore?"

"Doesn't matter. I think it's always full moon here. Let's get out of here before he wakes up. I don't think he's just gonna ask us for an aspirin."

"Right. It's always full moon *here*," said Claire, a mischievous gleam in her eyes. "What if we drag him into a world where it isn't a full moon?"

"Oh, I see," said Roger thoughtfully. He shrugged. "Guess there's only one way to find out, isn't there?" He grabbed one of the werewolf's legs and started to drag it to the door. Claire grabbed the other to help out. The dog looked at them like they were crazy.

In the hallway, there was no immediate change to the unconscious werewolf. The dog followed them in eagerly enough and began to smell around the hallway, his tail wagging once again. Claire and Roger opened the nearest door without more than a cursory glance at a morning desert scene and shoved the werewolf through and closed the door. They then collapsed onto the carpet in sweaty exhaustion.

"I need a shower," said Roger.

"I need two showers," said Claire.

"Woof,' said the dog.

"You know, we might owe this dog our lives. Give him some more jerky, Roger," said Claire while petting the dog affectionately on the head. Roger obligingly dug into his backpack and tossed a chunk of jerky to the dog. "We can't keep calling you dog, can we, boy," she asked the dog who was too busy wolfing jerky to respond.

"We found him in the Halloween world," said Roger. "I vote we call him Weenie." Claire giggled and clapped her hands.

"I like it. I christen thee Sir Weenie!"

"Woof," said Weenie.

Chapter Eight: Ramses

The ships hung in the sky in much the same way that bricks don't. – Douglas Adams, The Hitchhiker's Guide to the Galaxy

"You realize we will have to go in that door relatively soon, right?" Claire asked Roger as they both reclined in the hallway, trying to gather enough energy after their long run to do more than just breathe. Roger grunted. "What do we do if there's an irate werewolf on the other side, ready to tear us limb from limb?"

"Well, I think there's a better chance that a naked bloke with a horrible sunburn will be lying in the sand begging us for a drink of water," he replied deadpan. "But I suppose we could open the door with a crossbow pointed through it. If we had a crossbow… I forgot about that piece of junk." He sucked on a long cut on the back of his hand that he had just reminded himself about. He mumbled something unintelligible.

"What? Get your hand out of your mouth. And where's your walking stick?"

"I said we could use some more of whatever is in that can you unloaded on that wolf in the doorway. Just a touch of mist got on my hands and I didn't realize it until I stuck my hand in my mouth just now. Whew, that was a mistake. And I dropped the bloody stick in the park. I mean cemetery. Whatever, I lost it."

"Well, we're not going back for it. You'll just have to find another. That stuff is called bear spray. It's like pepper spray only a lot stronger. Dad keeps it for when he goes camping and hiking in the mountains. And we're out," she said shaking the empty can to demonstrate. Roger held up his hand and she tossed the empty can to him. "I doubt we'll be able to find any more."

"Something will turn up, no doubt," he said while reading the can. "Capsaicin? What's that?"

"Some chemical in plants, like peppers that trick your heat receptors in mucus membranes into thinking you're on fire."

"It works. Jeez. I could use a glass of water. I was thirsty already but now my mouth is on fire, too," said Roger, making a show of fanning his open mouth.

"Water won't work, in fact it will make it worse. Milk or bread; stuff with sugars and carbohydrates will help, but not a whole lot. It'll die down in a little while. You're lucky you didn't get a face full of the stuff. Your whole face would turn red and swell up, you'd be blind and feel like you were covered in lava."

"An experience I prefer to avoid, I dare say," said Roger. "I could do with a bit of shut eye, I'll tell you what."

"Not here, Roger. Time is passing while we're lying about in the hallway. If we are going to get some sleep, it should be in one of the worlds where we only use up an hour."

"Good thinking. Which one would you like to try?"

"Not that one," said Claire indicating the door through which they had heaved the unconscious werewolf a little while earlier. Just pointing at the door made Weenie growl softly, but without lifting his head off his paws. He was as worn out as Claire and Roger.

"That leaves those two," Roger said, pointing at the other two closest doors. "And I would prefer not that one because I don't have the strength for the fairy tale castle."

"Well that narrows it down nicely," said Claire, heaving herself up off the carpet which had begun to feel entirely too soft and inviting. It wasn't actually particularly soft or inviting, but she was bone tired. Without even reading the plaque next to the door they had chosen, Claire opened it and peered through. Roger and Weenie crowded in next to her and looked out at some sort of control room. Monitors, gauges, buttons, levers and dials adorned nearly every surface. A lattice work of Velcro on the walls held a wide assortment of tools and gadgets, both mechanical and electronic. A plain old crescent wrench was next to a piece of gear that Claire couldn't identify but reminded her of something out of Star Trek. She spotted one thing that had value: an electrical outlet. Claire jumped through the door and went to the outlet where she dug in her bag and plugged in her phone to charge.

"What are you doing, Claire?" asked Roger.

"Charging my phone, doofus. What's it look like?"

"Oh, that wacky gadget. I didn't know you had to charge it up. For all I knew it was nuclear or something."

"Now, that'd be worth having, for sure," said Claire and meant it. "Any idea what any of this stuff does? Or where we are for that matter?"

"I'm not the one that rushed in here without looking things over, toots," Roger replied, peering intently at several different monitors and meters. Weenie was sniffing a cabinet drawer intently. After a few good sniffs he started trying to open the drawer with his teeth with no luck. "This is a power gauge. It shows amperage and voltage, both of which are sitting in the green with… large numbers. Numbers that start with mega and giga. Wow. Maybe this is a nuclear power station or something?"

"Would a nuclear power station have readouts for internal pressure and…" she tapped on one readout speculatively, "local gravity?"

"Gravity? Cool. What's it say?" exclaimed Roger.

"It's a dual graduation. Two sets of numbers. Top one says '1' and the bottom one says '32.' The top one must be in g's, so one

93

is one Earth gravity. The bottom one must be in feet per second per second, because Earth's gravity is 32fps/s."

"Is there a dial or something to adjust gravity or is it just measuring?"

"I dunno," said Claire, using a built-in trackball to select menus on the display. "I can't find anything and I'm not sure what any of this does. I probably shouldn't be messing with it."

"Look at this," said Roger indicating a monitor that showed a video feed of a laboratory of some kind. Claire came over and stood by Roger, looking at the monitor. Loads of high tech lab equipment covered every convenient surface in the room shown on the screen, but no scientists used any of it. The room was vacant. "I think it's some sort of live closed circuit TV system." He pressed an arrow beside the video display and the picture changed to a cafeteria, also vacant. Roger pressed it again and it flipped to something that he was having a hard time interpreting. It looked like the outside of some metal box with lots of protrusions and equipment stuck to it. But there was no ground; the box was against a lot of black with some small lights dimly visible in the distance. The label indicated this was from camera 'Exterior 1.'

Claire who had seen plenty of sci-fi movies said, "Roger, that looks like the outside of a spaceship. I... I think we're in space."

"No way," Roger said hoarsely. "Where are all the people? And how do they keep the gravity on?"

"Both good questions. But a more interesting question is where are we besides in space? Is this a space ship or a space station in orbit? Is this the actual future or are we in some science fiction book?"

"Who knows," replied Roger. "But I found the people." He pointed at the screen which showed a sharp, clear digital video of several people in blue flight suits in a room that looked like a hangar. There was some sort of ship sitting in the middle of the floor, which was also what most of the people were doing. A couple of them were walking around, looking at stuff but they all seem bored. They looked like prisoners in an exercise yard. It seemed a bit odd to Claire that all of the personnel were apparently located in the same room. Shouldn't some of them be doing jobs somewhere else?

"You think maybe they're trapped down there?" asked Claire. The downward angle from the camera influenced Claire to think of the room as 'down there' without even knowing where the room was in relation to her. Or even where down *was* for that matter. In space, she supposed down was a very nebulous concept. All of a sudden she wanted to know where the Earth was and she looked around for a window but couldn't find one in the control room. Not knowing where she was in relation to her planet made her feel like she was on the verge of flying off into the nothingness of space. There was a moment of vertigo but it passed when she closed her eyes and mentally oriented herself towards the door. Technically there was Earth through that door. Claire felt a bit more connected to reality. She opened her eyes to find Roger looking at her with concern.

"All right, lass?" he asked Claire solicitously.

"Lass? You're not that much older than I am, *Laddie,*" Claire responded indignantly. Roger looked confused for a second but then grinned broadly.

"I guess I look fifteen or sixteen, don't I?" he asked.

"Well, yeah. You do. I assume you look that way because that's how old you are."

"Not exactly," Roger responded. "You don't age during the time you spend in the worlds in the hallway. At least I didn't, until I stayed more than a year in the lighthouse. I must have passed ten years or so exploring and whatnot. So, even though my body looks like I just got my driver's license, in experience I'm more like in my mid-twenties. Come to think of it, I never did get my license to drive a car." He laughed.

Claire was stunned. "Why on Earth did you not tell me that?"

Roger shrugged. "It's not something I think of often. It never really came up and one tends to assume their age is apparent to other people. Sorry, I didn't mean to mislead you or anything."

Claire thought about it for a few seconds. He was right, it would be odd to have to think about explaining your age to someone. She figured it was quite a bit less an issue than it would be if he had been trying to make her think he was younger. "I'll get over it," she told him. "But if you have any more big secrets that haven't come up, like maybe you're a Martian prince or a raccoon belly dancer in disguise, you should probably tell me now."

"Raccoon belly dancer?" he asked incredulously and started giggling.

"Idiot," she muttered and punched him in the arm. He stumbled backwards, still giggling and sat down on a console covered in buttons and switches. There was a loud shriek of electronic feedback. On the monitor, heads turned and stared at the camera. Several people leapt to their feet and started running.

"Oh, we've done it now," said Claire. "They're going to be here any second, screaming for blood and shooting laser cannons at us or something." She turned toward the door, planning a hasty exit, when there was another feedback shriek but not as loud or long and a female voice came over a speaker on the panel Roger had just gotten his butt off of.

"Hello?" said the voice tentatively. "Is someone there?" Claire hesitated but then started for the door again. "Hello? Please... somebody be there," the voice pleaded. Whoever owned the voice sounded desperate and completely devoid of hope.

Abruptly, Claire changed her mind and went over to the panel where Roger was staring at the controls in an apparent attempt to locate a mic switch. She selected a button that was labeled '1MC' because it had a toggle next to it that said 'XMIT.' Claire pressed the button and a short burst of feedback was replaced with the slight hum of an open mic. There was no microphone visible, but a little panel in the center of the console had a grate in it like one you might see at a fast food drive through. A little green light blinked on next to it. Before she could figure out what to say, Roger spoke into the grating.

"Somebody's here," was all he said and his amplified voice boomed from a loudspeaker mounted overhead and they could hear it from a speaker mounted outside the exit as well. After a short pause to look at the screen where the peoples' faces all wore similar looks of stunned disbelief, he said "We're here," and Claire released the button with a short burst of static. Someone screamed and someone else started jumping up and down. The lady who had spoken and was staring at the camera looked like she might start crying.

"Thank God," was all she said.

Claire and Roger looked at each other quizzically. Weenie gave a short bark and wagged his tail. The people in the hangar were going nuts, hugging each other, laughing, crying and generally celebrating.

"We're very glad a rescue mission was able to get here so quickly," said the woman in the video feed. "We thought we would all be dead long before anyone could get out here from Earth." She frowned. "You can't have come from Earth specifically to rescue us," she said. "Who are you?"

"Well this is going to get real interesting," said Claire to Roger without activating the com panel. "Can you think of a convincing cover story?"

"What? That two teenage astronauts with no space suits and no ship just showed up on this ship or station or whatever it is to save the day because it's a free day from school and we had nothing else to do? I'm sure whatever we come up with will be convincing," he said sarcastically.

"I see your point. What do you think we should tell them?"

"As little as possible." He leaned over and pressed the 1MC button. "I'm Roger and my companion here is Claire." Weenie woofed. "And our dog, Weenie." On screen, the woman looked at the camera in disbelief and sudden distrust.

"Is this a joke? How are you tapped into the internal coms? You can't be. You've got to be inside the station. How did you get here?"

Claire had a bit of inspiration. She pressed the button and said, "That's classified." Roger guffawed after she released the button.

"That'll do'er," he said with a wink. The woman frowned in annoyance.

"What are you doing on *Ramses*?" the woman asked, her voice all official sounding.

"Hold on, mum. You want to be rescued or don't you?" asked Roger. She took a couple of seconds to think about it. Several of the people had grouped around her by the camera and Roger and Claire could see them discussing the situation but not hear them. A lot of the jubilation had been replaced with confusion and impatience. One of the men activated their side of the connection.

"Yes, come let us out!" he said enthusiastically. The woman shoved him away impatiently.

"First of all, stop using the 1MC, it's a ship wide public address system. Hit the 'isolate com' button and select 'hangar'. Now, you'll have to turn off the radiation protocol, before you can get us out," she said to the mic. Roger and Claire exchanged glances.

"How do you think we do that?" Roger asked Claire.

"More importantly, why is the radiation protocol active?" asked Claire right back. "If there is a radiation leak, we could get cooked. Start looking for a radiation meter." She started looking at labels on a nearby panel.

"Or we could ask Captain Priss down there why it's active," suggested Roger.

"Good point," admitted Claire. Roger hadn't waited for a response before pressing the buttons the woman on the screen had specified.

"Oy, what's got this radiation protocol all bolloxed up in the first place?" This time his voice didn't come from any speakers mounted near them. Apparently they were only being transmitted to the hangar now.

"The coronal mass ejection from last week, of course. You guys have to have been in space at least a month in order to get out this far, so how did you ride out the CME?"

"We travel a lot faster than you give us credit for," said Roger. "How do we turn off this radiation thingy?"

"It should have discontinued automatically when radiation levels dropped below the danger threshold," replied the woman on the screen. "What's the meter say?" Roger started looking again for a radiation meter even though he had no clue what one might look like. He was concentrating on things that might be bright red or blinking. Claire, meanwhile was much more familiar with computers and had pulled up a radiation report on one of the monitors. She pressed the switch to answer the question.

"Alpha, beta and gamma levels are all in the acceptable ranges except in a room called 'Primary Reactor,' where they are elevated. It's neutron radiation that is through the roof according to the readout," she said.

"Well, that's not good," said the astronaut. "Neutron radiation indicates a reactor leak." Roger groaned loudly.

"Hell and breakfast," he said enigmatically. "That sounds B-A-D, bad. I think you were right the first time and we should leg it."

"And leave these people to probably die a long tortuous death? Besides, what if my brother is on this station somewhere? I think we should see if there is anything we can do to help."

"Normally, I'd agree that we should help get these peoples' kit un-banjaxed but the idea that *we* can fix a bloody reactor leak is a bit warped, yeah?"

"No clue what you actually just said, Paddy, but I think you're all for running out the door. Literally. You're probably right and we can't fix a reactor leak, but we should at least try to help before we abandon these people to die." Roger blushed, whether from being called 'Paddy' or from being shamed, she couldn't tell. "You'll have to remind me about that 'banjaxed' word. I like it."

"Oh, you're a thran redser, ain't you," muttered Roger under his breath in an accent so thick Claire couldn't understand what he was saying. She figured he was poking fun at himself. "Righto," he said in his more usual pronunciation. "Let's ask Captain Priss what she wants us to do." Claire nodded her approval.

"So how do we get you out of the hangar if there's a reactor leak?" Claire asked the stranded crewmember.

"That depends on whether there's actually a reactor leak and how bad it is. If the reactor is venting neutrons and it can't be stopped, we may have to abandon ship. First, let's hope the system is malfunctioning and can be reset." The woman, whose name turned out to be Commander Julianne Otto, not Captain Priss, walked Claire through how to do a master reset on the computer that controlled environmental monitoring systems. The hope was that the coronal mass ejection had overloaded some of the radiation detecting equipment and a reboot would force it to recalibrate itself and the system would back off radiation lockdown. After the reboot, it was apparent that the system was not simply overloaded and the lockdown stayed in place. There were a limited number of doors that could be unlocked from the command room, however.

"Seems a wee daft that there's no backup to let you out of the hangar in case of a foul up, doesn't it?" asked Roger at one point, his accent thickening up as he got more frustrated. "There's no, uhm, manual override, or whatever?"

"Well, yes, there is. We tried that immediately, but with no joy," replied the commander. "The system kept returning a message I'd never seen before. It said something about function disabled by command authority. But since I'm the command authority that didn't make any sense. I certainly didn't disable the manual override."

"There's no physical lever to open the door?" demanded Roger in agitation. "What kind of eejit designed this place?"

"The kind that didn't want us to open the door and die of radiation poisoning," replied Commander Otto, wryly.

"Well, couldn't you put on a space suit and go outside, walk around and come back in the front door?"

"Not if there's nobody there to open the door for us. We could go outside, yes, but all the entry doors are sealed. We would have to cut a hole in the hull.." she trailed off, looking thoughtful.

"How would a rescue team get in, then?" asked Claire.

"With a manual override…" began the commander

"Which is disabled by command authority." Finished Claire.

"Bollox," said Roger.

"Woof," agreed Weenie.

"You really have a no kidding dog in here with you?" asked Commander Otto incredulously.

"Yes… he's a mission specialist," said Claire. Roger laughed. The mission specialist had finally managed to wrestle the drawer open and was assaulting a silvery vacuum packed dehydrated space meal. He snuffled eagerly as a small tear released tantalizing smells of waterless food powder. He's welcome to it, Claire thought. She noticed that along with the vacuum meal, the drawer contained several metal brooches of some sort. Since she had a passing familiarity with the Star Trek shows that her dad was always watching, it occurred to her that those things looked like some sort of communicator. She grabbed a few and shoved them in a pocket and looked at the video feed to see if the trapped crewmen were wearing similar gadgets. They were.

"What if I reset the command override from here?" asked Claire. Commander Otto appeared dubious.

"I would have to give you the command codes," replied Otto hesitantly. You would have complete control of the ship." She bit her lip in consternation.

"I'm guessing that beats starving to death in the hangar," said Roger from across the room where he was examining a sliding door in the wall.

"He's got a point," affirmed Claire. "I don't see another way."

"I can hardly surrender the codes to people I don't even know. I don't even know how you got on this ship. For all I know this is some kind of trick to gain control of the *Ramses* remotely. I'll have to confer with the command team." She cut the audio and gathered several other officers together where they could be seen gesticulating and arguing vociferously. Both excellent words.

Claire joined Roger in examining the door that wouldn't open. There was a keypad to the right of the door. Two lights at the top of the door frame glowed green and a third one was a bright red. Roger typed in some random numbers on the keypad, prompting the red light to flash twice and a low buzzer to sound.

"Well that's not gonna work," said Claire. She went back to the master terminal and pulled up a schematic of the ship. She found the command deck where they were and tapped on the door depicted on the touchscreen. A little red lock icon popped up and she tapped

102

it again and the lock icon opened and turned green. The third light over the door switched to green and the door slid open with a whoosh reminiscent of the elevator doors but a bit more Star Wars-ish sounding. Roger jumped back, startled and turned to glare reproachfully at Claire.

"'Spose I could have warned you. Sorry," Claire said, chuckling. "You looked pretty funny just then, though."

"No worries," said Roger as he stuck his head out the door and looked around. Weenie padded over and poked his head out as well. The outside corridor was very obviously part of a spaceship, dimly lit with panels that slowly flashed a dull red to indicate some emergency condition.

"I'm not sure you should go out there, though," said Claire. "What if there are lethal radiation levels outside this room?" Roger jumped back.

"Good point, mate."

Claire spotted a large plastic box mounted under one of the consoles printed with the words 'Emergency Gear' in bright red. She popped the lid off and rummaged through the highly organized contents. After a few seconds, she came up with a package that read 'Radiation Dosimeter w/Aural Warning.' She opened the package and pulled out a black badge with Velcro on the back. She thumbed a switch on the back to 'on' and pressed the test button. All the LED's lit up and it peeped excitedly. 'Test Passed' appeared on the display and double zeroes registered in green.

"Here, catch," she said to Roger and tossed him the dosimeter. "Keep it with you. It will alert you of dangerous radiation levels. If the numbers change color or it makes distressing noises, come back. Oh, and take this with you. If I can figure out how to work it, it might let us talk to each other more easily." She tossed him the communicator.

"Right," he said and tried to stick it to his shirt and failed. He considered it for a second. "I'll just hold it. Come on, Weenie. Let's go exploring." With that, Roger and Weenie disappeared and the door closed behind them, cutting off Claire's view of Weenie's wagging hindquarters.

It was kind of creepy on the command deck alone with nothing to keep her company but softly glowing screens and blinking lights and the almost inaudible whirring of the air circulation fans. Claire pulled up the schematic again and in a moment of paranoia, locked the door to the command deck again. For good measure, she changed the access code to the door as well.

She took a few minutes to pull up likely menus until she found one dealing with the communicators. A map displayed where all the comm gadgets were located on the ship and a label with the names of who it was assigned to. Several were showing as located on the command deck with her and the tag 'inactive.' She located the inactive one that was heading down a hallway just outside the command deck and activated it. She set its label to 'Roger.' Then she activated her own and set it to her own name. On a whim, she activated another one and set it to Weenie. Now she was bored again. With nothing better to do, she started cycling through the video feeds, looking for Roger. She was cycling through the different cameras so quickly that when she found him, she passed him up and had to press the back button to get back to the video with him in it, but before she did, the screen showed a man in a suit similar to the ones in the hangar walking through a corridor that was definitely not the hangar. When she cycled back, he was gone.

"Well, consider me officially freaked out," she said to nobody in particular. She cycled back to see Roger and found the intercom button that corresponded to the label on the video feed.

"Hey, Roger, it's me, Claire." She grinned as she saw him jump on the screen. He turned around until he located the com station and the camera. He waved to her and toggled the comm.

"What's up?" Roger asked, looking at the camera.

"Have you seen anyone else?" she asked.

"Not a soul. Why?"

"I could have sworn I saw a man in a corridor on the video feed," she said and cycled back to the screen where she had seen the man. "He was in corridor A15," she said and consulted the schematic of the ship. "That's a corridor that runs parallel to yours about twenty meters away."

"You sure, Claire? I mean you weren't just seeing things all by your lonesome, brickin' it in the command center or whatever that place is?"

"Bricking it?"

"Never mind, lass."

"I'm sure, Roger. Be careful down there."

Claire toggled back to the hangar view where the officers of the *Ramses* were still conferring, and by the looks of things it was starting to get heated.

"Hate to interrupt, guys," Claire interrupted, "but we may have a situation." Commander Otto came back to the com port and keyed her mic.

"What's the problem Claire?" she asked, visibly irritated by her recent conversation.

"Is there anybody else aboard that you neglected to mention to us?" asked Claire with a hint of irritation in her own voice.

"No…," began the commander. "Well, not unless you count the recently deceased," she finished uncertainly.

"I see. Any chance they were only mostly dead?"

Commander Otto considered for a few seconds. "Possibly, I suppose. That might explain some things. Why?"

"I saw someone in one of your uniforms on the video feed. You said it would explain some things. Like what, exactly?"

"Well, it would explain how the manual override was disabled. And how a reactor leak either happened or was faked."

"Where was the body?" asked Claire grimly.

"It was in the freezer in the galley. There are actually shelves in the freezer designed for, uhm, casualties. Just in case. Someone's bound to die onboard eventually, so it makes sense if you think about it," said Commander Otto, sounding like she was trying to justify the macabre (awesome word) shelves to Claire.

"OK," said Claire. "I'm checking the galley feed now, but there's nothing on it that would prove anything either way. Too much to hope for that he would leave the freezer door open or a note or something. I'm going to get Roger to detour over there and give it a looksee. Oh, by the way, what was this guy's job?"

Commander Otto looked sheepish and sighed deeply. "He was the chief engineer."

Claire said a couple of words that she wasn't supposed to know and were never going to be in any spelling bee sponsored by the school. That ruled out using the communicators, since it was likely the chief engineer could listen in on them. She toggled over until she found an obviously nervous Roger tiptoeing through the darkened corridor, looking cool and goofy again in his magic shades. He was outside a door marked 'BIOLAB' trying to look in without exposing himself to hostile intent from within. He looked like a six-year-old playing soldier. Weenie was sniffing a fire extinguisher attached to the wall, unconcerned by his nervous partner. She found the com for the biolab and toggled it.

"Hey, Shaggy," she said. "I got a job for you and Scooby." Predictably, Roger jumped as her voice scared him yet again. He grimaced at the camera when he found it.

"Zoinks," he said in a decent Casey Cassum voice. "What's up, Red?" Claire explained about the supposedly deceased engineer and gave him directions to the galley. It was going to take a while because a straight course was blocked by a couple of doors she

106

couldn't unlock because of the radiation protocol. "Seriously? This is getting worser and worser every minute. Alright, boss-lady. On my way. Come on, Weenie." He broke the connection and began skulking about like a clown 007, hamming it up for his audience. Claire couldn't help but laugh at his antics.

Monkeying around with the computer paid some dividends. She was able to get the screen to partition itself and display multiple camera angles. She parked the hangar feed in the corner and brought up the camera with Roger and Weenie and put it in another corner. Since she knew the way to the galley from the biolab by looking at the schematics, she was able to anticipate when to change views to keep following them. She kept cycling the other cameras, looking for her elusive engineer. She still hadn't found him by the time Roger arrived at the galley but the point was moot because the red light over the door blinked twice and the buzzer sounded indicating that it was denying an entry attempt. It looked like the engineer had found her first.

Quickly, she found the camera for the corridor right outside her door and was rewarded with a view of a tall, lanky man in his thirties wearing a *Ramses* uniform and frowning at the access pad to the door of the command deck. He brushed his too long blonde hair out of his eyes and found the camera. He looked right at it, seemingly to stare into Claire's eyes, although she knew he couldn't see her. He keyed the mic.

"Thank goodness! I'm glad you're here, whoever you are. There's a reactor leak and I'm going to need help containing it. Let me in while there's still time." Claire decided he was probably lying and that answering him would be pointless so she ignored him. On her screen, Roger and Weenie were exploring the galley. Roger opened a large stainless steel door to a massive walk-in freezer and disappeared from view. Once Weenie felt the cold floor at the entrance, he declined to enter no matter that he could smell all kinds of tasty things in there. Roger came back out in just a few seconds and went to the com station.

"Any popsicles in uniform in there?" asked Claire.

"Nary a one, lass. But Scoob and me might take a minute and make some samiches," Roger said, ostentatiously licking his lips.

"No time for that. The dearly departed engineer is huffing and puffing and threatening to blow my house down," said Claire. "I think I can keep him from getting in for now, so you don't come up here yet. See if you can find a way into the reactor room."

"What? And get turned into glowing green mush?" Roger screeched, sounding particularly antsy.

"Anybody home in there?" asked the engineer outside her door, using his hand to knock loudly.

"I think it's a fake leak but be careful anyway. Mind your dosimeter. I'll be in touch," she said quickly to Roger then toggled over to the hangar. "Your dead guy is trying to get in here," she told the commander and the small entourage that had gathered anxiously around the com console in the hangar. She continued to ignore the engineer who the camera now showed was fiddling with some connections under the access panel.

"There's nothing you can do to keep him out," said a burly officer whose shiny bald ebony head reminded Claire of an 8 ball, his expressive face wrinkled in disgust and anger. "He's the chief engineer, if he wants in, he'll get in. Goodness knows he made fools of us, I don't see how you would be any different."

"Why isn't he in already?" asked Commander Otto, motioning for the black officer to be quiet.

"I locked the door and changed the password and I think I have an idea on how to discourage him," responded Claire. The knot of officers seemed impressed that she could accomplish such a complex task as locking a door. "The key difference is that I know he's up to no good, whereas he took you guys by surprise." She toggled back over to the com station nearest where Roger was skulking about outside a door emblazoned with the universal

108

radiation symbol of three upside down triangles. Red letters declared this to be the Primary Reactor.

"Hey, Nancy Drew," she said to Roger who didn't jump this time but did stick out his tongue at the camera.

"Don't make me come up there, young lady," he said in a mock stern voice, shaking his finger at her and frowning. It made her chuckle despite the stress of her current situation.

"That's precisely what I need you to do, sir. I'm going to lock the three doors leading into the corridor where this dude is at the moment. Then I'm going to open the one nearest you long enough for you to toss in those smoke bombs I know you're carrying in your backpack. What about that door you're looking at? Can you see anything? What's your dosimeter doing?"

"Whoa, slow down, girly," Roger responded holding both hands up to the camera. "First, this door isn't budging. Every time I try to get it to open it blares at me and some beour starts in about radiation and warnings and whatnot. As for this gadget," he held up his dosimeter, "it's still green zeroes." He rummaged in his back for a few seconds. "You mean these?" he asked, holding up two smoke bombs.

"Yessireebob. I mean those two. Now get a move on before this dude breaks down my door. As for the dosimeter, it just kinda confirms our suspicion that the leak was a sham. When you get up here, the door to the corridor will be closed. I'll give you a countdown and when I open it you have those bombs lit and toss them in. Alright?"

"Gotcha. On my way. Come on, Weenie." This last was to the dog who was laying by the radiation door, gnawing on a bit of plastic he found on the floor somewhere. Weenie looked up at his name, woofed once and followed Roger.

Claire pulled up the schematic again and selected the door to the command deck. Instead of allowing her access to its status and password, the computer turned the icon grey and informed her that it was out of service and under repair. She figured there wasn't long until the engineer got in so she decided to talk to him to try and stall him while she got the other three doors closed, preferably all at once. She selected the com station just outside the door.

"Who's there?" she asked, even though she knew perfectly well who was there. On camera, she was rewarded with a view of the man looking up from his work on the door.

"Someone's in there?" he asked the com station. "I thought the door was malfunctioning and I was attempting to repair it. Why didn't you let me in?"

"I don't know how the door works," she lied. "It kept telling me that it was locked."

"Yeah, it told me the same thing," he replied as he bent back to his work on the access panel. "Don't worry, miss. I'll be in there in a jiffy and we can talk about this." She didn't like the sound of that. She could see Roger was almost in position. With a final keystroke she closed and locked all three doors leading into the corridor just outside her door. He looked up at the doors in surprise and then sneered disdainfully.

"What's that supposed to do? Scare me?"

"I'll open it in ten seconds, Roger." On screen, Roger nodded and held his lighter up to the two fuses. They sputtered to life and began to burn down. Claire tried to count to ten but the fuses looked too short so she opened the door at six and Roger tossed them through. She immediately closed and locked the door again. The engineer looked bewildered.

"What in the…" he began but cut off as all hell broke loose.

Both smoke bombs began to belch copious quantities of acrid white smoke amid a small shower of sparks. Neither had much time to emit significant quantities of smoke before the small corridor was filled with the reeking, choking stuff. Almost immediately an earsplittingly loud klaxon began to sound all over the ship and an automated voice announced very loudly that there was a fire in section C6. It then announced that in one minute the atmosphere in C6 would be vented to space.

The engineer was coughing and gagging on the smoke and could no longer see well enough to continue hacking into the door controls. He switched to pleading and pounding on the door. Claire was in a panic. She certainly didn't mean to kill the man, just to frighten him and get him to leave her door alone. Perhaps she hadn't thought this all the way through.

"Roger!" she screamed into the comm. "I can't get this door open! Without the engineer you can't get back in here, so you'll have to drag him out before the atmosphere vents!"

"Perfect. Just bleedin' perfect. Ok, hurry it up!" She opened the corridor door Roger had lobbed the smoke bombs through and Roger grabbed a fire extinguisher off a nearby rack. He didn't use it to extinguish anything, but instead hit the surprised and gagging engineer on the head with it, then dropped it and with surprising strength put the slumped engineer in a fireman's carry and ran back through the door. Claire closed it behind them but the smoke was already filling the next section and Roger kept running until he got past the next door which Claire also closed. There was a loud whoosh from outside the door, followed by the klaxon going silent. Only then did Claire notice that the officers in the hangar were clamoring for her attention. With a sigh, Claire closed her eyes and took a minute to let the tension drain out of her tired and over-taxed system.

Chapter Nine: Ramses II

Claire was sorely tempted to let herself drift off to sleep. It seemed to her she had been running on too little sleep and too much adrenaline for far too long now. Come to think of it, make that *no* sleep. The last time she was asleep seemed like ages and ages ago. So, comforting, the thought of a little nap. She could put her head down on the console and…. But no. Too many things demanded her attention at the moment. Wearily, she opened her eyes and stretched. Then, she unmuted the hangar comm.

"Crisis resolved, everybody."

"What are you doing up there? Did you set my ship on fire?!" screamed an almost incoherent Commander Otto. Her face was in danger of turning purple and exploding, it looked to Claire.

"You're going to give yourself a stroke, Julie," admonished Claire in a voice that suggested she didn't care much either way. "It was just a smoke bomb. Your dead but not dead engineer has been incapacitated. No harm done. Well, unless you count the hallway outside vented to space, that is."

"Who has smoke bombs on a space ship?" asked one of the officers next to Commander Otto.

"Apparently, this young lady turned pirate who is demanding the command codes," she said to the man who asked the question but loudly and with the com active so that Claire would hear her. "And if I don't give you the codes, what happens? You vent the hangar to space?"

Claire rolled her eyes. "Oh, spare me the drama, ma'am. I'm just looking for my brother. I need the codes to get you out of the hangar, remember? You don't give them to me and I go about my merry way. I'm beginning to not care one way or the other. One question, though. Why would your engineer fake his death, hack into the computer, fake a reactor leak and lock you in the hangar?"

"To steal our cargo, obviously," said one of the officers whose tone suggested Claire was an idiot. Commander Otto must have thought that *he* was the idiot because she elbowed him in the ribs, hard.

"Oh. Interesting," said Claire. "And what would this oh so valuable cargo happen to be?"

"That's classified," said Commander Otto.

"Right. Not that I care unless it's my brother or a working crystal ball. Or a soft, comfy bed." said Claire, mostly to herself as she glanced at the display for the corridor where Roger and Weenie were tying up the engineer with a length of electrical extension cord. She glanced up and noticed one of the officers in the hangar was donning a spacesuit. Next to him was a portable welding rig. Holstered on his hip was what appeared to be a gun of some sort. A blaster pistol or something equally futuristic and lethal? "I see you're about to cut your way out of the hangar."

"Unfortunately, that's impossible. The door and walls of the hangar are made of a cobalt steel reinforced ceramic that's made to withstand the temperatures produced by a crashed, burning or exploding shuttlecraft," responded Commander Otto.

"I see. So, that guy over behind you is about to spacewalk over here and cut into the command deck, then?" Commander Otto

113

blushed but didn't say anything right away. Claire toggled over to talk to Roger.

"Roger, I think it's time to leg it, as you so eloquently put it earlier."

"Finally, the girl talks sense. But what made you change your mind? Was it the murderous traitor? Or the potentially deadly radiation?"

"It's the officers in the hangar who are about to break out of the hangar with a cutting torch and guns and have taken a dislike to little ole me."

"You're joking. No, of course you're not joking. Ok. How do I get back to you?"

"Working on it. Meanwhile, make sure that guy is tied up good and see if you can get into the cargo bay. There's something valuable in there that these people don't want us to find. Maybe see if you can get Weenie to guard that guy."

"Regular space pirates, then, are we? Sweet, I'm on it."

She gave Roger directions to the cargo bay and then Claire turned her attention to getting the atmosphere restored in the compartment outside the command deck and to getting the door to work again. It took her several frustrating minutes of navigating menus and pull-down screens before she got the computer to re-pressurize the corridor outside. Getting the door open was another matter entirely. The schematic doggedly insisted the door was out of service and under repair. Claire began to wish she had a cutting torch of her own. She finally gave up in disgust. That door was going to have to be opened by someone else. Probably the engineer.

She checked on Weenie who was standing inches from the engineer's face, softly growling and drooling slowly onto his chin. The officer looked terrified. And like he had a terrible headache, but that might have been Claire's imagination.

Roger was at the cargo bay but couldn't get the door open. Claire was able to unlock it from the command deck and Roger entered a cavernous space lined with crates, boxes and barrels. Red lights flashed on and off on the ceiling and walls, indicating the current radiation emergency. His dosimeter was still in the green, though. He walked around the bay for a bit, looking at the containers.

"Any idea what I'm supposed to be looking for?" he asked Claire via the wall mounted com.

"Not a clue. Look for something labeled secret or classified or in a locked container of some kind. I'll see if I can con it out of the people in the hangar." She toggled over to the hangar but nobody was by the com and she couldn't get anyone to answer her. The man in the space suit was ready to go and they were all clustered in the shuttle while he tried to get the hangar to depressurize and open. Claire pulled up the schematic and saw the doors were just waiting on depressurization before they opened. She locked them and then changed the password for good measure. She smiled as all the lights over the hangar door went red. That should stall them. She hunted around the console until she found an external com panel for the radio and selected a channel labeled 'shuttle net.'

"Yoo-hoo," she said into the mic. "Anyone home in the shuttlecraft?"

"This is shuttle Cleo, go ahead, Ramses," came the reply in terse radio-speak.

"Guess what we found in the cargo bay?" she asked coyly. Silence was the only response she got. They were skeptical. "Be that way, then," she said. "But I would like to know, what in the name of creation were you planning on doing with that thing, Julie?"

"It's Commander Otto, to you, pirate. You'll be in our custody soon, Claire and then we can talk about how you got into my ship."

"Doubtful. Oh, by the way, I locked the hangar door, so good luck with that. Don't worry, we'll be leaving soon and if I can think of a use for it, we'll be taking your little box of weirdness with us."

"Claire," came the voice of Roger over the internal comm. "I think I found what was so interesting." She looked at the screen where he was visible in the cargo bay, standing beside what looked like a pet carrier cage. Inside was what looked for all the world like a blue scaly monkey.

"Jackpot," she told Roger. "Can you lug that cage back here? And you'll have to convince that engineering traitor to open this door so you can get in." On the screen, Claire saw Roger put the cage with the weird monkey creature onto a floating anti-grav dolly of some kind and push it out of the cargo bay. She turned her attention back to the hangar where the air had been evacuated but the space-suited astronaut couldn't get the door open. She knew it was only a matter of time before Commander Otto got the door open with her command codes, but Claire figured Otto wouldn't want to broadcast them where they might be overheard or otherwise intercepted. Sure enough, she was soon rewarded with the sight of Otto herself in a space suit emerging from the shuttle and making her way to the hangar door.

Claire resisted the impulse to urge Roger to hurry up. He was already going quickly and badgering him would just make him anxious or angry. Or both. She checked on Weenie only to find to her horror that the dog was murdering the engineer. Or so it looked at first. The dog appeared to be trying to tear out the man's throat, but it was just his hand that Weenie was biting. No telling what the fool had done to provoke the dog. She toggled on the com in that section.

"Good dog, Weenie," she told him through the mic. "But back off, ok? We don't want him hurt too badly. Down, boy. Sit." Weenie took a second to release the crewman's hand but then he backed off out of kicking range and sat on his haunches. He woofed softly at the camera and turned his attention back to his ward. "That is one smart dog," Claire said to herself.

Roger got back to Weenie and the engineer at about the same time Commander Otto overrode the password and opened the hangar door. She couldn't help herself and gave in to the urge to key the mic.

"Time to kick it into high gear, Roger. We're about to have company."

"On our way, Claire," he responded. "But I don't know if this eejit will cooperate."

"Can he hear me?" On screen Roger shoved the glaring engineer closer to the camera and nodded. "Good. Listen up, pal. In a few minutes a man with a cutting torch is going to slice through the skin of this ship just a few feet from you. When he does, the atmosphere will vent and you will die horribly. Regrettably, so will Roger and our dog, Weenie. So, we need your help. Don't help and you go splat. Get this door open and we will take you with us so you can avoid being shot for the traitor you are. Got it?" The man appeared to consider it for a precious few seconds. Claire couldn't see the man spacewalking outside with the weaponry because he wasn't in the field of view of any of the exterior cameras, but she imagined him clinging to the ship feet from her, firing up his torch. Claire realized she was sweating through her shirt. "Well? What's it gonna be?"

"Alright," he croaked, holding up his blood caked hands. "I'll get it open, but I need to be untied. And you promise to take me with you on your ship."

"Untie him, Roger. Any funny business and not only will you try breathing vacuum but Weenie will bite off your face first," she promised grimly. He nodded resignedly as Roger started unwinding the electrical cord from his hands. When his hands were free he all but ran back to the door and took up where he had left off, hacking the door. Roger and Weenie followed with the monkey thing. Claire toggled back to the external radio.

"Looks like you're going to lose this race, Julie," she said via the radio link. "We're going to be out of here in minutes and we're taking your little pet with us."

"We'll see about that, Claire," came back Commander Otto's voice, hard as steel and angry in the extreme. "Garcia is already cutting and he reports your ship is nowhere to be seen. Looks like you're stranded and unless you have a space suit on, you're going to get very cold soon. Sorry, but I don't like pirates." As if to punctuate this grim message, an alarm sounded indicating that the atmosphere was venting in corridor C6. The same three doors that Claire had closed to trap the engineer were closed by the computer to keep the entire ship from losing its air. The people just outside her door were about to be in serious trouble. She turned on a camera in the hallway and saw a glowing gash where the torch was cutting through the hull. She could see detritus and debris being sucked out of the growing rent in the wall. Weenie was barking excitedly and Roger was banging on the door. The engineer continued working as quickly as he could.

"Is this blue monkey critter an alien?" she asked, not really hoping for an answer, but too curious not to ask.

"That's what makes it so valuable, of course. We found them living in caves on one of the moons of Saturn, Enceladus. Quite extraordinary. They can breathe a wide range of substances, including carbon dioxide. That 'critter' as you call it is worth billions. Fortunately, it can survive in a vacuum much longer than you can. See you soon. Cleo out."

Roger's eyes were bulging from the decreased pressure and Claire was starting to think that they might have lost the race, when the third light over the door turned green and it slid open, equalizing the pressure between the two spaces with an explosive gush. Her ears popped painfully. The engineer and Roger were blasted backwards by the air rushing out of the command deck through the doorway, but it only lasted a second and they ran into the room with her, Roger hauling the cart with the monkey. Weenie quickly followed and the door slammed shut again. This time the second light turned red, indicating the pressure outside the door was unsafe. For the second time in half an hour, the hallway outside the command deck was filled with nothing but cold vacuum.

All the new arrivals were gasping for air and sucking it in gratefully as the ventilation system pumped the pressure back up in the command deck. The engineer's eyes roamed over the gear littered room, obviously looking for the way out and not finding it.

"I assumed you had cut a hole in the ship to get in here. Where's your ship? How are we going to get out before they get here? You crazy girl, we're trapped in here!" The engineer was clearly freaking out. This close she could see his name tag read 'Simpson.'

"Calm down, Homer," said Claire. She shared a knowing smile with Roger. "Our escape route is through that door," she waved her hand at the only other door in the room, the one they had come through from the grey hallway in search of Nick. It was smaller than a normal door and the stenciling on the front clearly proclaimed it to be emergency suit storage. The engineer's face flushed with rage. He stomped over to the door and wrenched it open to reveal a small closet with two pressure suits and helmets inside.

"You stupid little girl!" screamed the engineer. "You've killed us all with your ridiculous foolishness. I ought to strangle you with my bare hands before they get in here." He took a step toward Claire but stopped abruptly when Weenie bared his teeth and started to growl low in his throat. Mr. Simpson unconsciously rubbed his bitten and bleeding hand. He also couldn't fail to notice Roger holding the telescoping steel pole he had retrieved with his backpack and fought the urge to rub his head too.

"Step aside, please," said Claire calmly, in her best royalty voice. He complied, glaring at her murderously the whole time.

Claire collected her iPhone and charger and then walked over to the door and closed it. She waited a second and opened it again, then climbed through the doorway into the corridor beyond. Roger shoved the wide-eyed staring engineer who followed her through in a daze. Roger motioned Weenie through and then picked up the pet carrier with the alien in it and stepped through himself. As he cleared the door, the other door beeped and opened as the man outside it entered the command override codes. Immediately, air started howling through the open door until Claire reached over and closed it from the inside with a quiet, final click.

"Well, what a menagerie we have here," said Claire with a laugh. "But I think our party is too large by one, sir." She indicated the engineer with her finger. "You are going bye-bye, I think."

"Where.. what… Is this your ship?" he finally managed to say.

"Not exactly. Although it does have the ability to take you a lot of places."

"I'll say," said Roger.

"Where are you taking me?" he asked. His panic was beginning to subside and Claire could tell it wasn't going to be long before he was a problem. Since he was the largest one present, he had the capacity to make quite a nuisance of himself.

"You're a nautical type guy, I think," mused Claire aloud. "What do you think, Roger?"

"Definitely nautical,' he agreed with a wide smile. "I think I know what you're thinking. Blackbeard?"

"Oh, aye, me hearty," she said in a passable pirate accent. She was trying for Johnny Depp's Captain Sparrow but fell short of the mark. She pointed down the hallway. "That way, Mr. Simpson, if you please. Briskly now, time is short." She could see him thinking about trying to overpower them or make a run for it. She pulled out her silver hairbrush and noticed it still had werewolf blood on it. "Don't make me use this," she threatened ominously.

"You're insane," he protested but not vigorously and he started walking in the direction indicated. It wasn't long before they came to a door what had a plaque that read simply, 'AARR.'

"Stop," she said and he did. "You can't open any of these doors, if that's what you're thinking. Try this one." Obediently, he grasped the brass handle and attempted to open it but of course she was right and he couldn't.

"Allow me," she said and easily turned the handle. The door opened on a room made entirely of wood. A lamp swung gently from a hook in the low ceiling over a table covered in old parchment charts and a bowl of moldy fruit. The soft gentle sounds of planks and ropes creaking competed with the susurrus of waves rasping against wood. The engineer looked in with curiosity.

"What is this room? Some sort of ship simulator?" asked the engineer with evident wonder. "Is it real or is it holographic?"

"Go in and find out," said Roger gruffly. "Not even joking, mate. Get in."

Chief Engineer Edwin Simpson lately of the Starship *Ramses* stepped into the captain's cabin of the *Queen Anne's Revenge.* He turned to look back just in time to see Roger close the door in his face. Roger dusted his hands dramatically.

"Good riddance to bad rubbish," he said and held his hand up.

"Amen," responded Claire as she gave him a high five. "Now let's go find Nick."

"Good God, girl. Can't we sleep a wee bit first? I'm bloody knackered, here." Weenie agreed with a soft woof. The alien just looked at them curiously, his pink eyes making spooky spirals in their sockets.

"Good idea, Roger," Claire agreed. "But like I said last time, not in the hallway. Let's go get some shut eye in the fairy tale."

Roger groaned to show his displeasure with that particular world. "Fine. Lead on, oh great and wise one."

"And don't you forget it."

Chapter Ten: My, What Big Teeth You Have

"If you want your children to be intelligent, read them fairy tales. If you want them to be more intelligent, read them more fairy tales." - Albert Einstein

"What are we going to do with this creepy little blue monkey?" asked Roger as he poked his finger into the carrier cage. The little alien studied the finger with seeming interest but made no move toward or away from it. Weenie was also curious and poked his snout in between the bars, sniffing at the creature within. Claire studied it from afar, trying to assess its value in her search for her brother. At the moment she couldn't see much point in lugging it around, but that didn't mean it didn't have any value. Better to keep it and not need it than to let it loose in a random world and wish she had it later. She certainly wasn't going to let a cave dwelling alien loose. But she didn't feel bad about keeping it in a cage because if she had left it in the space ship cargo bay it would no doubt get dissected by curious scientists.

"I'll think we'll take the little guy with us," she said. Roger stopped trying to poke it with his finger and stood up. Weenie got a good whiff and backed off, rubbing his snout and whining softly. Apparently, it didn't smell like something dogs liked. It continued to sit quietly in its cage and show not much interest in its surroundings. Roger offered it a piece of jerky which it ignored so he gave it to Weenie who made it disappear.

"Should we let it out of the cage, do you think?" asked Roger as he examined the latch on the cage which was fairly simple and not locked.

"Heck no," she said vehemently. "Who knows what this thing is capable of. It could be poisonous to the touch or have a taste for human blood. It might even spontaneously combust. No way to tell but better safe than sorry, don't you think?"

"Yeah, I should stop acting the maggot once I've had a kip."

"What? That made no sense, Roger."

"Sorry. I mean I'm tired and not thinking straight."

"Ok. Let's get into the fairy tale world and we'll uhm, have a kip did you say? I assume that means nap."

"That I did, Claire. And that it does. Alright, let's get a move on."

Retracing their steps to the area where they had been wasn't hard since they hadn't gone far to drop Simpson in to see Blackbeard. They didn't waste any time deliberating when they got to the door they needed. Claire turned the handle, opened the door and they all trooped into the fairy tale world, Weenie bringing up the rear and Roger toting the weirdo in the cage. The door deposited them outside a homey cottage with a thatched roof and wood smoke merrily drifting from the chimney. It looked to be midmorning and a warm sun and gentle breeze engendered a sense of peace and well-being. Weenie immediately went to a picturesque stone well and hiked his leg up to claim it as his own. The entrancing smell of something savory cooking wafted out of an open window. Claire felt her tummy rumble and heard Roger's do the same. Someone was happily whistling inside the picturesque little house.

Claire approached the brightly painted blue wooden door and knocked loudly and the whistling instantly ceased. A moment later the door was opened from the inside by a chubby little lady wearing an apron and a chef's hat. Her eyes lit up and he mouth creased in a big smile when she saw the strange group outside her door.

"OOOO! Visitors," she crooned. "Come in, come in!" She motioned for them to enter and threw the door wide. Claire tried to ask about her brother but the strange woman shushed her as she ushered them into her home. Inside the cottage the cooking aroma was much stronger and it set the group's collective mouths to watering. The plump little cook clapped her hands in delight and led them to a table that dominated one half of the only room visible in the cottage. "I hope you kids are hungry! I have stew and muffins and apple pie just begging to be eaten. And fresh milk, don't forget the milk!" She beamed at her visitors happily.

"Uhm. We're looking for my brother, Nick," said Claire as she pulled out her phone to display his picture.

"Eat first, questions later, dearie. No good gabbing away on an empty stomach now is there? Why look how thin you are!" She pinched Claire's cheek between her thumb and forefinger and clicked her tongue. "Auntie Ginger will fatten the lot of you up, don't you worry." She pulled out chairs for Claire and Roger and got out a bowl and placed it on the floor by Weenie. Claire and Roger shared a perplexed look before Claire shrugged and they both sat down at the table and Auntie Ginger placed steaming bowls of stew on the table in front of them, all the while whistling and talking to herself.

"Fatten us up?" Claire mouthed silently to Roger who looked at Auntie Ginger suspiciously for a moment then at his stew and back at Claire.

"You're killing me, Claire," he said, exasperated. "We're dying of hunger and sheer bone tiredness. We're knackered, the lot of us. Let's just eat and see if we can catch a nap somewhere soft. This biddy isn't going to eat us today. Don't look a gift horse in the mouth and all that, what?"

Claire was tired and hungry, too. Very much so. She felt bad that she was driving Roger so hard. He deserved a break. Heck, they all did. Maybe she should just count her blessings that this nice woman was offering them such great hospitality.

"Thank you, ma'am," mumbled Claire around a mouthful of steaming hot stew.

"Don't you worry your head, little one. Auntie Ginger is going to make it all better. Here, have a muffin."

The muffins were delicious. The stew virtually exploded on her taste-buds with a sumptuous (great word, thought Claire) blend of spices that she had never had the equal of. The meat was tender and delicious, the vegetables succulent but not overcooked or mushy. She had two bowls full of stew and three muffins and a slice of apple pie. With each bite she got a little sleepier so that by the time the delectable taste of the apple pie was more a memory than fact, her eyelids weighed ten pounds apiece and she couldn't keep her big ole heavy head upright. Roger was already asleep, head down on the table. Even Weenie was curled up beneath the table, twitching and snoring as he romped through his doggie dreams. Only the alien monkey thing and Auntie Ginger remained awake. It was a toss-up as to which was more strange: the alien with the googly eyes or the creepy cook who whistled while she washed her dishes and sharpened her knives.

Claire dreamed of her brother, Nick. In the dream she couldn't say his name, but kept calling him horrible things that she had at one time or another actually called him. Things like troll and fart-face. Every time she tried to say his name or tell him she was sorry, another horrid insult would come out instead and Nick started to cry. She tried to calm him down but instead called him a dingle-berry and a cry baby. With a look of wounded horror Nick turned and ran from her, disappearing into a dark, spooky maze and vanished into mist.

Claire ran blindly into the mist filled maze, screaming insults as she tried to call to her brother but she still couldn't say his name. Out of the maze came a strident beeping, piercing through the roiling fog. Like a too fast heartbeat it stabbed into her brain. She turned toward the sound and followed it into the maze at a run, thinking it might be Nick or something that was dangerous to him. As Claire ran, with the BEEP BEEP BEEP BEEP pounding into her head, a hazy light wanted to break through the mist if only she could... open... her... eyes. She finally managed to crack one eye and the dim light of evening washed into her brain, burning away her sleep and thrusting her back into reality. Claire realized she had been dreaming and that horrid beeping was the alarm on her phone that was in her pocket.

She didn't remember lying down, but she was laying on the floor by the table. Roger and Weenie were likewise sleeping on the floor. They were both protected from the evening light by the shadow of the table. Claire was the only one upon whom the sunlight fell with any force. She blinked against the glare and tried to sit up only to realize her hands and feet were bound with rope. When she looked more closely at Roger, she saw that he too was tied up. Weenie didn't appear to be restrained but Claire didn't think he would be much help getting them untied. With much difficulty she managed to lever herself into a sitting position and only got a muscle cramp in her butt to show for it. It took her a while but she was able to get her phone partially out of her pocket and silence the oh so annoying alarm which shouldn't be going off in the first place.

Claire didn't remember setting her alarm. Besides that, her phone wasn't able to tell time when in other worlds. So, the alarm shouldn't be able to work at all. This was a mystery that would bear some thinking. As she thought that she heard a strange giggle from under the table. She looked into the shadows where the sound came from and saw the googly eyes of the alien monkey-thing lazily spinning in circles. It made her vaguely nauseated. An odd thought came to her: what if that alien heard her thoughts? It made another gurgling noise.

"You can hear my thoughts?" she whispered at the alien. Its eyes flashed green for a second. "Whoa, that was freaky," she said. "Does green mean yes?" Another flash of green. "What means no?" The alien's eyes flashed red. "Good thing I'm not color blind." The alien laughed again in it's strange way that sounded somewhat like a baby giggling if it was giggling under water. "Did you make my phone's alarm go off?" Green. "Cool. Can you get us untied?" Red. "Shazbot."

She nudged Roger with her boot and he didn't stir. She kicked him harder and was rewarded with one tiny moan. That crazy lady must have drugged us, she thought. That would explain the headache and the mild nausea. Roger ate more than she did this morning and Weenie was a lot smaller than either of them. It might be a while before either of them were able to wake up. She wouldn't be awake herself if it wasn't for the sunlight on her face and the alarm in her pocket. She wondered how long she had before the mad poisoner realized she was awake. There was no sign of her but that didn't mean she was far away or would stay gone for long. Better get a move on.

Claire was able to get her hands on the corner of the table and lift enough of her body weight to get her feet under her and stand up. She hoped there was a knife or something sharp on the table that she might be able to use to cut he bonds, but no dice. Insane and evil the plump little chef might be, but she was undoubtedly tidy because the table was spotlessly clean. She took a tentative hop away from the table toward the kitchen and almost fell on her face. Precariously, she stood in place, swaying, while she regained her balance. The next hop went better and the third was easy. Claire bunny-hopped with increasing facility into the kitchen-side of the cottage in search of a cutting implement. There, she was rewarded for her efforts.

There was a dizzying array of cutlery available in the kitchen. This kitchen was obviously owned by someone who believed wholeheartedly in being prepared for any contingency that required cutting. There were small knives, large knives, fillet knives, cleavers, carving knives, etc. You name a kitchen utensil with a sharp blade and it was in that room. Claire selected the first knife she could reach and immediately cut her wrist trying to free herself. The pain of cutting herself caused her to drop the knife on the ground where it clattered on the stone floor. As she grabbed another knife awkwardly with both hands she heard the distinctive whistling of Auntie Ginger outside the cottage. It was a merry, happy tune that was catchy like a commercial jingle. Her brain automatically added some words, "Buy

Auntie's Apple Pie and You Will Surely Die…" Claire was certain it would be stuck in her head for days. More worrisome was the fact that it was getting closer.

Claire's second attempt to cut her hands free was going better than the first, meaning she didn't cut herself or drop the knife. Fortunately, the sound of whistling stopped somewhere outside, maybe at the well or a flower bed. Her mind's eye pictured Auntie Ginger happily pulling up some weeds from amongst the cheery flowers by the door. Claire's hands were free now and she was sawing on the bonds around her thighs, then her ankles. The whistling stopped altogether and Claire paused, listening for any sound that would betray Auntie Ginger's whereabouts. The whistling was replaced by humming that came clearly through the kitchen window. Thinking the nasty hag was just outside the window, Claire crouched down to avoid being seen and finished sawing away at her ankle restraints. She was free!

In four giant steps she was at Roger's side and working on the ropes binding his wrists. At the same time, she was whispering urgently to him. "Wake up, Roger, you stupid oaf. Open your eyes!" He moaned in response. She cut off his leg restraints just as Auntie Ginger opened the door to the cottage and breezed in, humming and carrying a basket of vegetables in one hand and some cut flowers in the other. She stopped mid-step when she saw Claire was awake and busy freeing her captives.

"Oh! I, uh… see that you're finally awake! You must be starving. Let me get you-" she started in her cloying happy voice. Claire was having none of it and cut her off.

"Shut it, you old bat," she hissed, brandishing the knife with one hand and slapping Roger across the face with the other, leaving a bloody smear from her cut wrist on his cheek. He opened his eyes for a moment and stared at Claire with blank eyes empty of understanding and then his eyelids slid closed again. "What did you drug us with?" She spat at Auntie Ginger.

129

"Drug? Oh to sleep? Just some herbs to help you sleep soundly, child," answered the crazy woman sweetly, taking a tentative step toward Claire. "You were so obviously in need of rest, I just wanted to help."

"Help, my eye," hissed Claire. "You don't tie up people you're trying to help. Don't take another step, you nutjob or I'll cut out your gizzard."

"Such strong words from such a little girl," said Auntie Ginger reprovingly as she took another step in Claire's direction. "No need to be violent, little miss. It was for your own protection. The herbs I gave you often cause sleepwalking and I didn't want you to wander into the forest and get lost or hurt." She spread her hands to demonstrate how non-threatening she was and smiled broadly, displaying teeth that had no business being that large or pointy.

"My, what sharp teeth you have, grandma," said Claire softly.

Auntie Ginger's lips closed over her teeth quickly and she reddened with anger. "I didn't point out how many freckles you have, why comment on my teeth? Are you always this rude?"

Claire fought an irrational impulse to apologize. Her second impulse was indignation in the extreme that this *kidnapper* would dare call her victims rude. She pushed aside her anger because she knew she had to think clearly if she was going to get out of this mess. Claire was tempted to try and use the knife on Auntie Ginger but knew she was no knife-fighter and didn't feel confident in her ability to inflict enough damage to make the woman leave them alone. Then a thought came to her. Maybe apologizing might be the right thing to do after all. It would certainly be unexpected and the lady just might be unhinged enough to buy it.

She dropped her hands down to her sides and let the tension out of her stance. "You're right, Auntie Ginger," she said, trying her best to feign sincere contrition. "That was rude of me and I'm sorry. I'm sure you were just trying to help and I'm being very ungrateful, aren't I?"

Auntie Ginger stopped her slow advance and her face betrayed a moment of surprise before a huge smile spread over her features and she practically glowed with pleasure. "It's ok, child," she crooned. "You're still tired. And hungry, too, I'm sure. And thin… so thin. Auntie Ginger forgives you. Now, come and let me get you some warm milk and a slice of pie to settle your nerves." She turned toward the kitchen and beckoned Claire to follow her, smiling her jagged, toothy grin. Claire did so, surreptitiously (a very difficult word to spell) sliding the knife into the back pocket of her cargo pants.

Auntie Ginger led Claire to a corner in the kitchen where a stone lid covered a cold larder where she produced a jug of milk and a slice of apple pie. She put the pie on a cute plate covered in crude depictions of kittens frolicking and poured the milk into a ceramic cup which she warmed on the still hot stove for a minute and then let Claire take them back to the table. Claire made a show of eating and drinking but tried her best to not ingest any of the stuff for fear it would knock her out again. She smeared the pie around the plate as much as possible and when her hostess wasn't looking she poured the entire glass of milk on Roger's face in the hopes that it would wake him up. It didn't; although it did produce some signs of life when the warm liquid got in the gash on his forehead. He sputtered and groaned and rolled over in his sleep. Claire gritted her teeth in exasperation. Auntie Ginger disappeared for a moment through the only other door in the cottage and returned with a vase into which she put the cut flowers and placed them on the table.

"There! That's much brighter, don't you think?" she asked with disgusting cheerfulness. Claire wanted to stab her in the eye but instead she nodded her head with enthusiasm and agreed with the crazy lady. "How's the pie, dearie? Good isn't it?"

"Oh, my, yes," agreed Claire in a voice so dripping with sweetness and innocence that there was no way Auntie Ginger would take it at face value; except she did. Satisfied that all was right in the world, she began to unpack her basket of vegetables and resumed her insipid whistling. Claire wiped the fork clean on her napkin and was about to put it in her pocket along with the knife but instead she stabbed Roger in the rear end as hard as she could with it. That worked like magic.

With an earsplitting yell of pain Roger launched himself off the stone floor and blearily looked around him for the source of the injury. Claire quickly plucked the fork from where it was quivering, stuck firmly in the meat of Roger's buttocks. He screamed again as she pulled out the fork and hid it behind her back. Auntie Ginger was running back to the table in alarm, brandishing a carrot.

"What's going on?" mumbled Roger incoherently.

"Sorry, I didn't mean to step on you, Roger," she said sweetly. Auntie Ginger looked on suspiciously. "Tell Auntie Ginger how sorry you are that you startled her with your yell, Roger. She's been very helpful. She put 'special herbs' in our food to help us sleep and restrained us so we wouldn't hurt ourselves sleep walking. We are ever so thankful, Roger. Aren't we?" This was delivered in the same sickly sweet voice that she used with Auntie Ginger. Even in his sleepy drugged state, Roger couldn't help but see what she was getting at, surely.

"What are you getting at?" he asked, too foggy-headed to catch her drift. Auntie Ginger looked at her with increasing suspicion and as her brows knitted Claire knew she had only seconds to convince this child eating villain that she was as harmless as kittens and warm milk.

"Calm down, Roger," she said in the same voice of extreme innocence. "You must have had a bad dream. There's nobody *evil* here, just *Auntie Ginger*. Come, sit with me and have a nice piece of pie. That last piece was so good, Auntie! Can I have another glass of milk, please?"

Roger looked at her like she was a few fries short of a happy meal but Auntie Ginger was lapping up the wide eyed waif act. "Of course you can have another glass of milk, child. Here, let me get it for you." Whistling again, she grabbed Claire's empty cup and headed for the kitchen.

"She's insane and planning on eating us," Claire hissed in a hoarse whisper. "I woke up all tied up and I had to cut us both loose. The food is drugged, don't eat it. Oh, and the alien is psychic."

"Well, shouldn't we get out of here, then? I don't feel like being served with a side of pie, myself."

"Definitely, but Weenie is still asleep. We can't carry both him and the alien and run from Auntie Ginger." Claire shivered as she said the name of their captor.

"I could hit her with my pie plate," offered Roger groggily. He was having trouble keeping his eyes open again as the pain from his backside faded a bit. "Why did you have to stab me in the arse for anyway?"

"You wouldn't wake up, Roger. You sleep like a log. Heck, you didn't even wake up when I poured a whole cup of milk in your face."

"Well that explains why my shirt is so wet. Great, I'm going to smell like sour milk in a little while." They straightened up from their conspiratorial posture with their heads together when they heard Auntie Ginger returning from the kitchen with a tray holding plates of pie and cups of fresh milk.

"Be ready. I have an idea," Claire muttered to Roger just before Ginger came within range where she would hear. Then she turned toward the lady and put on her innocent act again. "Roger said he's really thirsty and the thought of milk makes him ill. Could he have some cool water instead? We saw a well outside and thought maybe you wouldn't mind…"

Auntie Ginger set the food on the table and considered for a moment, frowning. Claire could practically see the gears turning in the woman's head. Then her smile returned. "Of course, little miss.

133

It will by my pleasure. You eat your pie. I'll be back in a jiffy." With that she trooped out the front door to the well. Claire got up and followed her when the door was closed and eased it open a crack so they could see Auntie Ginger at the well. Roger went with her to the door.

"What's the plan?" he asked a little too loudly.

"SHHHH," hissed Claire in annoyance. "When she leans out to get the bucket from the well, we will rush out and push her in."

"Seems a little violent, don't you think?" asked Roger as he grasped the doorframe to keep from swaying.

"She was going to freaking eat us, you dork." Outside, Auntie Ginger was slowly but steadily turning the handle that sent the bucket on the rope down to the water and then after what seemed like forever, she turned it the opposite direction to bring the bucket back up. "Ok, get ready," she said very quietly. The chubby lady leaned out to get the bucket and Claire threw the door wide and yelled, "Now, now, now!" And rushed out at the plump lady's behind that was in the air. But she rushed out alone because Roger was asleep on his feet, head leaned against the wall next to the door. Auntie Ginger screamed as Claire bounced off her beefy butt and rebounded into the dirt. She teetered on the edge of the well, one foot barely in contact with the ground with both hands windmilling in an attempt to shift her center of gravity back from the tipping point.

At first, Claire thought Auntie Ginger was a goner but with incredible swiftness the balance seemed to shift back and it was obvious that the cook was not going to fall into the well. Claire was lying in the dirt, a little too far to reach her in time to shift it back and Claire knew with horrifying certainty that there was nothing she could do. All seemed lost until a victorious 'woof' rang out as Weenie launched himself out of the doorway and directly onto Auntie Ginger's extra wide bottom and rebounded much like Claire had but managed to keep his feet instead of sprawling in the yard. His momentum was enough to topple the cannibal into the well,

134

where she stuck like a cork a few feet from the top. Her wide bottom was too big to let her go down any further and her feet were just even with the top of the well where they pumped back and forth in a swirl of pink petticoats. Muffled screams of fury rose from the well, but it seemed that Auntie Ginger wasn't going to be eating anyone anytime soon.

Tail wagging, Weenie came to where Claire was lying on the ground about to cry from relief and licked her face. She hugged Weenie tightly, face buried in his fur and said over and over, "Good dog, Weenie. You're such a good dog."

"Oy, what happened?" asked Roger who stood blinking in the waning sunlight. "What'd I miss?" Claire pointed at the wriggling black leather shoes peeking over the stone rim of the well.

"You missed that, you lazy bum. I thought we were done for. Why didn't you help me push her in?"

Roger scratched his head and looked a trifle befuddled. "Musta nodded off. Sorry 'bout that. I'm going back to sleep." He turned around and walked back into the cottage, his feet shuffling tiredly. Now that the adrenaline was draining from her system, Claire felt she could sleep too. Besides being tired, the drugs weren't completely out of her system.

"Come on boy," she said to Weenie and they both went back into the cottage, where they found the other door led to a comfortably appointed bedroom, leaving Auntie Ginger screaming incoherently into the darkness. And they slept like babies.

Chapter Eleven: Highwayman

"I came from a real tough neighborhood. Once a guy pulled a knife on me. I knew he wasn't a professional, the knife had butter on it." — Rodney Dangerfield

Claire dreamed of Nick again. This time she was shopping in the bazaar world, her motley collection of coins jangling in her pocket, begging to be spent on all the weird and wonderful stuff that was on display. She saw a beautiful leather jacket that looked so soft and pliable that she just had to have it. Claire grabbed the butter-smooth leather and held it up to look at it and saw that it was her brother's skin with his face still visible in the grain of the leather. His eyes opened and she tried to throw the jacket down but couldn't let go. Then his mouth opened and he said her name…

"Claire!"

She screamed and tried to run and found herself tangled in a quilt being held by Roger who was saying her name.

"Nick," she said vaguely. "Nick, oh my brother. He's lost and my dream was so bad." She was blabbering and realized she was crying uncontrollably. Roger stroked her hair and murmured reassurances in her ear. She pushed him away and quickly dried her eyes, disgusted with herself and embarrassed. There was no time for this. While she was uselessly crying, her brother was maybe being made into a leather jacket somewhere.

"I'm fine," she said. "Give me a minute to get myself straightened out. My hair's a mess." It was indeed a mess. While she got her emotions under control, she sat in front of a mirror at a dressing table and put the silver brush to its original purpose and gave her hair a hundred strokes. It was calming and gave her time to gather her reserves so she could face the world. She put her unruly but brushed fiery tresses into a severe pony tail using about a hundred elastic bands and ventured forth from her solitude.

"Let's see if our kind hostess has any food that isn't poisoned. I'm starving," she said to the house in general as she walked out of the bedroom. Weenie was awake and rummaging through the kitchen cabinets with canine gusto. Claire walked into the kitchen and found his tail protruding from a cabinet and wagging enthusiastically while munching sounds emanated from within.

"Anything good in there, Weenie?" Claire inquired of the wagging tail.

"Woof," came the muffled response.

Claire opened a cabinet which hadn't been obviously pillaged by the apparently ravenous Weenie. Inside was a large basket full of ripe fruit. She recognized apples and pears but there were some other types of fruit with which she was unfamiliar. She underhand tossed one of the strange fruits to Roger who had entered the kitchen behind her and then she selected a yellowish pink apple for herself.

"I don't see how she could have tampered with an apple," said Claire as she bit into the juicy delicious fruit.

"You never saw 'Snow White?'" asked Roger, rubbing the unidentified fruit on his jacket sleeve and peering at it suspiciously. Claire nearly choked. Snow White had indeed been poisoned with an apple. But she was hungry, and what were the odds? She looked at the apple and with a mental shrug, took another bite. It was too good to waste.

"I almost threw this at you, you, you... baboon butt."

137

"Baboon butt? I have no words," laughed Roger. "Your eloquence astounds me. What the heck kind of fruit is this anyway?"

"Dunno. Try it and see if it's any good."

Roger sniffed the purplish fruit and took a bite. Its skin was thin and the meat was juicy and flavorful and very sweet. "Mmmmm. That's good. Like mom used to make." Roger grinned broadly with purplish juice running down his chin until Claire threw a towel at him.

"Cretin," she muttered just loud enough for Roger to hear who grinned even wider in response. Claire stuffed some of the fruit in her book bag and tossed a couple more to Roger to put in his backpack. Weenie came out from the cabinet snarfing down something that he found tasty, his entire muzzle covered in what looked like sugar. Claire laughed and petted his sticky head. She opened another cabinet and dropped her backpack in shock. Inside the cabinet were kids' clothes and toys and other gear that obviously belonged to children. Some of the stuff was from the world they were in, like small crude leather shoes. Other stuff was obviously not; like a plastic Transformers lunchbox and a Toronto Blue Jays baseball cap… and a creamy soft leather jacket.

Claire's hands shook as she picked up the jacket, half expecting to see her brother's dead face in the grain. When she held it up and saw that it was just a normal leather jacket that any boy might have worn and not the one in her nightmare, Claire started breathing normally and only then became aware she had been holding her breath.

Weenie barked loudly and Roger looked up and saw the panicked look of shock frozen on Claire's face and rushed over to her.

"What's wrong?" he asked excitedly, apparently ready to start smashing heads with his extendable baton which had appeared as if by magic in his hand.

"These things," she explained with a raspy voice that betrayed that she was on the verge of losing it again. "I think they belonged to people. To little kids that monster… that hideous *hag* abducted. And ate? Oh my god. I think I'm going to be sick." She rushed outside and threw up her recently ingested apple in the flowerbeds all over the too bright flowers next to the door. She looked up with hate smoldering behind her purple eyes at the shoes still peeking over the lip of the well. They were no longer moving. Claire wanted to set them on fire and listen to Auntie Ginger scream. She wiped her mouth and took a step toward the well, murder on her mind, when Roger's hand fell onto her shoulder and he held her back.

"She's brown bread, leave her be."

The odd usage distracted her from her obsessive hateful intentions. "Brown bread?" she asked.

"Yeah. You know. Dead. Brown bread. Like apples and pears for stairs. Like that."

"No, you weirdo. I do not know. You say the strangest things, Roger." He shrugged in response. With effort, she turned her back on the well and its macabre contents and went back inside. Roger followed her back into the cottage. She went back to the cupboard with the grisly souvenirs and started sifting through the things methodically, trying not to think of her brother Nick being captured by this evil woman.

"Why don't you leave it, Claire? No sense in torturing yourself like that," suggested Roger softly.

"I have to know, don't you see?" she asked plaintively. "If the search ends here, I have to know. I can't leave until I know if I have to go home and tell my mother that her only son was cut into chops by an overweight clean freak with a baking fetish!" Her voice rose steadily until she was almost shouting. Roger's face betrayed his sympathy and she felt sorry immediately for yelling at him but she was too emotional to apologize so she just went back to sorting through the contents of the cabinet. Without saying anything, Roger

139

started helping her separate and sort through the junk. He didn't know what might have been Nick's but he was able to cull out the stuff that obviously belonged to a girl or to a lower tech world. They didn't find anything that was recognizably Nick's and Claire felt a little better, but you can't prove a negative and a niggling doubt refused to be dispelled from her heart.

Claire had a sudden inspiration and rushed back to the alien in the cage with hope surging in her soul. "Hey, little guy," she panted, an eager smile twitching her lips at the thought that it might be so easy to find Nick. "You're a psychic little bugger aren't you?"

"What malarkey is this, then?" asked Roger who had followed Claire to the cage side.

"He's psychic, Roger. Maybe he can help us find Nick."

"Are you having me on? Or are you a nutter?"

"Neither. Now be quiet and let me talk to this little googly eyed guy." She turned back to the alien who looked at her a little sadly. His ears were drooping which lent an air of moroseness to his demeanor. He looked lugubrious, Claire thought, also thinking that this was the first time she had ever actually seen someone or something that had that particular quality. It's a great word but more suited to Dickens novels than real life, Claire had found, much like her mother had said.

"Can you hear me, little guy?" she asked. His mesmerizing swirling eyes flashed green. Yes, he could hear her. Roger gasped in disbelief. "Sweet," she smiled broadly. "Was Nick ever here, in this cottage?" He shrugged expressively. This was obviously the 'I don't know' signal. Her hopes fell. "Is he here now?" The eyes flashed red. That's a no. "Is Nick in this world?" Shrug. She steeled herself for more disappointment. "Is he alive?" Green.

Claire whooped with joy at the confirmation that Nick was alive. She didn't know why she believed the little monkey-like creature so readily, but she did. She grabbed Roger and danced him around in glee. He looked perplexed in the extreme. Claire calmed down and explained how the alien had helped to wake her up and how they came up with a system of communication and his apparent psychic abilities. Roger was dubious and wanted to test this assertion with some mind reading demonstrations but with the answers limited to 'yes,' 'no,' and 'beats me,' Claire didn't feel it would be time well spent.

"Take my word for it, Paddy," she said. "We need to get a move on."

They searched the place as quickly and efficiently as possible. Claire refused to take any food that was meat-related for fear that it might not be from an animal and she didn't want to find out the hard way that little brothers taste like chicken. They did find a couple of useful items in Auntie Ginger's room. One was a small orange beaded bag with a clasp that looked both horribly ugly and cheap. Claire was inclined to ignore it but out of curiosity Roger opened it and found that it could hold a lot more than should have been possible. In fact, the only limitation that they found was contents had to fit through the small mouth of the bag which limited the diameter of any object to just a few inches. But if you could fit it in, the bag would hold it and without getting any heavier. Roger kept calling it a bag of holding. It lightened their load considerably.

They also found a rusty cavalry saber with an ivory handle and a leather sword belt. Claire thought it was ridiculous to be lugging around a sword, especially since neither one of them knew how to actually use one. But Roger insisted on strapping it on and admiring himself in the mirror.

"I'm for sure keeping this baby. Makes me look dashing, doesn't it?"

"A sword, Roger? Really? You're more likely to hurt yourself with that thing than an opponent. And if you cut yourself, you'll likely get an infection and die. I'm guessing you haven't had a tetanus shot lately."

"Oh, come off it, Claire. I look quite the figure. People are likely to run from the mere sight of me in this rig."

"Or collapse laughing. Fine, keep it. Maybe we can sell it or something."

It took them longer than they would have liked to be ready to go. Claire was obviously impatient and kept urging Roger to hurry up but he was insistent about being thorough. When they had taken everything of value that they could carry conveniently, including a fair amount of assorted coins, they took their leave of the quaint little cottage and followed a weed-grown track that lead to a wider road that in turn led in the general direction of a castle that they could see on a hill in the distance. Claire spared a single look back at the cottage with its well and the feet of the cannibal hag protruding from it. Shameful waste of a perfectly good well. She also noted the location of their doorway to home, which looked like it led into a woodshed.

"Let's take a dander down the boreen, lass," suggested Roger which was clear enough to Claire what he meant. They used a good ground-eating pace and were soon well out of sight of the cottage. Claire's mind turned to the task ahead.

"So, swashbuckler," began Claire as they walked toward the castle, taking turns carrying the alien's cage while the intrepid Weenie ranged ahead, sniffing and peeing on anything of interest. "This castle we're heading for. Who lives in it?"

"Well, it's been a donkey's years since I was here, gingernut. But as I recall, there was a King and he had a son and a daughter. His wife was a right feek but a bit of a lady muck if you get my drift."

"No. No, I don't get your drift. English, please?"

"Right. I forget you can't talk proper." Roger grinned at Claire's irritation which made her even more irritated. "Ok. The King's wife. The Queen, I suppose is the kids' stepmom. She's a fine looking lady but severely full of herself, I guess you could say.

She's got the King under her thumb and she treats the kids none too well."

"How old are these kids?"

"Haven't got a baldy." He looked askance at Claire's cloudy expression. "I mean it's tough to say. They were younger than we are, last I was here, but they could be all grown up by now. Who knows? Time being what it is for us and all."

"The king was a decent enough guy, though?"

"I suppose he was. Bit berco, letting his wife run the show and all."

"So, what's the plan, Paddy? We just march up to the front gate and demand to see the King?"

Roger refused to let Claire get to him and showed no reaction to being called Paddy. He couldn't help it if his speech was seasoned and flavorful whereas hers was irritatingly proper and correct. Dull, even. But he toned down his accent. "Getting in might get problematical. Knocking isn't likely to get us arrested, but we probably won't be invited in, either. It's the King's bleeding castle innit? Besides, why would we want to see the King at all? Surely, if your brother is here, someone in the village will know about it."

"There's a village by the castle?" asked Claire.

"That there is. Place called Aulin or something similar."

"You've been there, I take it? What's it like? Where should we start looking?"

"I've been there. It's a bit whimsical, but it's got all the same stuff as any other town. I figure we do the same thing we did in Weenie's world." Weenie looked back at them and pricked his ears up and gave a short woof. "No, we're not talking about you, boy," Roger called to him with a smile. "I think we should check out the local pub."

"I'll try to forebear from suggesting that you want to start at the pub because you're Irish, Roger." Claire made a drinking motion with her hand and Roger scowled. "But I was thinking we could see if there are any shops that he might have gone into. Toy store or something like that."

"Nothing to keep us from doing both. And I'll try to *forebear*," he placed a lot of emphasis on the word to rub it in that Claire used unwieldy vocabulary the way a carpenter uses a hammer: Often and with force. "from suggesting that you want to go in shops because you're one who could never resist a display window." Now it was Claire's turn to scowl.

"I resent the implication," she intoned in her best royalty voice with her nose high in the air.

"There's a lot of that going around, sure."

The road they travelled was pretty much the opposite of the road to The Hollow. The sun was up and poured its warmth on them while a soothing breeze kept it from getting too hot. Flowers grew in the grass lining the smooth and rut-less path and bees and butterflies were industriously adorning the scene. Weenie leapt and pounced in the high grass, joyously chasing bugs and phantom scents, woofing with delight whenever he caught either. The trees were a riot of vibrant green and white as the magnolias and dogwoods bloomed. Claire deeply breathed in air heavy with the perfume of springtime. Roger duplicated that feat and promptly sneezed violently several times in a row.

"Bless you," Claire said politely.

"Than's," Roger replied with his nose crinkled like he might sneeze again. "Loo's li' I migh' have allergies." He pulled a hanky out of one of the pockets in his jacket and blew his nose loudly and long. "Sorry," he said, his voice much improved.

"Never mind," said Claire waving her hand at Roger distractedly. "It looks like Weenie may have found something

144

interesting." Weenie was growling and tugging at something hidden in the high grass and wildflowers.

"If you consider a cow patty interesting..." Roger remarked under his breath.

Claire ignored Roger and ran over to the spot by the side of the road where Weenie was worrying something they couldn't see. It turned out to be a short little man who was trying ineffectually to hide even though Weenie had him by the pants leg and was alternating between trying to tear off his pants' leg and trying to drag him out of the grass. When he saw that he had been discovered by more than just a dog, the wee man stood up and brushed himself off, or tried to. Weenie still had hold of his pants at the ankle and the man only came up to Claire's shoulder, so he was about to topple over every time Weenie shook his head.

"Alright, you got me. I surrender," gasped the diminutive man with no trace of humor in his voice. He was dressed in an odd sort of camouflage, matching pants, jacket and hat that closely matched the greens of the grass and weeds with the odd splash of color to mimic flowers. Random twigs and bits of grass were sewn onto it. Claire looked at him curiously but was aware that the man wasn't even looking at her in return. His gaze was at Roger behind her who, she saw when she turned her head, had out his new sword and was holding it in a distinctly threatening manner.

"Whoa, Roger," exclaimed Claire, alarmed at his hostility. "What are you doing?" He didn't answer her directly but instead pointed at the strange little man with the tip of his sabre and waggled the sword expressively.

"Drop the wand," Roger said in a voice edged with steel. Claire looked more closely at the little man who was indeed holding a carved and polished stick in his upraised hand. "Do it now, ya wee blaggard."

Claire could see the calculating look in the man's eyes and knew a split second before he acted that he wasn't going to drop the

145

wand. Weenie realized it too and as the man shifted the wand to point at Roger, he was upended by the Dalmatian who charged him, all flashing teeth and deafening bark. A blistering, sizzling bolt of *something* shot out of the wand and missed Roger's head by mere inches, making his raven hair stand up on that side with static electricity. In a split second Roger was standing on the man's arm with the point of his new weapon touching the man's neck. Claire quickly grabbed the wand out of their assailant's hand and held it up to the bright sunlight to examine it when it was apparent that the brief scuffle was over.

The wand was made of some dark, tightly grained wood and was very smooth to the touch, either from careful polishing or by long years of being handled. Arcane symbols were carefully carved in relief along the shaft and it seemed to weigh a lot more than it could if it was made only of wood. She pointed it at the ground by the man's head and tried to make it shoot something out, but with no success.

"Alright, mate. What's the story?" Roger asked the man he was standing on. Just then, Claire screeched loudly and incoherently. "Wha?" he asked her, taking his eyes off the man.

"Backpack!" she nearly screamed in his ear in between inarticulate screeches.

"Keep your Alans on, love." He looked where she was gesticulating and saw a faded red backpack with some robot on it. "It's just a satchel all a flitters."

"It's NICK'S backpack. I'd recognize that tattered old Ironman anywhere!"

"Weenie," Roger called to the dog, "Let go of the bugger. Good boy. You stay there and be ready to bite his face off."

"Woof."

"Now, you," Roger continued as he backed off a pace and gestured with his sabre. "Stand up slowly. Any more tricks up your sleeves? I'm tempted to slit you open and see if there's any more surprises on the inside." Roger grimaced horribly and ran his free hand over the hair on the side of his head that was still standing straight up. The little man stood up like he was told and held his hands out in front of him.

"Please, I surrender," he began in a much softer voice from the one he had used just a few seconds ago. "You wouldn't hurt me?"

"Shut up," said Roger roughly. Claire had already reached down into the grass and pulled up the Ironman backpack by one of its frayed and faded straps. She held it up and looked at it. It was much as she remembered it and Claire was certain that it was Nick's. There was no obvious damage to it beyond what two strenuous years on the back of a rambunctious elementary school boy will cause. No blood or scorch marks or elephant foot prints or anything else to indicate trauma to its wearer.

"Where is the boy that this belongs to?" she asked the man in camouflage much more calmly than she felt. Her hand around the strap of the backpack squeezed and relaxed and clenched again in an ominous rhythm.

"Don't know nuthin bout no boy, miss," he said with a smug grin on his dirty, scruffy face. "Bought it off a man in Aulain. Cost me two coppers. It's mine."

A tear leaked out of one of Claire's eyes and slowly meandered down her check. She made no effort to wipe it off but let it make its salty way to her resolutely set chin. She turned her face to Roger who saw that despite the tear she was very much in control of herself and the situation.

"Roger, I am not satisfied with this little pig's answer. I'm going to ask him again and if I remain unsatisfied, I'll need you to hurt him."

"My pleasure," he responded grimly. "Chancy eejit nearly took off me head."

147

"Sir," she addressed the little man again. "This belongs to my brother and I desperately want to find him." She held up the backpack. "So I'll ask you again. Where is the boy that this belongs to?"

"Tojer," he said defiantly. "Bought it off'n a man," he was interrupted when Claire nodded curtly to Roger who without any hesitation at all hit the man across the face with the fist holding the hilt of the sabre. The sudden brutal violence of the act took Claire by surprise but she didn't let any emotion show at all; her face remained as impassive as the sunlight and just as merciless. The man fell backward and collapsed in the grass with a grunt of surprise and pain. Weenie instantly was on him, his teeth clamped on an ankle; growling and worrying.

"Back, Weenie," Roger told the dog. "We'll feed you any of the parts we cut off." He reached down and grabbed the man by his shirt and hauled him back out of the grass and onto the road where he shook him and let him stand on his own which he managed, just barely.

"Don' feed me to your monster!" gasped the man as he spit out blood and a broken blackened tooth.

"We've no time for these…" Claire groped for a word, "shenanigans." Roger snickered. "If I don't like your answer this time I will have Roger cut off whichever part of you he wants and feed it to Weenie. And we'll know if you're lying. Roger, hand me the lie detector we found on the Ramses that you have in your pocket." Roger looked at her blankly for a second then he grinned in understanding and took out the dosimeter and placed it in her outstretched hand.

She walked over to where the alien sat complacently in its cage, eyes swirling sickeningly. Claire leaned down and whispered to it, "I don't want this scum to know you have psychic abilities. The fewer that know, the better." Its eyes flashed green. Apparently, it agreed with her. "Can you tell if this guy lies to me?" Green again. If it had been red, she would just have had to bluff, but this was much

148

better. "I know you can manipulate electronics. Can you affect this gadget?" In answer the numbers went from zero to 99 and it gave a loud chirp. "Perfect." She walked back to where Roger and Weenie were guarding their now terrified captive.

"Let's test this shall we?" The man eyed her suspiciously. "What's your name?" she asked him. He spat out more blood.

"Rupert," he said reluctantly. The machine didn't respond.

"So far so good," she said happily. "What do you do for a living?" He hesitated until Roger started to pull his fist back in obvious preparation to hit him.

"I sell odds and ends to those that want em." The machine displayed a 50 and gave a lower pitched chirp.

"Well, that's obviously only part of the truth. Where do you get these odds and ends?"

"Find em," he said sullenly. The impromptu (very good word) lie detector showed 99 and beeped loudly again.

"Try again," said Claire.

"Buy em wholesale," he lied. Claire nodded to Roger who without any preparatory drawing back of his hand, backhanded Rupert across the face hard enough that the rogue went sprawling on the road, limbs akimbo. Weenie again grabbed him by the ankle more quickly than a snake. This time Rupert was out cold and it took a few minutes to revive him. By the time he came around, Claire was considering dragging him behind them her impatience was so great. Instead she calmed herself and opened Nick's backpack to see what might be inside.

There was a change of camouflage outfit in the bag and a bar of soap. Some coins of predictably odd denominations jingled in a side pocket, including two dollars in quarters that her mother had given Nick for the candy machines before he vanished. Tears welled up and blurred her vision, but she pressed on, hoping for a clue as to where Nick might be or at least where he had been. There was a packet of M&M's, a small ivory figurine, two cheap watches, a pair of dice and a can of mosquito spray. She had almost given up hope of finding clues when she found a rolled up piece of wide ruled notebook paper with Nick's writing on it. It didn't seem to make a lot of sense. Written on the paper was a long sequence of letters and numbers down the left side, close to the margin. It was mostly L's an R's but with a smattering of S's and some of the L's and R's had 2's and even a couple of 3's beside them. She couldn't make much of it and showed it to Roger to see if he could puzzle it out.

"Dunno, Claire. I would say the L's stood for left and the R's for right, but what's with the S's and numbers?" He shrugged. "Maybe this muppet will have some idea. And maybe he'll make us beat it out of him. Oh, what craic we'll have then, lass." There was something decidedly unpleasant in the gleam in Roger's eyes, but Claire figured her own eyes weren't expressing anything cheery of late.

"You're not going to have any teeth left if you keep telling fibs, Mr. Rupert," said Claire in a patently false pleasant voice when the nasty little man was finally with-it enough to make sense of what she was saying. He glowered back at her. "Let's try again, shall we? Where do you get the stuff you sell?

With a resigned sigh that spoke volumes all by itself and quick glance at Roger who looked disappointed that he probably wasn't going to get to smack Rupert again, the robber said, "Fine, alright? I take them off people what has 'em."

"You steal them, you mean."

"Yar. I steals em."

"And where is the young man from whom you stole this item?" asked Claire while holding up the backpack.

"I don't know," he said and immediately cringed from the expected blow from Roger but Claire put out her hand and the blow never came. Rupert opened one swollen eye and seeing that he wasn't about to be hit in the face, continued. "I don't know where 'e is. Because he done runnoft." Claire checked and saw he was telling the truth.

"Fine. You don't know where he is. But under what circumstances did you obtain this backpack?"

"Er. Circumstances was that I knocked him down and told 'im to give it me an' he did," Rupert said, evidently surprised that they hadn't figured that part out yet.

When Claire heard that she wanted to hit him again despite the fact that he was telling the truth but restrained herself on the theory that such an act would be, at the best, unhelpful, and at worst downright dishonorable. But she still wanted to do it. The picture in her mind's eye of this stooge knocking down Nick and robbing him brought out all the defensive big sister feelings. Like a lion tamer with a whip and a chair, she forced her more ferocious instincts into the background. "Ok," she said. "Then what happened?"

"I asked him what all the trash in his pack was an' I dumped it out. He were most unhelpful. Then he throwed dirt in me eyes and runnoft. Dirty rat." He seemed strangely offended that his victim would dare to harm him and run away without being helpful.

Claire help up the paper with the letters and numbers. "Before he, uh, runnoft, did he tell you what this is?"

"Oh, that," said Rupert. "He said it were the directions to the middle of the minotaur's maze. I kept it in case it were valuable."

"Maze? Where is this maze?" asked Claire.

"Beats me. He didn't say. He up and-,"

"Runnoft, yeah we got that much," Roger cut him off. Rupert nodded.

"Well, can you at least tell us which direction he ran?" asked Claire in exasperation.

Rupert pointed down the road in the same direction they were going. "Hied off down the road toward Aulain, quick as a flash, he did."

"And this was today?" asked Claire hopefully.

"Wut?"

"Today, sir. Did you rob my brother today?"

"Nar. It war mont's ago, it war." Hope fizzled in Claire's breast. But at least this fool had supplied the first tangible clue as to Nick's whereabouts.

"See? Now wasn't that easy?" asked Claire in a voice that her mother would have recognized as her own and Claire had last heard a week ago when she had to be asked to pick up her wet towel off the bathroom floor. "Now take off your clothes."

"Wut?" This seemed to be Rupert's favorite word or at least the one he was most familiar with. The little man's eyes got really wide really quickly at the order to disrobe. Roger couldn't suppress a startled chuckle. Claire almost smiled at the look of comic surprise on the highwayman's face but managed to maintain her stony visage.

"You should know the drill, Rupert. You hide on this road and waylay passersby and take their stuff. If Weenie hadn't been alert enough to find your sorry butt in the weeds, we probably would have been robbed just like my brother, maybe even fried by your little toy. Well, the tables are turned, buckaroo. Consider yourself out-robbed. Now take off your clothes before I have Roger knock you senseless again. Looks like he wants to, doesn't it?" Roger tried to look fierce but the effect was spoiled when he sneezed violently and had to blow his nose again.

The little man whined and complained worse than her brother at bath time but ultimately Rupert's protests subsided when Roger made exaggerated preparations to punch him in the face again. With black looks and much muttering, the robber stripped off his camouflage outfit and soon was standing on the side of the road in nothing but an incongruous pair of Sponge Bob Square Pants boxer shorts that he took from God knows who. Claire stuffed his clothes in Nick's backpack while Rupert stood shivering despite the warm sunlight. He looked pathetic and quite sad with the blood drying on his face and ankle and his skinny shoulders already starting to turn pink in the sun.

"Aw, come on, miss," complained Rupert when they were about to leave him practically naked on the lonely roadside. "At least gimme my shoes? There's stickers in the grass!"

"I'll tell you what," Claire told him after a couple seconds of thought. "I'm looking for my brother and if you can give me any kind of clue as to where I might find him, I'll give you your shoes back. Although I doubt they are actually yours."

"Ah course I dunno where he is, but if anybody knows it'd be the queen. She keeps a sharp eye out for goings on round here." He held out his hands, hoping of the shoes. Claire dug them out of the backpack but didn't hand them over. Instead she dangled the black Converse All Stars just out of reach.

"Not quite good enough, Rupert, my boy," she said teasingly. "But if you tell me how to use the wand I took off you, I'll be generous and give them to you anyway."

"I dunno how to work it for most things," he said dully. "Just that saying 'fritters' makes that lightning stuff shoot out of it." He shrugged. Claire pointed the wand at a bunch of wild flowers.

"Fritters," she said forcefully and was rewarded by a sizzling bolt of energy that leapt from the wand tip and fried the flowers to a blackened crisp.

"That was almost my noggin," whispered Roger in astonished anger as he rubbed the side of his head where the hair still stuck up in unruly spikes. Rupert had the good grace to look ashamed. Claire threw the shoes at him and they hit him in the face and knocked him over into the grass where they left him.

"Come on, guys. Let's go meet the queen," Claire remarked and started down the road whistling 'If I Only Had a Heart.'

"Why not?" agreed Roger as he followed her.

"Woof," chimed in Weenie.

Chapter Twelve: The Queen

As a child, I was as intrigued by the Evil Queen as I was charmed by Snow White. --Stephane Rolland

The crew made good time despite the fact that they were weighed down. Claire was now toting two backpacks; her own and now Nick's. Roger was solely responsible for lugging the alien in the cage in addition to his own pack and the sabre which banged awkwardly on his thigh.

"Screw this," he said after a mile or so of fairly rapid but uncomfortable progress. "Claire I'm going to let this little wierdo out of the cage. We'll both be more comfortable if he just sits on my shoulder."

Claire had no objection and they made the adjustments. They left the cage in a clump of distinctive flowers so they could retrieve it should the need arise. Once again they were on their way into the unknown, Claire with renewed hope, Roger with a rising sense of adventure, Weenie with the same fierce loyalty and happy go lucky unconcern as always and the no-name alien with a new perch and the same googly eyes.

"We named Weenie," said Claire to break up the monotonous silence. "But we haven't named our little alien psychic gonzo."

"Are you suggesting that we give the little bugger a name?" asked Roger.

"Well, yeah. I guess I am."

"Did it occur to you that he might already have a name? Maybe we should just ask him what it is."

"Good, point, Roger." She slowed her pace a bit until she and Roger were walking abreast and turned to look at the rider on his shoulder. "Hey, there, Crazy-Eyes. Do you have a name or what?" Its eyes flashed green. "You do? Awesome. Can you tell it to us?" Red. "I see. Is that because we can't pronounce it or that it isn't a sound or something like that?" Hesitation, then green. "Would you like us to come up with a name for you ourselves?" More hesitation, then it shrugged in an incredibly human way. Claire grinned. "Ok, then. I'll call you 'Spanky the Wonder Monkey.'"

Roger's laugh was cut off by a deafening high pitch scream that didn't so much seem to come from the alien as from the air around them. It was obvious that it was originating from him, but just not from his mouth. It was so head-splittingly loud that it drove Claire to her knees with her hands clasped desperately over her ears which did absolutely no good. Roger looked down at her in apparent confusion and Weenie trotted over and licked her face in concern. It went on for what seemed an eternity to Claire whose discomfort progressed to pain and she scrunched up her eyes and put her head on the dirt. About the time she was becoming concerned that she might die of a hemorrhage (terrible word to spell), it stopped and was replaced by Roger frantically saying her name over and over.

There was no ringing in her ears afterward, just silence. She stood up on the wobbly legs of a newborn foal and fought down the urge to technicolor yawn for the second time that day. Claire looked at the alien's stoic face but couldn't do it for long because the eyes going in spirals were not helping the nausea situation.

"What in the blazes was that?" she asked.

"What was what?" returned Roger. "You just fell down with a horrid look on your face. I thought you had a rupture. I was brickin it for sure."

"That little demon nearly killed me," she exclaimed, pointing at Spanky the Wonder Monkey. "You didn't hear anything?"

"Maybe he didn't agree with the name you gave him, Claire," suggested Roger warily, trying to keep an eye on the alien on his shoulder and succeeding only in turning part way round. "And he displayed more of his psychic repertoire?"

"Talk about your extreme reaction," she said. "Fine, I won't call you Spanky the Wonder Monkey." His eyes flashed green. "I'll call you Ramses after the ship we found you on, ok?" Green again. She found herself pathetically eager to please in order to avoid the horrific mental screeching experience. After she steadied out and stopped shaking and feeling like she was going to urk, they got back on the road but most of her trust and affection for the little creepy alien had evaporated like the morning dew. As a far as Claire was concerned, any goodwill he had earned with waking Claire up and being a living lie detector was very much cancelled out by the tortuous mind-scream.

Once they got to moving again, it wasn't long before they came to the abrupt beginnings of a village. It began abruptly because there was a wall with a gate which clearly defined where the village was and where it wasn't. It wasn't a huge medieval wall, but it was taller than either of the human members of what Claire was beginning to think of as her 'crew' and presented a significant obstacle to their progress. Fortunately, there was an open gate that the road ran right in through. Nobody was guarding the gate so they sauntered on in unimpeded.

Once inside the village, the road was cobbled and ran straight as an arrow to a spacious town square situated around a fountain depicting two women with buckets pouring water out of jars, which disgorged an unending deluge of sparkling clear water into the fountain pool with a pleasant gurgling sound. The town square was dominated by a massive stone cathedral on one side and a half timbered inn on the other. The inn was declared to be "The Queen's Colors" by the sign out front. The sign, the doors and the window shutters were adorned with pink, lavender and green stripes. Claire shuddered to think what kind of unhinged mind would pick such a hideous motif as 'their' colors. There were a number of other businesses arrayed around the square; most of the expected variety like a cobbler and a cloth merchant. There was one that stood out both because it had a neon sign out front and because that sign proclaimed in glowing red letters that the establishment was "Mad Mike's Marvelous Mysteries."

"Queen's Colors," said Roger.

"Mad Mike's," said Claire at the same time. They frowned at each other.

"Rock, paper, scissors," suggested Roger. Roger won with scissors versus Claire's paper. Claire stamped her foot in frustration but Roger wasn't paying attention. He was already halfway across the square to the inn/pub when she jogged to catch up with him. Weenie was greedily lapping up water out of the fountain and had to hurry to catch them, his muzzle dripping and his tongue flopping happily.

"Oaf," she said under her breath.

"Sore loser," Roger returned. Well, he had her there, she guessed.

The Queen's Colors was pretty much the exact opposite of Happy Jack's, much like the difference in the paths to town. It was full to bursting with loud, merry folks drinking, eating, talking and being boisterous. The smell of something fried and presumably tasty permeated the thick atmosphere of the common room and mingled with the smoke of numerous pipes and cigars. Apparently, word hadn't spread to this little world that tobacco smoke was harmful. The barmaids wore horrible garish dresses in the aforementioned colors and were as busy as bees. Nobody seemed to notice when Claire and her motley assembly came in through the front door and made their way to the central bar where a voluptuous middle aged woman in the queen's colors tended bar with a huge smile stretched

158

across her jovial face. She greeted them warmly and impossibly, her smile got bigger.

"What can I get for you fine folks today?" she asked them pleasantly. Claire was over her earlier nausea and her tummy was rumbling in protest to the emptiness it was experiencing. By the look on his face, Roger was likewise famished.

"I'll have a milkshake, please," said Claire, her mouth beginning to water with anticipation. The woman behind the bar looked at her oddly.

"A what? You want milk, you said?"

Roger nudged her and said out of the side of his mouth, "No ice cream because there's no ice, dummy."

"Oh, right," said Claire, her hopes of a tasty treat cratering in a heartbeat. "Uhm. Something that tastes good and will fill me up, then," she told the barmaid who nodded like she got that particular order all the time. She filled a tankard with a thick foamy substance and placed it in front of Claire with a grin.

"Try that on for size, honey. That'll be four pence." Claire was familiar with the copper coin known as pence. It was about four times as large as a penny and made from pure copper. She dug a handful of pence and US pennies out of her pockets and placed them on the bar. The barmaid grunted in acceptance and took what was owed, leaving the rest.

"And for you, sugar?" she asked Roger as Claire took a first tentative sip of the frothy drink in the pewter tankard.

"MMMMM!" Claire said with enthusiasm as she took a second, larger gulp of the drink that tasted a bit like cream soda, but thicker and with an unidentified tang to it. It burned slightly as it slid down her throat, leaving a warm sensation in her stomach and a pleasant sweet aftertaste in her mouth. "That's good!" she said, wiping a foam mustache off her upper lip.

"One for me too, then," said Roger and in no time the barmaid had another foam covered drink on the bar and had subtracted the appropriate amount from the pile of coins.

"Enjoy. Let me know if you need anything else," she said helpfully and moved off to wait on other customers. Roger took a good long drink of his beverage and when he was done he wiped off his own foam mustache and gave an appreciative sigh.

"Oy, that's the good stuff, that is. Almost as good as a pint of Arthur's."

"What do you mean?" asked Claire after another long sip. Her thoughts were becoming a trifle fuzzy around the edges. It wasn't an entirely unpleasant sensation, but a corner of her mind was a little alarmed.

"The bevvies, I mean the drinks," explained Roger. "They're a bit strong, but good. Careful, or you'll get proper buckled on this."

"Buckled?" Claire said, laughing. Everything seemed a little more humorous than it should all of a sudden. The alarmed part of her brain got her attention. "You mean drunk?! What? Oh, no, I don't have dime to be trunk. I mean," she started laughing so hard at her switched consonants that she couldn't finish her sentence.

"Oh, here's a lightweight for sure," muttered Roger. "No more of this for you, coppertop. Another slug o that and you'll be scuttered."

Claire looked at the empty tankard in horror, her giggling fit fading away and leaving nothing behind save one forlorn hiccup. How did all that get into her stomach so fast? And why did everything seem slightly off center? Roger waved the barmaid over.

"Rosie lee and some chips for the ginger," he said, his accent thickening up of its own accord.

"Sorry," said the barmaid. "I didn't catch that."

"Tea. A cup of tea, please. And a plate of something fried."

"Sure thing, sugar. Coming right up."

When the tea and fried rings of something that wasn't onion but was still very good arrived, Roger got Claire to start putting it away so there would be something in her stomach to absorb the too-tasty drink she had drained in a hurry. Roger asked the alien on his shoulder if he/she/it was hungry but got no response. He offered a fried ring of some sort on a fork to the little monkey alien who dropped the fried ring on the floor and contentedly munched on the tin fork. Roger shrugged. What do you expect an alien to eat anyways? Weenie made quick work of the fried thing on the ground.

Once they were all busily engaged with munching on the inn's heart attack special, or the cutlery as taste dictated, Roger called over the barmaid again. She sidled over to Roger's end of the bar after she filled someone else's order and batted her eyelashes at him.

"What can George interest you in, now, sugar?" she asked in a very friendly tone of voice.

"George?" asked Claire in confusion.

"George Martin at your service, sugar," said the waitress and blew a kiss at Roger.

"That sounds like a guy's name," said Claire.

"It's not," insisted George.

"You ever think of going by your middle name instead?" suggested Claire, while licking golden foam off her lips.

"Why? You think Raymond sounds better?" asked the barmaid.

"Ahem, well. Right," said Roger, flustered. "My friend here is looking for a boy."

"Aren't we all, dear?" asked the barmaid playfully.

"Yes," he began. "I mean no. It's her brother we're after. He's runnoft, I mean he's lost and we're looking for him. He had an unfortunate run in with this chancer down the road who robbed him. Claire, hand me that infernal gadget of yours what has the picture on it," he finished, turning to Claire who took time out from stuffing greasy fried food into her mouth long enough to fish out her phone and show George the picture of her brother.

"Cute kid," George said politely. "But I haven't seen him in here. Tell ya what, though. If anyone knows, Ed will. HEY ED!" She yelled across the common room then put her fingers in her mouth and whistled piercingly. When it got relatively quiet in the room she yelled for Ed again. In a few seconds a man in a garish military uniform in the queen's awful colors worked his way to the bar where Roger and Claire were sitting. "This is Ed," George said, pointing to the man in the putrid uniform, sprouting braid and ribbons from every available surface. "He's a lieutenant in the Queen's Guard. Ed, these two are looking for the girl's brother. Said someone robbed him on the road here." She showed him the picture on the phone. "Seen him?"

"I saw one of these thingamajigs in Mad Mike's a couple weeks ago," Ed exclaimed as he took the phone from George who went back to the business of the bar. "It didn't work but it looked just like this. Mike wanted twenty gold eagles for it. This one would be worth a fortune, I'd wager." His face transformed from wonder to serious when he saw the picture on the screen. "You know this boy?" he asked Roger.

"Personally, no, I've never met the lad," said Roger as he tried to puzzle out the change in Ed's expression. "But his name is Nick and we're looking for him, seeing as he's lost and all. He's Claire's brother," he added by way of explanation.

"Your brother, miss?" asked Ed as he handed Claire's phone back to her.

"Mmmhmm," she mumbled around a mouthful of deep fried goodness. "These are good! 'At's my bruzzer."

162

"I think her majesty would be interested in making your acquaintance, miss. Why don't we mosey on down to the castle and see if we can get an audience?" Roger was immediately alarmed but seeing the look on his face, Ed calmed him down. "It's not like that, sir. Nobody's in trouble. But her majesty would be greatly interested in meeting anyone that could tell her about Nick." Ed quickly motioned to a subordinate who was hovering just out of conversational range. When he came over, the lieutenant whispered in his ear and the aide jogged off in a hurry.

"Was e done, my bruzzer?" asked Claire whose head was buzzing like a log full of bees. Ed looked at the empty tankard.

"Little too much honey cream ale, miss?" he asked in an understanding tone. Roger nodded. "A nice walk will help you clear your head, miss Claire. Here, let me help you up." When Claire stood, she almost collapsed onto the floor but managed to stand with Ed's help. She grabbed the last fried thingy and her cup of tea and they made their way out of the hustle and bustle of The Queen's Colors.

The walk to the castle did wonders to sober Claire up, just as advertised. Roger never seemed to show any affects from the honey cream ale, but then he was larger, heavier and older than Claire. And Irish, but Claire thought it would be impolitic to point that out again.

The castle itself was a massive stone pile that rose up on the east end of the village like a mountain of grey stone blocks. Flags in the queen's putrid colors flapped gaily from the battlements and the towers, merrily clashing with every other color on earth. The crenelated curtain wall enclosed an enormous amount of land that contained a small village in its own right that existed to serve the castle and its occupants. They walked through the portcullis with their uniformed escort and followed a cobbled pathway into the main hall of the castle where Claire was overawed by the massive silk and wool tapestries draped over the walls. From there, they were ushered into a smaller room, paneled in a dark, burled wood and covered with carpets and rugs. A banked fire in the hearth provided warmth in a room that was chilly despite the fine spring day outside.

Claire, Roger, Weenie and Spanky the Wonder Monkey cum Ramses the alien took seats in finely upholstered, overstuffed couches and chairs in the wood paneled room. The comfy furniture, warmth radiating from the fire and the dimmed, shadowy lighting soon had Claire gently snoring; her head resting on the back of a couch. Weenie curled up on a bearskin rug in front of the fire and promptly began emulating Claire. Roger sat Spanky/Ramses down on an end table and began exploring the room. The alien began nibbling on a brass candlestick with an awful metallic grating noise. Roger discovered a hidden door behind a wall tapestry and opened it for a quick look that revealed an unlit stone staircase that spiraled upwards into darkness. He quickly closed the door and came out from behind the tapestry when he heard footsteps approaching. A liveried servant opened the door ceremoniously and bowed.

"Her Majesty, Queen Beatrix," announced the servant in a stentorian voice that vibrated Roger's toenails. Claire snorted and sat up. Weenie twitched in his sleep and passed gas. The alien took another bite of brass. Roger hastily knelt and kicked Claire in the foot.

"Kneel, you twit," he hissed at Claire from the side of his mouth. Claire stared groggily for a second and started to get off the couch.

"No, no. This isn't formal. I've surprised y'all. Chillax," said Queen Beatrix in an East Texas drawl as she waved one manicured hand at them lazily and made her way to a chair by the fire where she unceremoniously tossed herself and curled her legs under her. "I don't stand on ceremony when I can get away with it," she said to Roger and gave him a knowing wink. "You must be Roger and Claire and this beautiful dog (she pronounced it dawg) is surely Weenie." Claire slowly relaxed back into her spot on the couch. The queen lazily reached down and patted Weenie's head like he was her favorite pet. Weenie opened his eyes and wagged his tail eagerly

164

while licking the queen's hand. She smiled radiantly, displaying perfectly aligned brilliantly white teeth.

Claire was struck by both the queen's nonchalance and her resemblance to Claire's mother. It wasn't a perfect likeness, but the queen and Deborah Grant could easily have passed for sisters. They had the same handsome facial structure with high cheekbones, same colored eyes and hair, similar cupid bow mouths. The Queen's nose was a little longer than Claire's mom's but it wasn't unattractively large by any means. The unexpected likeness made Claire realize how much she missed her mother even though it had only been a little over a day since she had last seen her. Claire had been away from her mother for much longer periods, but the continual stress and strife of her current situation quite simply made part of her want her mommy. The queen noticed Claire's appraising look and cocked her head to the side curiously.

"Pence for your thoughts," said Queen Beatrix in a pleasant, familiar voice. This was something her mother often said, only with 'penny' instead of 'pence' of course. The continued unexpected familiarity startled Claire and she felt her eyes get big and forced a more natural look onto her features.

"Nothing much, er... Your Majesty. You just remind me of someone I know."

"Someone beautiful and downright awesome, I'm sure," joked the queen. Claire was fascinated and a little taken aback by how down to earth this young queen seemed.

"Roger mentioned that he had met you, but he didn't say how young and pretty you were," remarked Claire, still a little in awe and was even more surprised when the queen blushed at the complement.

"Actually," said Roger, "I did meet you, but you were only a princess at the time. Your stepmother, Queen Stephani held your current title." Roger's accent and inflection had lost most of its earthy Irish flavor and sounded much more cultured than it had recently. At the mention of her stepmother, the pleasant features of the queen darkened slightly and her mouth seemed to frown a bit without actually making any movement that Claire could discern.

"Ah, yes. My dear step mum," said the queen in a slightly less than pleasant tone. "That would be why I'm interested in your brother, Claire. A little over a year ago, he showed up at the palace and was quite" "Wait. A year? That can't be. He just went missing yesterday," broke in Claire. She pulled out her iPhone and brought up the picture of Nick. "This is Nick. Are you sure it's the same boy?"

The Queen studied the picture briefly. "Quite sure. That's definitely little Nicky."

"But that can't be," began Claire.

"Sure it can," said Roger. "You forget how time works differently amongst the worlds in the corridor. He could have spent just under a year here, and only an hour would have passed outside."

"Oh. Wow. I didn't think of that." Claire had a hard time wrapping her mind around the possibility that her little pest of a brother might have survived and even thrived on his own in strange worlds for so long. She was even a little envious.

"As I was saying," continued the queen, "Little Nicky was quite entertaining and charismatic. When he heard about our predicament, he-."

"What predicament?" asked Claire causing Queen Beatrix to frown in obvious annoyance at the interruption. She decided against questioning the charismatic part.

"I assumed you had heard…?" prompted the queen. Claire and Roger both shook their heads.

"I see. For the past three years everyone in the royal family save myself has been frozen in time, unable to move a muscle. Not even to blink their eyes. Nobody knows if they are conscious or not."

166

"That's horrible," said Claire.

"How typical of a fairy tale world. I hate these places," said Roger softly enough that Claire hoped the queen didn't hear him.

"We were able to learn of a possible way to return them to active life," continued the queen.

"Kissed by a prince?" ventured Roger.

"Hardly. Don't be silly," chided Queen Beatrix. "There is a horn that when it is sounded, will cancel all spells over anyone that hears it."

"Convenient," remarked Roger. The queen's eyes narrowed slightly, making her look annoyed. Claire wanted to throw something at Roger. They were all distracted for a second by the hideous teeth grating sound of Spanky tearing off a bit of brass candlestick with teeth that must have been as strong as steel.

"Please forgive Roger, Your Majesty," said Claire solicitously. "He was hit on the head recently and hasn't been right since." Roger's gaped-jawed stare of incredulity helped to reinforce her assertion that he wasn't all there. The queen nodded with understanding. Claire continued, "So, you were saying? A horn?"

"Right. The minotaur's horn is the only cure I can think of. Of course, we know the minotaur in question keeps it at the center of his maze, but other than that, we know very little. Nobody even knows where the maze is."

Roger and Claire exchanged glances. Could that piece of paper from Nick's backpack be the key to the maze Queen Beatrix was talking about?

"How does this pertain to my brother, miss er. Uhm. Your Majesty?" asked Claire, stumbling over the unfamiliar honorific.

"I was getting to that, Claire," replied the queen, a touch of irritation showing through her relaxed demeanor. "Anyway, when we learned about the possibility of the horn curing my family, Nick swore he would go and find it. That was months ago and we haven't heard from him since, I'm afraid."

"What caused this coma or whatever?" asked Roger. Claire caught a glimpse of more annoyance flash across Beatrix's face.

"We think it was a curse from a sea hag that was seeking revenge for the death of her mate. She blamed the royal family, although I'm not sure why," explained Queen Beatrix. Out of the corner of her eye, Claire noticed Spanky's eyes quickly flash red. Muffled by the pocket of her jacket, the dosimeter in her pocket gave a quick yelp. Claire doubted that anyone heard it but her. The queen was lying.

"I don't see why Nick would stay here, knowing that his family would be worried sick about him," opined Claire. "He's an irresponsible little brat sometimes, but even he's not that callous." Claire was sure she saw the queens eyes narrow and her jaw clench.

"Nick told me quite often that he was much happier here than at home where he was unappreciated. I mean no offense, but he didn't seem to believe you cared much for him."

Despite herself, this accusation caused intense feelings of guilt in Claire. She didn't want to break down in tears in front of the queen and fortunately she was distracted by Spanky the Wonder Monkey's eyes flashing again and another little chirp from her pocket. This time, the queen noticed the eyes of the alien flash as well. She shifted her gaze from Claire to the crazily swirling eyes of the strange little creature that had just finished eating one of her antique candle holders.

"Oh, what an interesting creature," she exclaimed with pleasure. "I would love to have one like it in my menagerie. What's his name?" asked the queen as she reached out her hand to pet the alien on its little scaly blue head. At this point, things got weird and Claire was a bit disoriented. Time seemed to hiccup and proceed at ¾ speed as Claire watched, unable to move faster than molasses. Spanky sank his razor sharp teeth into the Queen's hand and clamped down with incredible force. The sound of a bone in Beatrix's hand being broken was amazingly loud but was quickly drowned out by the earsplitting scream of agony that erupted from the queen's throat. Blood splattered in slow motion over the couch in startling ruby red droplets as the queen tried unsuccessfully to dislodge the alien from her hand. Almost instantly, the door burst open as a ridiculously attired guardsman charged in with his very un-ridiculous halberd leading the way.

Claire noticed something odd about the queen. As she struggled with the alien causing her so much agony, she seemed to *ripple*. Like the surface of a puddle disturbed by a pebble, her face looked wavy and distorted and then with a *pop* she was clear again. But she wasn't the same person. The woman screaming in pain no longer resembled Claire's mother. She was still quite beautiful, but her hair was raven black and her complexion was white as a corpse and looked even more dramatic framed by that black hair. Her eyes went from cornflower blue to the grey of old ice. With the glamor gone, a great deal of the empathy Claire felt for the woman before her vanished and she realized that she had been duped by magic. Time hiccupped again and the world jerked back to normal speed.

Queen Beatrix patted Spanky on his scaly head with a very un-bitten hand and cooed at him in the voice people reserve for lap dogs and babies. There was no blood on the couch and the door remained un-burst-through by poorly dressed halberd wielding men. Beatrix looked at Claire expectantly as Claire gaped back, slack jawed and mute with shock.

"Eh?" she finally managed in a weak, strangled voice.

"Does the adorable little guy have a name?" The queen asked Claire. She was back to resembling Claire's mother, but Claire could see through the magical disguise. It was like a transparent overlay that covered but failed to conceal the real queen beneath. Whatever had happened seemed to have rendered Claire immune to whatever charm the queen was using to deceive her. Claire hoped her newfound awareness didn't show on her face or in her voice.

"Oh," she managed, attempting to sound normal. "We named him Spa- I mean Ramses after the ship we rescued him from." The Queen went back to petting Spanky, and Claire shot a look at Roger to see if he had been similarly affected. By the look on his face, he had. His eyes were wide and beads of sweat stood out on his brow.

"What was that?" she mouthed silently at Roger. His only response was a minute shrug.

"Well, I'd love to hear all about your adventures and your adorable brother but I can see y'all are all tired out. How about I let you rest and freshen up and we reconvene over dinner in a few hours? I'll have Rackles, my seneschal, show you to your rooms if that's ok?" She picked up Ramses and perched him on her shoulder where he sat, apparently content, passive as ever, his inscrutable eyes spiraling dizzily.

Claire cast a quick glance at Roger who was no help. "Sure, that'd be great, er, Your Majesty," said Claire uncertainly. She wasn't sure she wanted to be the guest of someone who was deceiving her for unknown ends but didn't want to make a powerful monarch angry, either. For now, she would play along.

Chapter Thirteen: The Eye of Connix

"Knowing it and seeing it are two different things." — <u>Suzanne Collins, Mockingjay</u>

Rackles, a portly, snobbish man who had avoided being tricked out in the queen's vomit inspiring colors, led them up several flights of stone stairs and showed them to a suite of rooms that included two bedrooms with bathrooms that actually had running water. Claire had a deliciously hot bath and fell asleep in the capacious tub. She awoke all wrinkled and pruny in lukewarm water. The towels were thick and luxurious and made the clothes she put on seem stiff and scratchy in comparison. She frowned at the reflection of her side in the mirror. Where the werewolf had hit her, her skin was a mosaic of beautiful colors that shouldn't be on human skin. She guessed she was lucky no ribs were broken. She got a fresh shirt out of her backpack and got dressed. As she sat in the central room of the suite, brushing her damp hair and humming softly to herself, Roger came in, also freshly bathed and looking quite refreshed.

"Roger," she said to him as she picked bright red hairs out of the antique silver brush and frowned over a spot of dried werewolf blood. "What happened to the queen earlier?"

"That's a darn good question, Claire," he responded as he sat on a leather ottoman next to her and started pulling on his boots. "What did you see?"

"I saw Spanky bite the crap out of her hand. And then it was like it never happened."

"I saw the same. Anything else?"

"Yes," she said, her purple eyes narrowing in suspicious dislike. "I saw her glamor slip. At first she was like my mother and then after the, uh, event, I could see through it. She looked creepy under the illusion."

"I saw the same. Good to know I'm not off my nut. The woman under the glam, that's the old queen. The stepmother of Beatrix. I wonder why she's pretending? I thought she seemed awfully like my mother, too. Before, that is. Not after." Roger gave a shudder at the thought of the corpse white woman looking like his mother.

Claire giggled. It felt good to laugh, but it didn't last long. "Do you think she was telling the truth about my brother?"

Roger shrugged. "Probably some truth in it. I'm sure he was here and now he's not. Based on the paper with the directions on it, I'd say he was on to something to do with a maze, for sure."

"That horn story is probably reversed, if it's not made up entirely," said Claire giving her hair some more strokes and wincing because they were made a little too vigorous by her irritation. Roger looked at her expectantly, waiting for an explanation. "I mean, she's probably after a horn that will end the curse and wake her family, but I'm betting it's so she can hide it away or destroy it so nobody else uses it. I'm guessing she bewitched them all herself." Roger was nodding along.

"Makes sense, Claire. But it doesn't change much. We still have to find Nick and Nick's not here."

"What if he is, though?" asked Claire earnestly. "I mean, this evil queen lady seems like the type to have dungeons and torture chambers and stuff like that right? What if he's locked up in some dank, smelly dungeon under this castle?"

"You want to go sneaking about in the middle of the night, trying to break into the dungeons and rescue your brother, eh?"

"That's about the size of it. Meanwhile, we'll have a good dinner, not let on we know the queen is an evil witch, and try to get as much info out of her as we can."

"That sounds like a plan, especially the dinner part." He rubbed his stomach dramatically and licked his lips. "But by the looks of it, she's a right bad egg, that one. We'd better not bollox up our little chinwig or we'll be the ones in the dungeon needing to be rescued."

Rackles came and got them at dinner time and escorted them to an extravagant banquet hall heaped with a glorious feast. The smell of their dinner wafted out and greeted them warmly before they even made it into the room so they were salivating already when they walked through the door. Besides a guard at the door, the only people in the room were the queen, ineffective disguise in place and crazy alien on her shoulder, Lieutenant Ed with his gaudy uniform and the three of them. Of course, Weenie didn't get his own seat but seemed content to sit on his haunches between Claire and Roger and greedily accept table scraps. From above them on the wall, a somber king glared down on them from his ornate frame.

"So, about my brother," began Claire when there was a break in the ravenous stuffing of faces that commenced with their arrival.

"Mmm? You've thought of something relevant?" asked the queen between bites of sweet, smoky barbeque ribs.

"Yes, ma'am," answered Claire after she wiped her mouth with the pink, purple and green napkin. "When you saw my brother, did he have his backpack with him?"

"He did, indeed," answered the queen. "And it was stuffed full of anything he thought would be useful. I tried to make sure he was well equipped."

"How long ago was this?" asked Roger.

"At least six months ago, I'm sure," said the queen and then took a loud bite of sweet, buttery corn on the cob. Buttery juice dripped from her chin.

"Did he say where he was going?" asked Claire before tearing off a piece of honey glazed roll.

"Not exactly," answered the queen and took a sip of sweet tea. "He did mention something about a door. In fact, he said he would try the door with the black handle, whatever that means." Claire had an idea what it might mean and it wasn't good. It meant that Nick was going to look for the maze in another world. If the queen was telling the truth Nick wasn't in this world at all. Claire hoped she was lying. Something about a door with a black handle tickled the back of her mind, but she couldn't place it.

"How did you escape being turned into a coma patient, Your Majesty?" asked Roger rudely around a bit of baked sweet potato. "If you don't mind me asking," he added hastily.

"I was out of the castle at the time," she replied vaguely. "I've been awaiting news of Nick for forever it seems. Not just because he might find the cure for my beloved family, but because I worry about his safety." The disguise face was the picture of friendly concern and seemingly sincere warmth, but Claire and Roger could see the real face beneath and it showed barely a trace of humanity on its rigid corpselike features. She took a dainty bite of pecan pie.

"Her Majesty tried to send armed men with Nick to aid in his quest, but he was having none of it," volunteered Lt Ed who until now had eaten sparingly and maintained his dignified silence. "Said something about going places they couldn't. He was a bit mysterious." The queen nodded her enthusiastic agreement.

"Nicky was always mysterious. And brave. We all loved him here," said Queen not-Beatrix.

He was also nine years old, thought Claire. Who sends a nine-year-old on a mission to save a royal family? He was brave?

174

Hogwash. And nobody calls him Nicky. She didn't venture these thoughts aloud.

After a delicious dinner, they retired back to their assigned suite and Claire noticed with chagrin that an armed guard was posted outside their door. Even more ominously, Spanky stayed on the queen's shoulder.

"There's no need for you to stand guard all night," she told the guard. "It's not like we expect to be attacked in the night while we're in the middle of a castle!"

"Orders, miss," was the only response he gave.

Once inside, they rested while they waited for night and made their plans.

———————————

"Excuse me, sir," said Claire to the guard in the wee hours of the night. She could tell that she had startled the man who was probably half asleep on his feet. "My dog, Weenie, needs to go out and do his business." Weenie poked his head out of the door and looked with mute canine supplication at the Guard. At least, Claire liked to think that's what it looked like. The guard rolled his eyes in exasperation.

"It'll have to wait until shift change in three hours, miss," said the irritated guard. "When my relief shows up, I'll take him myself."

"Oh, no need," said Claire in a voice that was the picture of innocent naïveté, which is a French word and very difficult to spell for English speakers and Claire had a feeling it wasn't permissible for spelling bees. "I'll take him myself and she and Weenie took a few steps in the opposite direction of the guard.

The guard moved towards them, reaching for Claire's arm. As he stepped in front of the half open door, Roger stepped out of the darkened room and hit him with a very heavy bronze bust of some important person that history forgot. Unlike how things go in the movies, this did not knock out the guard, mainly because he was wearing a steel helmet. With a startled yelp, the guard dropped his halberd and fell to his knees. Realizing the danger, the guard tried to turn to see his attacker and roll away from the next blow. Fortunately for Roger, he was too dazed to do it quickly enough and Roger hit him again with a loud clang. The first blow smashed in the back of the helmet and deformed it enough that it didn't fit well anymore. It was turned a little sideways and down, obscuring the guard's vision. The second one came from almost directly above the guard's head and smashed the helmet onto his head with tremendous force. The helmet was so deformed that it was going to take a blacksmith a long time just to get if off the poor man's head. Then again, judging from the spreading pool of blood that was growing like a dark halo around the collapsed man, they might just bury him in it.

"Oops," said Roger. "That second one might have done for him." Weenie padded over and sniffed at the downed man. Then, he hiked up his leg and let loose a yellow stream on the atrocious uniform.

"Weenie," scolded Claire. "That's just not nice." Weenie looked back at her as if to say when you gotta go, you gotta go. Claire grabbed their gear from inside the suite and handed Roger his portion.

"Ok," said Roger. "We'll split up, yeah? I'll go this way and you take the other side. We'll meet back here. We've got three hours before shift change." He pulled the communicator they got from the Ramses out of his pocket and successfully got it to stick to his shirt front. Claire already had hers on. She tapped it and was rewarded with a beeping sound reminiscent of Star Trek.

"Cool," she said and then, "Roger," a little more loudly to the air and a half second later she heard her own voice come out of the matching com on Roger's shirt as the computerized device automatically routed her voice to the right com. She tapped it again and said, "Weenie." Once again her own voice sounded back at her but this time from the com she had tied around Weenie's neck.

Weenie cocked his head at the sound, momentarily perplexed. Claire smiled. "Keep in touch," she told Roger and turned and trotted down the hallway. Weenie followed her and Roger took off in the opposite direction.

Without much of a plan, Claire just kept jogging down the hallway which had many fewer doors along it than the corridor where the stairs don't go. When she did encounter doors, if they were unlocked she pushed them open to reveal mainly unused sleeping chambers and suites of residential rooms. Locked ones she didn't bother with. There was no time. When possible, she turned right and when she came to stairs she took them down, seeking whatever was on the lower levels of the castle. Only a couple of times did she and Weenie come across anyone. Whenever Weenie heard someone up ahead he would stop and woof softly and they would duck into the closest room and close the door until the way was clear.

It didn't take too long before Claire was glad they had all their gear with them because finding their way back to their rooms would be pretty iffy. Most of the castle was dark but not too dark to see. Widely spaced wall sconces provided enough light to move about safely without fearing running into a wall but it was still pretty gloomy. Eventually they found themselves in a part of the castle that was obviously not living quarters. It was dirtier and didn't have as much decoration. The doors were all ironbound and looked very sturdy.

They were passing one of the rarer wall tapestries in this part of the castle when Weenie stopped and sniffed at the elegant decorative wall covering. After a couple of good snorts at the corner he grabbed the edge of the tapestry and started trying to tear it away from the wall with his teeth.

"Whatcha got, there, boy?" asked Claire as she grasped the tapestry and helped Weenie peel it away from the stone. It was firmly secured and wouldn't budge. She didn't want to rip it so she quit pulling. "Give it a rest, Weenie," she said. "If there's something behind it, we'll have to find another way to get it loose. Let's look around." She examined the edges of the finely woven tapestry in an effort to see if there was a release of some kind or at least to see how it was attached to the wall. Weenie obediently let the fringe go and started sniffing around in the corridor near the wall hanging. Unable to find anything useful, Claire took a step back and studied the tapestry itself. Depicted in the weave was a massive red and gold dragon, breathing fire rendered in stunning detail with shimmering threads. Claire studied the regal creature, marveling at the detail and appreciating the craftsmanship. She noticed the beast's eyes. There was something intriguing about them. They seemed almost alive. On a whim she reached up and touched one of them and found a slight protrusion in the stone behind it. The other eye also had a slight bump behind it. She pressed both simultaneously and applied pressure. At first nothing happened, but then an entire section of the wall slid backwards to reveal a passageway.

"Awesome," breathed Claire. "Good job, Weenie. Let's see where it goes." They entered the passageway and it closed behind them after they had gone only a few paces. Unconcerned, they continued on. This passage was much narrower than the outside corridor and even darker. There were no torches or candles in wall sconces. The sole source of illumination were odd symbols high on the walls that glowed softly. They went slowly at first as the passage twisted and turned seemingly at random. There were no doors that they saw or windows. Finally, the passage ran straight for a while and ended at a small wooden, ironbound door. To the right was a staircase leading down and to the left was a pair of tiny holes in the wall at about eye level that let in twin beams of light. Claire stood on tiptoe and peered through the holes that were spaced just about perfectly. She was looking down on the banquet hall where they had eaten dinner. From what she could tell of the location of the holes, they were about where a life size portrait of a mounted knight hung high on the wall.

She pulled a flashlight out of her bag and shown it down the pitch black stairway to the right of the door. The stairs curved too quickly to see much so she turned her attention to the door. It was unlocked and swung open on well-oiled hinges.

The room behind the door was relatively small and cozy. Every inch was covered in some form of fabric. Plush crimson carpeting layered the floor and the walls were hung with silk curtains. Flags and banners of every color and with strange designs and symbols were suspended from the ceiling. In the center of the circular room was a table with one stool in front of it. Dangling from the ceiling over the table was a brass and crystal chandelier set with at least a dozen candles made of wax so dark it looked black and burned with an eerie blue light. The table was draped with gold satin and in the center of it on an ornate silver stand was what looked like a giant glass eye. In fact, it looked like the eyes depicted on the tapestry over the secret doorway. The eye was deepest red, shot through with veins of gold and black and the iris was vertically elongated, like a cat's. She and Weenie approached the table slowly and as she neared the eye, she reached out her hand to touch it but stopped when she saw something move within it.

At first she dismissed the movement as her own reflection in the glass but when she leaned closer she saw a tiny man move within. The man wore a long coat and cargo pants over black combat boots. On his back was a bulging pack and at the man's side dangled a cavalry sabre. He wore dark sunglasses despite the gloom through which he moved. It was Roger she was watching in the glass. She touched her com.

"Roger," she said and was rewarded with the beep of the com. In the ball, tiny Roger stopped and tapped his com in response.

"Is this how this thing works, then?" came Roger's voice from the com.

She tapped the com to reply but before she could, one of the silk hangings was pushed to the side and the Queen stepped into the room and stopped and stared at Claire in shock and horror. On her shoulder was Spanky.

179

"What are *you* doing *here?*" exclaimed the Queen. Wondering if Roger had heard that, Claire glanced at the ball where tiny Roger stopped in mid stride, then began to sprint down a stone staircase.

"I couldn't sleep," lied Claire. "I went exploring and just kind of wound up here, Your Majesty." She noticed belatedly that the Queen wore no glamor. Her eyes narrowed suspiciously when Claire recognized her.

"I see," she said contemplatively. "I see a lot. Almost as much as you, it would seem," The Queen looked at the crystal ball. "I also see you've found the Eye of Connix."

"Is that what you call it?"

"Yes. It is actually an eye. Its previous owner is depicted on a tapestry. One you've seen recently no doubt."

"It's, um. Very nice, I'm sure," Claire said unconvincingly. She was glad she hadn't touched the shiny ball. She had thought the sheen of the surface was just highly polished glass, but now she imagined it to be wet like a living eye. She shuddered uncontrollably.

"What did you see in the eye?" asked the Queen as she came closer to the middle of the room. Claire glanced back to the orb and saw the little Roger had vanished.

"See? I didn't see anything. Why? What do you see in the eye?"

The Queen's gaze flashed involuntarily to the Eye of Connix on the table and when she did a scene of horrible battle flashed in its depths. Two armies of awful creatures fought in the ball under the gaze of the wicked Queen.

"It always shows me that. I don't know why," admitted the Queen.

"Perhaps I could take it to someone who could use it to show me where my brother is," suggested Claire hopefully.

"I think not, fool," sneered the Queen. "Now that you know I have the Eye, I can't let you leave this castle. Not only is the Eye of Connix extremely valuable to my enemies, the knowledge of its existence alone is potentially fatal."

Claire wasn't exactly surprised the Queen turned out to be so evil. It was just that kind of week. "So, you were lying about my brother?" she asked.

"Mostly not," replied the Queen. "He did indeed go on a quest for me to find the minotaur's horn. His motivation might have been a bit different than what I let on, though. Just as my reasons for wanting the horn are not quite what you may think."

"Yeah, I guessed you're the one responsible for the royal family's predicament," said Claire stalling for time for Roger to find them. "But I don't see how you could convince my brother to abandon his home for your silly quest."

The queen laughed in a predictably sinister way. "The idiot boy thought he was saving you, girl. I put a glamor on Princess Beatrix to make her look like the person he cared about the most. To him, the comatose princess looked like you, Claire. He thought he was searching for the horn to awaken you. I would assume he's dead by now. Fortunately for you, you won't have to live with that guilt for long, I promise."

Claire sighed with resignation. She was actually getting quite weary of having to fight people, bad or not. She wasn't naturally a violent person and all the damage she and Roger had done to admittedly evil folks was starting to wear on her conscience. Maybe if she talked some more, the queen would see reason. Besides, she had more questions.

"So why on Earth did you invite us into your castle?"

"Simple, Claire. I wanted you to help me find your brother."

"But why? Surely you don't care about him."

"True. But he has something of mine and I want it back. And I want that horn. I think he knows where it is."

"Something of yours? Like what?"

"None of your business," snapped the Queen.

"What if I trade you the directions through the maze for the eye?" offered Claire.

"You're lying," said the Queen. "You don't know where the maze is, much less how to navigate it. Even if you did, it wouldn't matter. Enough talk."

"Look, lady," she said to the Queen. "You have to know this is going to go badly for you, right?" The Queen looked perplexed. "I'm going to walk out of here with the Eye of Connix," Claire continued. "And you are going to either let me take it or you'll be killed or something horrible is going to happen to you."

"You are threatening me?!" snarled the Queen. "How rich. I have an army, little girl. What do you have?"

"A loyal dog," replied Claire. Weenie snarled and showed his fangs on cue. "A good friend," she tapped her com before she continued so Roger would hear her. "Who even now is rushing to the reception room we were in earlier to the secret passage that leads to the corridor outside. Any second now he will burst through the door over there, with his sword drawn, ready to strike you dead."

The Queen glanced nervously at the door. Claire took a step toward the eye and pulled out her hairbrush.

"And I have a hairbrush. And a couple of magic wands," she continued calmly. "More than enough to deal with you, ma'am. Where's your army? I don't see it."

"What kind of a fool do you take me for, little girl?" said the Queen haughtily.

"An ugly one," she replied as she pulled a wand out of her bag with her other hand. The Queen's eyes widened in alarm and she raised one hand threateningly.

"Stop right there, missy, and drop that stick right now," ordered the Queen.

"Go soak your head, witch," replied Claire. She sat the brush down on the table and reached for the eye.

The Queen screeched something that Claire couldn't understand and a bolt of lightning shot out of her outstretched hand at Claire who threw herself to the side to avoid being hit. She had been expecting such an attack and she was blindingly fast. Even so, she wasn't fast enough to completely escape damage. The bolt hit her arm which immediately went numb and her jacket sleeve burst into flame as she fell. As she landed, she rolled and used the wand to shoot an icy missile at the Queen but it hit a protective shield of magic and shattered inches before reaching its target. The Queen laughed with derision at Claire's missile's failure but her laugh turned into a high pitched scream as the alien on her shoulder bit her ear off. Then Weenie knocked her from her feet as he bowled into her, teeth snapping. The alien and the Queen's ear went flying into the corner and blood sprayed from the gaping wound in the side of her head. Weenie grabbed her outstretched hand in his jaws and shook his head violently from side to side, sending blood and bits of torn flesh showering around the room. Claire pointed the wand at the Queen and shot a long jet of ice at her which unexpectedly didn't hit her as a missile but enveloped her in an icy casing. Weenie leapt back with a pained yelp from the cold.

Roger burst through the open door, panting from exertion and tried to draw his sabre as he came through but got it caught in some silk hanging from the wall, which tore loose and fell on him. Blinded and confused he tripped over the frozen Queen, still trying to get his sabre free, and collapsed on the ground, a gasping, writhing pile of pointy silk.

"About time, Roger," said Claire grimly. "You're my freaking hero."

"Give me a bleeding break," he said from under his silk prison. "And a hand, please."

Claire helped unravel Roger from the silk. He stood, chest heaving, observing the ice-bound Queen lying on the floor. He looked at Claire and swatted a smoking ember on her arm.

"You think she's alive in that ice?" asked Claire.

"Don't be thick, lass. It's a fairy tale world and she's the Queen. Of course the cailleach is still alive. We'd best leg it."

Claire grabbed her brush and shoved it in the tacky orange bead bag and then grabbed the eye. It was not slimy like she half expected it to be, but smooth and hard and it was warm and vibrated in her hand. She shoved it in her bag and rubbed her hand on her pants unconsciously.

"What's that, then?" asked Roger.

"It's a crystal ball, I think. Well, it's an eyeball, but I bet that witch in the Halloween world can use it. It's the key to finding Nick."

"Well, ain't that a bit o luck?"

"It sure is. But like you said, we better runnoft. Grab Spanky, I mean Ramses."

Roger looked around the room. "Where is the little bloke?"

"He's right over there…" Claire was pointing to the bloody ear on the ground, but Spanky was nowhere to be seen.

"Well, that's strange. He was right there, gnawing on the Queen's ear. Where'd he go?" mused Claire.

"Search me," said Roger. "But we have not got the time to look for him. He'll have to shift for himself."

Claire agreed. They trooped out the way Roger had come in and down the stairs to the wood paneled reception room. Roger peeked out the door into the great hall and found nobody there. They walked out the front door like they owned the place. The two guards at the front door apparently had no orders regarding exiting guests and ignored them as they left. Once out of the castle, they stepped up their pace and were fairly jogging by the time they got out of town. They stopped for a rest along the road about halfway back to the door. Thankfully, Rupert wasn't anywhere to be seen. Claire didn't feel like having to deal with the little toad.

While they rested, Claire's arm started aching and when she checked it she found that fortunately it was unbroken, but there was a nasty burn with blisters. She bandaged it with one of her shirts that she tore into strips and hoped it would be ok until she could get better medical care. Claire patted Weenie's head, avoiding his mangled ear, and told Roger what had gone down in the room with the Eye of Connix. When she told him about the part where Nick went on the quest because he thought he was saving Claire, she thought she was going to cry again. But she didn't.

Sensing her distress, Weenie licked her hand. Roger sat next to her and took her other hand in his. She was grateful for the support. Support that she had but Nick didn't. Claire was saddened by the suspicion that she was not a good sister. She promised herself that she would never insult her little brother again if she got him back.

In the distance back toward the village they heard some sort of siren wail, it's keening cutting through the still air like a scythe.

"Well, that's enough lying about," said Roger as he released Claire's hand, got to his feet and brushed off his pants. "Let's get a move on, shall we?"

Chapter Fourteen: A Clown, a Ballerina and a Donkey

"All the people like us are we, and everyone else is they." — <u>Rudyard Kipling</u>

They were in the grey corridor outside the Halloween door, trying to plan how they were going to get to the witch without being attacked by the first person to see them. Roger suggested they stay off the main road.

"Then how are we going to get into town if we stay off the main road?" asked Claire. Roger thought about it.

"We could move faster if we stole some horses," mused Claire.

"The only horse I saw was one spavined nag that looked nigh unto death," said Roger.

"We need to blend in," said Claire. "Too bad we're not monsters or zombies or look hideous in general. Well, I don't anyway," she joked.

"Hardy har har, redser," said Roger testily. "Still, that's not a half bad idea, Claire. We need disguises."

"There was a booth in the bazaar that sold disguise spells, wasn't there?" asked Claire.

A couple of hours later, they stood at the doorway again, all of them covered in disguise spells. Weenie was disguised as a tan and white donkey and it was quite convincing. When he tried to bark, it came out as a hideous donkey bray which confused him half to death. After a couple experimental barks, he shut up all together. Roger complemented Claire on her disguise as a thoroughly demented looking clown.

"Very spooktacular, Claire. Like Ronald McDonald on heroin meets the Texas Chainsaw Massacre. How do I look?"

When Claire looked at herself, she didn't see a clown. She saw herself. When she looked at Roger she saw… well, she saw a ballerina in a pink leotard and tutu. Claire managed to keep a straight face.

"Very uhm. Scary, Roger. Like Pennywise out of *It*."

"I'm a clown too? Creepy," said the ballerina in a very female voice, the Irish accent replaced by Russian. Claire clapped him on the shoulder.

"Creepy doesn't even begin to describe you," she said.

"Do you mean in general or right now?" he asked suspiciously.

"Both, dude."

"Don't make me turn you over my knee, sister," threatened the beautiful ballerina, her tutu flouncing saucily.

"Moving on….," said Claire. "I know how attached you've gotten to your little sword and all, but I'd like to make it in and out of this place without having to chop up anybody. Or burn down more of the town. Know what I mean?"

"I ken it, lass. I'm not a hard man and I feel right bad for that guard what copped it in the noggin. They leave us alone, we'll do the same, eh? Although, it's not fair to go blaming me for all the violence. You've made a hash of several people's days lately."

187

"True. I'll try not to hurt anyone, too. Sounds good, Roger," Claire agreed happily. "Let's light this candle."

There was nobody waiting in ambush when they came through the door into the cornfield. Besides some of the dry stalks crushed down where they had plowed through them, there was little sign that they had been this way a couple of days ago. The going was easier because of the crushed-down path they left on the way out last time and the trip seemed to go much more quickly, mainly because they were familiar with the route. The sign announcing The Hollow was right where they remembered it, but the night seemed to get darker. Something was blotting out the ever present full moon. Claire sniffed and realized that what was blocking out the moonlight was smoke drifting from the town.

"I hope we don't see anyone," opined Roger. "They're not likely to be in a good mood, seeing as it looks like we might have burned down the town and all."

"Let's hope it's not that bad," said Claire, digging one of her last sports drinks out of her backpack. "Let's keep moving; the faster we go, the less likely we are to have to test these disguises." They hadn't really stopped or even slowed down much, so Claire chivvying them along was just her nervousness manifesting itself. However, they were soon interrupted in their travels by a slight man in a strange camouflage outfit, leaping out from behind a tree next to a small pond filled with weeds, brandishing what looked like an ancient flintlock pistol.

"Hands in the air, girls!" shouted Rupert as he jumped out, a wild look in his eyes.

"Oh, come *on!*" exclaimed Claire, pointing at Rupert with the bottle of Gatorade she was drinking. "You gotta be kidding me."

"Don't this take all," said Roger in his girlish Russian-accented voice.

"HEEHAWW," added Weenie.

"How did he even get here?" asked Claire plaintively.

"There must be some other way to travel between the worlds. Some of them at least," said Roger musingly. "I know of more than one instance where multiple doors open into the same world." This was news to Claire but now wasn't the time to pursue it.

"I said hands up!" screamed Rupert, spittle flying from his sunburned lips.

"Look, Rupert," said Claire patiently. "Unless you want to end up naked on the side of the road again, why don't you just runnoft and forget you saw us, eh?"

Rupert's eyes got even wider, this time in shock and fear and Claire was mildly concerned that they might pop out of his head. But he shook off his astonishment.

"No idear what yer talkin 'bout, nope. Ain't never been nekkid on the side of no road, I ain't," insisted the little idiot, ignoring the fact that Claire knew his name. "Now gimme what's in yer pockets, yer dang ugly clown."

"Rupert," began Roger his hands spread in a conciliatory gesture.

"Don't yer 'Rupert' me, lady. Gimme that fancy tutu. It'll fetch a good price."

"Tutu?" asked Roger, looking at Claire for an explanation. She just twirled her finger next to her head to indicate Rupert was crazy.

"TUTU?!!" demanded Roger, his pretty features turning bright red with anger.

"Gimme what's in yer pockets!" screamed Rupert jamming the barrel of his old gun right in Claire's face. Claire grabbed the gun, wrenched it from Rupert's hand and threw it in the weeds beside the pond where it vanished with barely a rustle.

189

"Hey! Me gun!" exclaimed Rupert but his protests were transmuted to an angry, indignant squawk as the elegant ballerina grabbed him by the collar and the seat of his pants and heaved him after his gun, but a little off to the side. His noises turned to a scream of fear and were cut off by a large splash as he fell into the stagnant muddy pond. Instantly there was a great commotion in the water, splashing and screaming. Claire figured there might be alligators in the little pond. Oops.

"Manky git," muttered Roger the ballerina as he dusted off his hands. "Tutu?" asked Roger a third time as they started walking toward the smoke again. Claire sighed.

"Does it matter, Roger? I mean really. You're a very pretty ballerina. And nobody will recognize you. Unless you keep chucking people into reptile infested ponds, that is."

Roger harrumphed and walked on in indignant silence.

It looked like everything on the south side of the main drag through The Hollow had burned down. This included Happy Jack's, which was a smoldering pile of embers with a scorched "Happy Jack's" sign out front. The charred Steinway piano was still recognizable but no zombie sat at it and it was likely silenced forever. Claire wasn't exactly surprised because she had a hard time picturing a fire brigade of ridiculous Halloween creatures being very effective. Maybe it was a failure of imagination on her part or maybe not. The blackened evidence stretched before them. They got a few curious looks as they walked along the road, devastation on the left and less devastated spooky unburned town on the right, but nobody seemed to recognize them and they were unmolested. Fortunately, Elm Street ran to the north of town and the run down house at 1313 looked to be untouched by the conflagration. Devastated by time and neglect, perhaps, but not fire.

Claire brazenly marched up the steps and almost put her foot through the rotten decking on the front porch before pressing the doorbell which did absolutely nothing. Roger, who had followed her, but more gingerly, on to the porch, reached out and used the brass knocker to announce their presence. The metallic clanging that Roger produced echoed through the house and they waited on the porch, trying not to fall through the old rotten boards. The donkey sniffed dog-like at the hole where the clown's foot had gone through. The ballerina stood with arms crossed, looking tough.

After a while, Roger reached up to use the brass knocker again and almost grabbed the witch's nose as she opened the door abruptly. The witch jumped back in alarm at the fist almost in her face and then screamed in alarm when she saw the clown on her doorstep. She tried to slam the door, but the ballerina stuck her toe-shoe in the way and the door thumped against it like it was a steel toed boot. The witch was about to run when something made her look closer at the strange group on her front porch.

"Oh, I see. Disguises. Very clever," said the witch. "I hate clowns. They're so creepy. I dang near peed my pants."

"Sorry, ma'am," Claire said. "We didn't want to attract attention after all the commotion we caused last time."

"Very sensible. Come on in, the lot of you, before someone thinks I'm having a ballet slash rodeo on my front porch," said the witch and opened the door wide and led them into her ramshackle home. The clown sidled into the entryway, followed by a doggish donkey and the ballerina brought up the rear with a graceful pas de chat. The witch offered them seats on an ancient green chintz sofa covered in knitted doily covered pillows. "I would offer you refreshments, but I'd rather you not stay long enough for anyone to notice the infamous arsonists are in my house. So, state your business and begone."

"My stick," exclaimed Roger who had noticed an ornately carved walking stick with a dragon head sticking out of an umbrella stand that appeared to be fashioned from a moth eaten elephant's foot.

"Mine, now. Losers weepers and all that," said the witch. "Now spit it out, what have you come for?"

Claire saw the ballerina's fists clench in a very unladylike way and placed a cautioning hand on Roger's arm. She shook her head firmly at him and the fists relaxed.

"Keep it," he muttered.

"Our business," said Claire while digging in her bag, "is you finding my brother and yes, I know, your crystal ball was broken in a bowling accident or whatever. Will this work?" She pulled the Eye of Connix out of her bag and unceremoniously deposited it on the coffee table where it sat, glistening in the faint light, seeming to stare at the witch like a baleful... well, like an eye. The witch was clearly astonished. This was so clear because her mouth hung open like a broken mail box and her eyes were as wide as humanly possible. The old witch stared at the eye for what seemed like a long time but was probably less than twenty seconds before she switched her gaze to Claire.

"Where in all the heavens did you find such a thing, dearie? I'm not sure I can keep an artifact of that power in my house. I'd be afraid of being murdered in my sleep by someone who wanted it... or by it, itself."

"It's valuable, is it?" asked Roger.

"Is a soul valuable?" returned the witch in a soft voice heavy with dread. "Is an object so powerful that Merlin himself would only touch it with reverence valuable?"

"So that's a 'yes,' then," said Roger, smirking.

"Valuable or not," interjected Claire. "It's yours. Now, please use it to find my brother."

"First, answer my question, miss," whispered the witch. "Where did you get it? And more importantly, who is going to turn up here looking for it?"

"We got it a long way from here," said Claire vaguely. "And we took it by force from someone who admitted to not being able to use it. So I don't see how they could find you."

"You'd be surprised," said the witch, staring at the eye, entranced. "Not here," she said suddenly, looking at the window in apparent fear. She rolled the eye into a ratty old blanket and started out of the room. Claire and her gang got up and followed the witch down a hallway to a door that led down some rickety stairs to a basement furnished with shelves and a small round table draped with red velvet. The shelves were filled with glass jars containing all manner of weird things from roots and unidentifiable powders to small animals in liquid. Claire thought she glimpsed a head in one of them. The table had a black iron stand in the middle that looked like it was made to accommodate a sphere. The witch placed the eye reverently on the stand and slowly sat at one of the two chairs around the table. She gestured to Claire to take the other chair opposite her. It looked like a gypsy palm reader's setup. Claire sat.

The old witch bowed her head and started chanting nonsense words in a low voice that Claire had a hard time hearing. Slowly, the woman started speaking louder and faster, hardly pausing to take a breath, her words gushing out through clenched teeth. Claire thought she could make out some Latin in the string of words. She made out 'veritas' which she knew meant truth and 'carpe' for seize. 'Noctum' probably had something to do with night but most of them she didn't get. She gazed at the eye which stared back, passively, offering to yield no secrets. She searched its depths while the witch chanted, expecting and hoping to see Nick in the eye the way she had seen Roger: as a miniature of himself and a portion of his surroundings, like watching live streaming video on a smartphone. But nothing was happening and Claire was starting to think the old lady was a fraud.

Reality exploded out of the eye and enveloped Claire with its cold and dark. The eye reached for her and sucked her in, screaming in fear as the darkness touched her and held her and stroked her. It whispered to her.

"See….." it hissed in her heart.

Claire opened her eyes in the darkness and found that she could *see*. She was in a war camp, surrounded by vicious half naked warriors that looked piggish. Orcs. A volcano glowed softly in the dark distance. Tied to a log near a large fire outside a large tent of uncured hides and bleeding from several lacerations, gagged and unconscious was her little brother. One of the Orcs prodded Nick with a knife and he whimpered and tried to draw away from the torment. The Orc laughed at him and stuck him hard enough to draw more blood. Claire tried to reach out to him but she could not move; only see. She saw Nick open his eyes and he screamed. He screamed her name.

Reality convulsed and spat Claire back out in a blindingly bright darkness that oozed and melted and became a basement in a rundown house dimly lit by a lantern. A gorgeous ballerina in a tutu was shaking her.

"Claire," said Roger. "Wake up! I hear people outside. Oh for the love of-."

"I saw…" said Claire in a hoarse whisper, shaking her head to clear it. The old witch was face down on the table, unmoving.

"You saw what?" asked Roger. "Never mind. We'll talk about it later because I think we need to go."

"I saw Nick," she said. "I saw him and I know where he is, Roger. I know where my brother is."

"Great, Claire. That's great, it really is. But we need to get out of here, come on," Roger insisted and grabbed Claire by the arm and practically dragged her out of her chair.

"Wait," she said, noticing the witch. "What happened to her. Is she still alive?"

"Dunno," Roger replied while propelling Claire toward the stairs. "You were in this weird trance and she was muttering and screeching and then she just collapsed and didn't move no more."

"Oh, well at least let's see if she's alive," said Claire trying to turn back to the witch and the table. "We might be able to help her."

"I'm not sure we even have enough time to help ourselves, lass," said Roger mournfully as they emerged into the hallway. Claire heard it then: the sound of lots of people yelling and shouting outside. It sounded like they had the house surrounded.

"Burn 'em like they burnt the town," someone shouted angrily from somewhere outside.

"We're too late," said Roger dejectedly. Through the window they could see the wavering flickering light of torches moving in the darkness around the house. A lot of people were shouting and cursing and yelling. Weenie the donkey whimpered in a very doglike way.

"How did they find us?" asked Claire, feverishly trying to think of a way out.

"Haven't a baldy. But I think we're going to find out soon." He grimaced as someone pounded on the door.

"We know you're in there!" someone shouted through the door. "If you don't come out, we're going to burn down the house with you in it." It sounded a lot like the bartender from Happy Jack's.

"And burn down the rest of your crappy little town while you're at it?" shouted Claire through the door. Roger was looking through all the windows in the house on the ground floor, one after the other, looking for a way out.

"Claire," he yelled. "Come here, quick." She ran to the room where he stood next to a window, hiding himself behind the ratty black curtains. "Look out there and tell me what you see, lass."

Claire eased up to the other side of the window and peeked through the coarse, musty smelling material of the curtain. She saw the Frankenstein monster that had danced so slowly in Happy Jack's and a few feet away from him, holding a torch was Rupert looking damp and bedraggled. The monster appeared as distracted and listless as ever but was avoiding the flame dancing on the end of Rupert's torch. There were scores of other spooky characters in a ring around the house but Rupert and the monster marked a definite thin spot in the lines.

"I'd wager five quid to your belly button lint that maggot is the reason we're surrounded," said Roger grimly, fingering the hilt of his sabre nervously. "I say we break the window and bum rush the eejit and leg it for the cornfield quick as you like," suggested Roger.

"I think it's our best chance, Roger. Good plan. What do we break the window with?" From the front of the house whoever was yelling through the door was threatening to throw torches through the window if they didn't come out by the count of ten. Roger shrugged and pulled his sabre out of its scabbard.

"This'll do it," he said, grinning broadly.

Claire was expecting him to swing the sabre at the window like a baseball bat. Instead, he put on his sunglasses and dove through the window head first, leading with the hilt of the sabre, the blade laid against his left shoulder. Claire gasped at his unexpected maneuver and quickly dove through the broken window herself, trying not to touch the broken shards of glass but cut her hand and her eyebrow anyway. Claire's last thought as she dived through was 'Leroy Jenkins.'

As Claire hit the ground and rolled she saw two things that alarmed her and dumped several tons of adrenaline into her system. First, she noticed that Rupert was holding more than just a torch. In his right hand was the flintlock pistol from earlier and it was pointing directly at Roger. Second, seeming to assemble itself from liquid darkness rather than just emerge from the shadows was a massive black stallion bearing a rider with no head. The headless horseman was turning toward Roger, sword raised to swing. Time seemed to slow to a crawl as Claire's brain and nerves, steeped in fight-or-flight hormones, fired at a vastly increased rate. She forgot her pains and fears and focused on the threats before her. Ignoring the blood obscuring her vision, she was pulling a wand out of her bag and racing straight at Rupert at superhuman speed.

No matter her speed, she wasn't as fast as a bullet and couldn't cover the whole distance of the dusty back yard in less time than Rupert's finger could move half an inch of trigger pull. She never heard the shot, it blended and merged with the sounds of the mob and the tremendous pounding of her own heart in her ears. She saw the smoke erupt from the barrel of the old gun and the look of surprise on Rupert's face as Roger never slowed. Roger slashed down and sideways with his sabre and Rupert did nothing to block the glinting death that bore down on him. As he swung the sword, the ballerina disguise around Roger rippled and popped like a soap bubble. Knowing Rupert was finished, Claire switched targets and blasted a sizzling bolt of energy at the headless horseman who immediately burst into flame and fell off his horse. She felt her own disguise pop similarly to how Roger's had.

Claire used the sagging remains of a low picket fence as a spring board and leapt into the saddle and then held on for dear life as the stallion reared on its hind legs in terror. Claire looked and saw Rupert's severed head roll to a stop at the Frankenstein monster's feet who inadvertently kicked it into the ditch and started walking toward them, arms outstretched. He seemed reluctant to get too close to the burning body of the headless horseman that was writhing around on the ground soundlessly. Roger grabbed Rupert's torch from beside the little headless body of Rupert and stumbled to Claire, bent nearly double, the tip of his blood smeared sabre dragging in the dirt.

Claire grabbed the reins and brought the horse under control, barely. It was nervous and didn't like its new rider and kept stepping sideways and trying to turn around. She sawed on the reins and dug the bit into its mouth to keep its head pointing where she wanted it.

It neighed in protest and snorted but complied. They had to hurry if they didn't want to end up part of the new headless fashion trend. The mob, or at least the portion nearest them, was converging on them, albeit with a fair amount of caution. They were apparently building on an already solid reputation for being dangerous.

"Roger," she called down to him. "Quick. Hop up." She pulled her foot out of the stirrup to give a way to mount behind her and slid out of her backpack to make room. He leaned against the horse's flank, breathing heavily and gasping.

"Can't," he wheezed. "The poxy bollix shot me."

"You have to," she cried desperately. "Here, grab my hand and I'll help pull you up. No, put your foot in the stirrup first. The other one. Fast!"

She was finally able to pull him up onto the horse's back with her but she was alarmed at how much of his weight she had to lift. He was sweating and looked white as a sheet in the drab moonlight. He settled in behind her and she felt his head slide down onto her shoulder even as his arms circled round her stomach. The roaring mob was now very close and it was spooking the already alarmed horse. If it reared up, Roger would fall for sure. Not giving it a chance, she tried to spur it forward. She wasn't wearing spurs and Roger's leg was in the way but the horse got the idea anyway and surged forward eagerly, knocking a zombie into the gutter. A thrown pitchfork sailed entirely too close to them and clattered against the fence. Deja vu. She made for the main road and let the horse have its lead and they flew like the wind. Weenie the donkey slowly fell behind but kept following them. She heard a wolf howl up ahead, its ululating sound rising out of the night like an unwelcome specter, audible even over the pounding hoof beats and it sent chills up and down her spine.

As they turned on to a cobble stretch of the main road she saw glowing eyes in the near distance as a werewolf took up a blocking position in front of them. She reached up and pulled Roger's glasses off and he offered no protest as she slid them on her own face and the night jumped into bright clarity. The wolf howled its awful challenge and she urged the horse into a breakneck gallop, it's hooves striking fire from the cobbles. At the last second the wolf tried to jump to the side and rake the horse with its claws but Claire and the horse guessed which way it would leap and moved to the side to intercept it and they simply ran the werewolf down, it's body tearing and crunching like a paper bag full of popsicle sticks under the iron shod hooves.

The horse had unnatural stamina and barely slowed the whole way back to the door. Weenie fell farther behind but she still caught sight of him every few minutes trying to follow. They left any and all pursuit far behind and the night was quiet save for the blowing of the horse and the crunching of the trampled corn stalks underfoot. Roger was unconscious and getting him out of the saddle without hurting him took some doing and in the end he fell the last couple of feet anyway. He was just too heavy for Claire. She opened the door and dragged Roger into the corridor where she could see his wound better but left the door open for Weenie who she could hear coming closer through the corn.

Claire examined Roger's blood soaked shirt and found a half inch hole which she ripped to expose his bloody abdomen which also had a half inch hole in it. She fought the urge to vomit at the sight of the gory wound. She felt around his back for an exit wound and found none. The hole was just below his ribcage on the left side. Claire wasn't sure what was there. His liver? A kidney? Blood continued to flow freely from the hole in Roger and puddle on the grey carpet. She knew that if he didn't get expert medical attention very quickly, he would die. She wadded up a pair of clean socks from her bag and pressed against the wound and bound it with duct tape as best she could, trying not to panic at the dismaying sight of all the blood that was on everything. It covered her hands and her backpack. It was on her knees from kneeling in the growing puddle. There was no time to waste and she made a quick decision. Weenie trotted through the door, no longer looking like a donkey and with blood dripping from his muzzle. He sniffed at Roger's face and immediately howled, a long forlorn sound that felt like someone squeezed her heart. The tears weren't far away.

"No, Weenie," she admonished. "Stop that. He's not going to die. We have to hurry."

She shut the door and tried to lift Roger onto her shoulders but couldn't. With no other options, she grabbed him by the arms and dragged him, leaving a gory crimson streak glistening wetly in the unwavering light. She could imagine the noises of indignation and distress the cleaning robot would make when it discovered this mess. She dragged him all the way to the elevator and then into it. Weenie followed her and they all went down together.

"What do I care how 'e looks? I am good-looking enough for both of us, I theenk! All these scars show is zat my husband is brave!" — J.K. Rowling, Harry Potter and the Half-Blood Prince

As soon as the elevator floor indicator blinked on, Claire dialed her dad's cell number and pressed send. It went straight to voicemail. She tried it again and it went to voicemail yet again. She looked at her phone to see what time it was and saw that it was almost three in the morning. Had it been less than twelve hours since she set out to find Nick? She tried to do the math but her brain wouldn't work right. She didn't know if it was the next day or next week, but it didn't matter. Who to call if she couldn't get her dad? Not her mom. She would be no help and would flip out for sure. A friend from school? Yeah, right. What high school student is going to come running at 3AM to help rescue a kid and possibly get killed for the effort? Besides, none of her friends could drive yet. Ok, an uncle? Possibly, but which one? Uncle Derek might be helpful in getting Roger to a hospital but she nearly laughed picturing him in a high stress situation like facing an army of Orcs. Uncle Clark it was, then.

His number did not go to voice mail and only rang once before he picked up.

"Claire?!" he exclaimed when he answered the phone. "Where are you and Nick? Your parents are worried sick!"

"I need you to not talk, but listen, Uncle Clark," she said in her best no nonsense voice.

"What? Oh my god, were you kidnapped? Are they making you say that?"

"I SAID SHUT UP AND LISTEN!" she nearly screamed into the phone, her voice exploding with anger and frustration. "I'm sorry. There's no time. I need your help but you can't ask questions yet. I'll explain when you get here."

"Get where?" asked Clark, his voice calmer as he accepted the situation as something to be dealt with. He could always get angry later.

"How fast can you get to the library?" she asked

He considered for a couple of seconds. "Ten minutes," he said after taking in to account all the variables he could think of.

"Ok. I'll wait five and then I'm calling 911 for an ambulance for a friend of mine," she said. "Don't park at the library. Park down the street and run here. Don't walk, run. You have to get here before the ambulance. Got it?"

"Yep, I got it Claire. You have some explaining to do when I get there."

"Yessir. Oh, and Uncle Clark?"

"Yes?"

"Bring a gun." She hung up her cell phone. She went to the phone in the lobby and dialed 911. She explained there was a teenage gunshot victim on the steps of the library, then she hung up, contrary to the instructions of the operator. She unbuckled Roger's sword belt and removed his backpack, the knife in his boot, the communicator and the dosimeter from his pockets and put everything in the elevator. She checked his pulse and was relieved to find he was still alive.

"Stay here, Weenie, ok? I'll be right back." Weenie whined and tried to follow her as she dragged Roger out of the elevator on the ground floor of the library. "No, you stay. I'm coming back. Hopefully with help." Reluctantly, Weenie sat on his haunches by the pile of gear and gazed with infinitely sad eyes at the elevator doors as they closed.

Claire used her bag to prop open the door so she wouldn't get locked out. Then she sat Roger up on the steps of the library by the front door and got him to drink a little bit of water from his canteen, but he never fully came around to consciousness. Claire was mildly surprised to find the entrance to the library so normal and the night so calm. She didn't know what she had expected. Police tape over the door maybe? She had probably watched too many police shows on TV. She could now hear the sirens approaching and she was starting to get nervous that Uncle Clark wouldn't make it here in time and she would be forced to attempt Nick's rescue alone.

Clark Grant jogged up to the library carrying a Browning 30-06 rifle with a scope and with his Ruger .40 strapped to his thigh. He hadn't taken the time to look for suitable clothes and was wearing jeans and a t-shirt, but he was loaded for bear.

"You didn't say what kind of gun, Claire," said Clark gesturing with his deer rifle so I brought the little un and the big un." He grinned but then he saw Roger sitting in a spreading pool of blood. "Oh, dear God!" he exclaimed as he bent to examine Roger. "What happened to him?"

"He was shot," she said matter-of-factly. "No time to explain yet. You need to get inside the library and wait for me outside the elevator. Don't press the button or a dog will probably chew your face off. Seriously. I'm going to wait until the ambulance pulls up and then I'll be right behind you."

Clark looked at Claire with a measuring gaze as he tried to determine if now was the time to exert his authority or let her call the shots. His glance took in her stern expression, her scorched and bloody clothes, her cut up eyebrow and the red halo of frizzy hair that escaped from her ponytail, finally resting on the eyes of a determined and experienced adult staring out of his niece's face. Purple eyes.

"NOW, Uncle Clark," she insisted. "If we want to get Nick back alive." That did it. Clark nodded curtly and went inside the library lobby with a purposeful stride, avoiding walking on the bloody trail from the elevator to the front door. Claire didn't have long to wait. The ambulance jumped the curb and pulled up on the grass right by the front steps when they saw Claire waving frantically at them. They were followed by two police cars, sirens and lights splitting the night. As soon as the vehicle stopped, she disappeared inside the library, sprinting for the elevator. Another log of guilt piled onto the growing stack in her heart as Claire abandoned her best friend in the world to possibly die far from home. "Hit the button, Uncle Clark," she called.

As the elevator doors opened to reveal a growling Weenie, Claire rushed up and soothed him with a pat on the head.

"Get in quick," she said to Clark, digging the key out of her pocket. Clark stepped gingerly into the elevator trying to avoid standing in blood and to not get too close to the dog that was still showing his teeth. "Weenie, this is Uncle Clark. Uncle Clark, this is Weenie." Clark hardly noticed what Claire did to the service door and the button within. When the doors opened on the hallway, he took a step out before it registered what he was looking at. Claire and Weenie followed him and Claire dragged out all the gear on the floor. "You should take as much of this with you as you can. It's useful stuff and if we leave it, the cleaning bot will get it. Here let me help." She started buckling the sword belt around Clark's waist.

"Whoa, Claire," he said, stopping her from buckling the bloody belt. "You need to explain now. Start with this hallway that shouldn't be here."

"You have to promise to keep it secret, Uncle Clark," Claire half whined.

204

"Like Hell I do. There's a boy shot downstairs and your brother is missing with nothing but your strange call to your mom as a clue. You spill your guts right now, little lady. The police will be up here any minute anyway."

"No they won't," she said resignedly. "They can't get to this floor. See these doors?" she asked her uncle.

"I sure do. What are they? Some sort of book storage?"

"No, sir," she answered contritely. "Every door is a separate world. Some are based on books, some are the past and some the future. Some I have no idea what they are. Go open one and see, but don't step through." The closest door was the light house door and Clark opened it and peered into the lighthouse. His face betrayed naked astonishment and he backed away from the door when he saw the spray from the breaking waves through the window of the lighthouse.

"This makes no sense, Claire," he insisted. "I must be dreaming."

"You're not," answered Claire. "And Nick is trapped in a particularly nasty world. If we don't rescue him soon, he will be killed and possibly eaten." She started to break down at this point, the stress of the past couple of days plus the guilt of her brother and getting Roger shot were too much for her to bear at the moment. "You don't know all the horrible things I've seen and done lately, Uncle Clark!" Seeing her distress, Clark tried to comfort her. She was glad for the embrace and kind words, but found she would much prefer Roger. "No time," she mumbled, breaking the hug. "We have to go."

"Where exactly are we going, Claire?" asked Clark.

"First we have to go look at something. Follow me."

Claire marched off with a purpose, followed by a grim Weenie and a perplexed and awed Clark. She knew about where the door she wanted would be and it didn't take her long to find it. It had a black handle and she remembered the last time she opened it, she was nearly killed by an Orc warrior wielding an axe. She got out her iPhone and activated the camera before opening the door a crack and peering through.

"What's through there?" asked Clark, straining to look over Claire's shoulder.

"Ssshhhh!" she hissed and waved Clark back. She quietly eased the door closed. "I don't see anyone nearby so I probably have enough time to do what I need, but stay back from the door and be ready to shoot anything that comes through it besides me, ok?"

"Seriously?" he asked.

"Have you ever read *Lord of the Rings*, Uncle Clark?"

"I saw the movies," he replied while nodding his head. She rolled her eyes. Does nobody read anymore?

"That'll do, I suppose. Remember the Orc army in the movies?"

"Sure. Hard to forget. Those things would give nightmares to Freddy Krueger." Clark shivered for dramatic effect.

"Yeah, those are the guys," she agreed. "Well, there's about a million of them on the other side of this door. For real. Not movie monsters, real live, stinking, murderous Orcs and if they get a chance they will violently end your life. So if one comes through the door, I need to know you will shoot it dead with no hesitation."

"Uhm. Ok? Yeah. No problem." He leaned the rifle against the smooth greyish wall and drew his Ruger from its nylon holster and checked to make sure there was a round in the chamber and the safety was off. He thumbed back the hammer. "All set. Bring em on," he grinned. Clark was familiar with guns and was quite a good shot.

"That's the spirit, Uncle Clark," Claire said encouragingly.

206

"How bout we shorten it to just Clark for now, Claire?" suggested Clark. "In a pinch, saying 'Uncle Clark' might take too long."

"Good idea, Clark," she agreed with a grin. For the first time since they had entered the elevator, Claire thought maybe she made the right decision. "Ok, here's the plan. I need some pictures of where this door comes out in the Orc camp. I'm going to ease the door open, step through and take a few shots and then step back out without ever closing the door. If the door closes, an hour will elapse outside. OK?"

"I guess. You sure you don't want me to take the pictures?" he asked chivalrously.

"Yeah, I am. Sorry but I need pics of something specific."

It went according to plan, for once. She eased the door open, stepped through and took several pictures, then stepped back through without anyone noticing or trying to kill her. Maybe the orcs were less alert because it was daylight out. She closed the door with a profound sense of relief. Next she led them to a door with a beautifully filigreed silver handle.

"More pictures?" asked Clark.

"Not exactly. This one should be much safer. But if some short people with pointy ears show up and point bows at us, don't freak out. And let me do the talking."

"Elves?" he asked, with relatively little incredulity.

"Yes," Claire said as she opened the door with the silver handle. She motioned Clark and Weenie through into a lush forest alive with vibrant colors, rich smells and musical birdsong. She took a deep breath, savoring the invigorating air that she remembered so well. "If I'm right," she said to Clark, pulling out her phone and motioning him over, "then this is the same world that Nick is trapped in, just a different location." She pulled up the pictures she took in the Orc encampment and found one that featured the tip of a smoking volcano on the horizon. She enlarged that spot and held up the phone and compared it to the tip of another smoking volcano that just peeked over the trees in the distance. "It's important that that volcano is exactly the same. This needs to be not just the same world, but the same time."

"What good will that do us?" asked Clark as he studied the volcano and the picture of the volcano. Not only did they appear very similar, different only in angle, but some of the same clouds were in the picture that he could see on the phone. Claire had seen the same thing.

"Well, it wouldn't unless we can engineer a distraction from outside the camp. Something like say, an attack," said Claire as she pocketed the phone.

"By Elves?"

She motioned for silence. The last thing she wanted was for an Elf to overhear her plan prematurely and take offense at being used as a distraction. Claire pulled the golden chain out of her pocket and held it up for Clark to examine. He looked with obvious appreciation at the exquisite workmanship of the finely crafted golden chain web that glinted warmly in the sunshine.

"Alidraal," announced Claire.

"Alli-what?"

"Alidraal," said Claire again. "If you can hear me, this is Claire and I need you. Please, I need your help." Finished, Claire lowered the chain and looked around hopefully, half expecting the beautiful young Elven woman to step out from behind a tree like she had the first time they met. Of course, she didn't.

"Who is Alidraal and what makes you think she heard you, Claire?" asked Clark, not insultingly but genuinely curious.

"She gave me the hair chain and told me if I had great need, to hold it and say her name and she would hear and come if she could. I guess we'll have to wait. Let's find a site to camp. Watch out for direwolves."

Not far away from the tree from which they had emerged, they found a peaceful clearing filled with grass and flowers. Claire didn't think it was the same one she had done her homework in so long ago because there was no moss covered log, but there were plenty of idyllic (good word but hard to spell) spots to sit and wait. Claire wasn't sure how long they were going to have to wait for Alidraal to show up, assuming she was going to show at all, but she was content to put her brain in neutral and listlessly feed scraps of jerky to Weenie. Roger's jerky. Clark was less content and circled the clearing restlessly, peering into the surrounding vegetation for something that might need shooting.

Weenie was the first to mark the arrival of someone to the vicinity of their little clearing which he did by emitting a low threatening rumble as his hackles stood up. He stared unblinking into the underbrush, continuing to radiate canine menace in audible form. Claire patted him fondly.

"Weenie, that's no way to welcome visitors," she said loud enough to be heard by Clark on the other side of the clearing who looked into the forest even harder, a little alarmed. "You guys can show yourselves now, you know. Nobody here is going to hurt you."

"I can't guarantee the same for you," said an Elven warrior as he stepped out of the forest. Claire would have sworn there was nothing there the second before and now this Elf stood before her in what she could only call splendor. His clothes shimmered slightly and tried to blend into the background. His bow was strung but there was no arrow in it and his sword was sheathed. Claire thought he might be related to Alidraal because of his eerie hair color, an iridescent silver that caught the light and threw rainbows into the shadows when she didn't look straight at it. His features also bore some resemblance to Alidraal, although obviously masculine and rugged. He gave a polite little bow that was little more than a slight inclination of his head and upper body. His eyes flickered to Clark and the Ruger that was pointed unwaveringly at the Elf's center of mass. Claire saw a little red dot from the LED aiming pointer on the pistol was planted squarely in the center of his chest. Fortunately, he didn't seem to notice. "Your loyal companion has a good nose," he said with a slight smile that didn't last long. "My name is Requis. In gentler times I might welcome you to our forest home, but circumstances dictate I be a little more circumspect. Now, tell me who you are and how you came to be inside the sentries."

"Is this what passes for polite around here?" asked Clark, his wonder worn thin and replaced with irritation at being treated so brusquely.

"No," said Requis. "Unfortunately, manners must yield precedence to prudence. You will answer my questions or you will be killed."

"If you keep saying things like that, you will be the first to die," snarled Clark as he braced himself and Claire could tell he was seconds away from turning Requis into Swiss cheese and the Elf didn't have a clue how close to death he was.

"Enough!" announced Claire in her regal voice of command that she spent so much time practicing. "We are surrounded, Clark, and I have no doubt that you could kill this warrior but our deaths would be but a second behind. Lower your weapon and we'll answer his questions. After all, these are the very people we came to see." She inclined her head to Requis, purposely making it less of a bow than he had. She could be as rude as he if she wanted. "I am Claire and this is my Uncle Clark," she said, pointing at the man with the gun. "This is Weenie."

"Woof," agreed Weenie grimly, who then padded over to Requis, wagging his tail and licked the hand that was held out to him. Requis smiled. As unimpressed with humans as Requis was, it seemed he couldn't help but like Weenie.

"Alidraal can answer some of your questions, sir," said Claire. "But we don't have time to waste at the moment. My brother's life depends on us acting fairly quickly."

Requis frowned. "Be that as it may, young Claire," he replied. "We can't simply drag a royal princess out of the city and interrogate her. You must answer my questions. Here and now." There was still no sign of anyone else hiding in the forest, but Claire would have bet all the gold coins in her backpack that they were out there. She looked around nervously, hoping Alidraal would show up soon.

She dug out the chain hair restraint from her jacket pocket where she had put it after using it to summon Alidraal (hopefully). Claire held it up again so it twinkled and sparkled in the light. Requis sucked air through his teeth in astonishment.

"Where did you get that?" he demanded harshly, taking a step toward Claire and raising his hand as if to snatch the chain from her but his hand stopped short of touching it as if he revered it too much to handle it roughly.

"Alidraal gave it to me when I met her in this forest a while back," Claire explained. "I gave her a pen," she added a little lamely. Surprisingly, Requis nodded eagerly.

"Yes, I have heard of the wondrous quill that never needs inking. Alidraal submitted it for study to the Royal Academy of Wizards but nobody can match it or, indeed, even understand its magic." Requis paused. "But I still can't just let you wander loose inside our perimeter, no matter how powerful a sorceress you are. Perhaps especially since you're a powerful sorceress."

"Sorceress? Claire?" scoffed Clark in disbelief. "She's a sorceress with a pole vault or in a spelling bee, but that's about it."

"Hush, Clark," admonished Claire. "We'll talk about it later."

Requis looked suspiciously at Clark, who would dare belittle such a powerful sorceress and concluded he was probably even more dangerous than he looked. Requis was starting to look more worried than anything else.

"If you survive her wrath, you will face an angry monarch," said Alidraal as she glided out of the surrounding forest with catlike grace and spooky silence. "I will personally see the King knows of your insolence."

Clark stared with awe at the most beautiful woman he had ever seen and his pistol dropped several inches as his entire posture relaxed and his eyes followed her every move, enraptured. Claire shook her head in disgust. Requis went as pale as a sheet of paper and dropped to one knee.

"Highness," he said, lowering his head in subservience.

"Alidraal," began Claire, "Requis was just doing his job. I'm not offended by such dutiful service to his sovereign. He does his race proud."

Alidraal smirked. "I'm inclined to agree, Claire of the High School. And he was right that you must answer questions. One of burning importance. Why have you returned to our forest with such a fierce looking warrior?" She looked with undisguised appreciation at Clark. Claire looked from Alidraal to Clark in disbelief. There was no time for this.

"Your Highness," Claire addressed Alidraal, taking the title from Requis's earlier use. "I have come on a rescue mission. My brother is in great danger and I have brought my Uncle Clark here to help me rescue him."

"Rescue? Here? I know of no human being held by us," said Alidraal. "Requis. Have you taken a human captive?"

"No, highness," he responded, still on one knee with his head lowered.

"I didn't mean here as in your forest," explained Claire. "I meant here as in your world. I believe Nick is being held captive by the Orc army camped that way." Claire pointed toward the volcano smoking in the distance.

"Then he is dead," said Alidraal simply. "Orcs are not known for keeping prisoners alive long. I doubt he survived the first day after his capture."

"With respect, highness," argued Claire. "I know he is alive. I saw him in the Eye of Connix."

"I know not of this eye, Claire," said Alidraal.

"It is a powerful artifact. It's the eye of a dragon and with the right person using it, it can show you distant events. It commanded me to see… and I saw." Claire shivered with the memory of the traumatic experience using the Eye. Clark was now staring at Claire with something akin to horror. At Claire's pronouncement, silence descended on the group as they all regarded Claire with varying degrees of dread. The silence was abruptly broken by the pain filled scream of an Elf as it stumbled into the clearing and collapsed bleeding and broken. Over its crumpled form leapt a direwolf, hideous teeth and claws flashing as it bounded for Alidraal, whom it apparently remembered from the last time she was roaming the forest. Several ineffectual arrows protruded from its back, doing nothing to slow its insanely fast attack.

It was painfully obvious that neither she nor Requis were going to be fast enough with their bows or swords to stop the horrid beast. Claire's hand was already going for a wand but she knew she would be far too slow as well. Three rapid reports shattered the air, the Ruger's barrel erupting in fire and lead as Clark's steady hand and quick reflexes showed they were equal to the speed and ferocity of the direwolf. All three rounds found the animal's heart and it collapsed at Alidraal's feet in a cloud of spraying dirt, grass and leaves.

Graceful Elven Princess she might have been, but her stoicism wasn't quite up to such an event. Alidraal screamed in horror as the direwolf leapt at her and when it fell dead in front of her, she took an unsteady step backwards and sat abruptly on her dainty little butt.

"Dear spirits," whispered Requis as he looked from the direwolf bleeding out its last in the grass to Clark who stood resolutely, pistol smoking ominously in his hand. "To me!" he shouted and the forest virtually exploded as Elven warriors closed in from every direction and entered the clearing with weapons drawn, ready to face death at the command of their leader.

"A perimeter! Now! Protect the princess!" Requis barked to the newly revealed war band and they obeyed instantly, turning to face outwards and blending back into the forest on the edge of the clearing. Clark walked over to Alidraal and extended his hand to help her up. Requis looked like he wanted to protest but didn't have the courage.

"Princess," said Clark simply. She smiled in return and accepted his hand and stood with all of her previous grace and poise.

"That makes twice that you and yours have saved me from that particular direwolf," Alidraal said to Claire quietly.

"You think it's the same one?" asked Claire.

"Yes," replied the princess. "That's my arrow in its shoulder," she said indicating an older, blood caked arrow broken off in its thick, furry shoulder. "No doubt it was maddened by the pain of its earlier encounter with me… and you. When it caught my scent, no doubt it couldn't help itself. You have my thanks, sir," she added as she turned and addressed Clark. Her voice didn't try to hide her admiration for Clark. "And of course, we are at your disposal in the search for your brother, Claire. How could we refuse? What's your plan?"

Claire smiled a cold, dangerous smile that didn't reach her eyes. "I think we're going to kill a lot of Orcs," she said.

"Child Claire," said Alidraal grimly. "Our army needs no encouragement to do that. All they need is a reason and if you give them a good one, they'll probably erect a statue of you."

Claire told them her plan.

Chapter Sixteen: Nick

Cry 'Havoc,' and let slip the dogs of war --<u>*William Shakespeare, Julius Caesar*</u>

Claire quietly and carefully cracked open the door with the black handle and peeked through the slim crack with one eye. Nobody on the other side seemed to have noticed what she had done. Behind her, standing nervously in the otherworldly hallway was a small troupe of warrior Elves led by Captain Requis, and Weenie of course. With the door cracked, Claire activated her com.

"Roger, Testing, testing," she said. "Anyone there?"

"We're here, Claire," said Uncle Clark through Roger's com.

"We're in position and ready as soon as the area clears out," said Claire.

"That's a go," said Clark. "You should see results soon."

Claire didn't see anything happening through the slit. What few orcs were in view continued with their regular dusk activities, oblivious to the coming chaos. Smoke drifted lazily in through the door from countless fires that were being used to cook food and boil water in the massive encampment. Besides smoke, the smell of latrines and slit trenches, the stench of unwashed animals and the smell of death and rotting carcasses filled the air outside the door and drifted into the hallway, making Claire slightly nauseated. The Elves tried not to show their disgust but couldn't completely ignore the putrid smells, either.

At first she thought she was imagining it; a high pitched whistling sound grew slowly but steadily until an unearthly roaring scream filled the air and hurt her ears even through the cracked door. She caught sight of a massive ball of roiling flame that rivaled the setting sun for intensity arcing through the air, launched by an Elven wizard and hurtling toward a large formation of Orcs getting ready to go out on a raid. Burned and bleeding Orc bodies flew through the air as a massive explosion rent the evening. Screams of pain and anger followed and were in turn themselves followed by shouted orders and the harsh blaring of war horns. Claire peeked again and saw the area thinning out as the hordes of Orcs grabbed their weapons and rushed to repel the attack that Claire knew was even now slamming into their camp.

The Elvish army that attacked was relatively small and had no hope of actually defeating the Orc army in a pitched battle. But they had surprise on their side and they brutally carved a path of death and destruction through the flank of the larger force, taking no prisoners and burning as much as they could before retreating back into the forest. As the Orcs slowly began organizing themselves into some semblance of a military formation to fight off the bloodthirsty Elves, the area in front of Claire's door cleared of piggish warriors.

"It's now or never," she said and threw the door open.

Claire raced through the door, wand at the ready, followed by the squad of Elves who quickly moved to secure all the nearby structures and vantage points. Requis stuck by Claire, bow nocked and eyes scanning for threats. Weenie began sniffing the ground, trying to locate something that smelled more like Nick's backpack than Orc. Claire moved quickly, scanning the area for both threats and for the large hide tent she remembered from her experience in the Eye. Sounds of battle drifted from the east, screams and battle yells, explosions and ominous whistling and roaring made it sound like the end of the world was just over the horizon. She saw few Orcs but they were so intent on rushing to battle, they ignored her. Her Elven contingent turned a couple of them into pin cushions before they could raise an alarm.

She saw the hide tent she was searching for just as a group of Orcs armed for battle emerged from the tent next to it and spotted her. With fierce war cries they charged her and Requis, intent on slaughtering them where they stood. Most of them didn't even make it close to them as Elven arrows cut them down and sizzling energy bolts from Claire's wand took them out of action. Two got close enough to be a threat, with arrows stuck in their armor and wicked looking scimitars in their hands. Requis's sword moved too fast for Claire to even see as it first cut the inferior scimitars in half and then quickly dispatched the Orcs holding them.

Claire triumphantly sprinted to the tent and rushed inside ready for anything. Anything except the smoke filled gloomy stench of an empty tent, which is what she found. Nick wasn't in the tent. She cast about looking for anything that might give her a clue as to his whereabouts but came up empty. In her frustration, she shoved over the only piece of furniture in the tent. The cheap, shoddy cot collapsed to the side and underneath it sat a pair of beat up Nike cross trainers.

"Weenie!"

Weenie scrambled into the tent and eagerly sniffed the proffered sneakers deeply and then snorted with satisfaction. He put his nose down and immediately started following a scent out of the tent. Claire followed close at his heels. Requis stuck to her like glue and his soldiers prowled restlessly, clearing the way and efficiently killing any Orc they found.

When Clark gave the signal, the creepy robed dude unleashed a hellish ball of fire that roared away like a freight train to deliver devastation by the truckload. Clark whistled appreciatively. As soon as the raging ball of death vanished over the trees, an ordered rank of grim looking Elven warriors began to trot in the same direction.

Clark and Alidraal followed a few paces behind with the Elven general in command. Clark kept stealing admiring glances at Alidraal and she returned the favor.

When they reached the end of the tree-line where the forest gave way to a wasteland of ravaged nature that had been pillaged of all useable or edible material to feed and sustain the Orc horde, they stopped on command. Not too far away, they could see the encampment boiling with activity like an ant bed disturbed by a boot. Only, the boot that had disturbed this particular ant bed was a fireball that left death and smoking wreckage in a wide swath. Another command was barked out by the general and as one the Elves drew their bows and unleashed a deadly rain of finely wrought arrows onto the heads of those ants that were actually Orcs who died in large numbers.

But not large enough. War horns and battle cries rang out from the outraged ranks of the brutalized Orcs as they formed a loose formation and surged forward with their weapons brandished threateningly and their faces contorted into rictuses of hate. The Elves had time for two more volleys of deadly accurate arrows that left huge gaps in the advancing Orc formation. Clark unslung his deer rifle and lay down on the barren ground and rested the 30-06 on a stump. He racked the bolt and slid a round into the chamber and searched for anyone in the horde that looked like a leader. He spotted a massive black Orc in shiny lacquered armor and with a helmet that looked like a skull and sported a black plume. The Orc officer's sword flashed darkly in the waning light as he gestured towards the Elven line.

Alidraal looked at Clark curiously as he acquired his target through the Leupold scope and took a deep breath and slowly released it. The crack of the rifle was by far the loudest thing on the battlefield and everyone nearby blanched in startled surprise. The Elven wizard's spell failed and the lightning bolt fizzled and died before it reached its target. The range was less than 100 yards and the bullet Clark's rifle fired was suited for killing elk at four times that distance. Clark's target's head virtually exploded as his round took the Orc in the eye. As the Orc collapsed like a sack of jellyfish, Alidraal looked at Clark with renewed appreciation. She imitated his earlier whistle. He winked at her and picked out another target.

The Orc swarm finally reached the waiting Elves' disciplined ranks to find they had dropped their bows and were wielding long deadly halberds with expert skill. Two more officers' heads exploded as Clark finished out the three rounds in his magazine and pulled out his Ruger. He ran up to the line where the action was because a .40 pistol isn't a distance weapon. He was vaguely aware of Alidraal running with him, razor sharp sword in hand, but lost track of her whereabouts as he emptied his gun with chilling accuracy and cleared the immediate area of threats in a matter of seconds. The Elven wizard was staring at him in absolute horror. He smiled at the wizard and looked around for Alidraal.

The Elven princess was fighting two orcs at once as her sword danced and flowed like smoke and then she was fighting nobody as the Orcs fell to the ground to bleed at her feet. More were coming at her and she set her face grimly as she faced them. Two more Elves moved up beside her to protect their princess and they were joined by Clark, with Roger's sabre in one hand and his Ka-bar knife in the other. Clark didn't have much skill or experience fighting with edged weapons but what he lacked in finesse he made up for with enthusiasm. In a lull where he actually had time to think, he thought that he had found his calling.

They followed Weenie's nose in between tents and shelters and pavilions; past campfires and slit trenches and wagons full of supplies. Claire almost didn't believe her eyes when they ducked under a rope hung with skins and carpets hung to dry and saw Nick tied to a roughly hewn wooden frame. Nick was filthy and covered in dried blood. What were left of his clothes hung off his emaciated frame in tatters. His eyes were closed and his mouth was stuffed with a foul rag. Weenie ran up to him and began to lick his face enthusiastically. Even though Weenie had never met Nick, he seemed to understand that this was the object of their search and at long last it was over.

Claire rushed to his side and started struggling with his bonds. Nick's eyes flew open in wild panic. Claire tried to reassure him that it wasn't an Orc come to torture him, but his sister bringing rescue but his wild eyes just got more frantic and he was trying to talk around the filthy gag in his mouth. Claire pulled the gag free.

"It's a trap! Run, Claire!" screamed Nick as soon as the gag was removed.

"No way am I running, kiddo," she said to him grimly. "Watch for an attack!" she yelled to Requis as she pulled out Roger's boot knife and made short work of the bonds securing Nick to the frame. When the last one supporting him was cut, he sagged against Claire, unable to stand and his limbs numb from lack of blood flow. Warning yells came from the Elven squad. Claire put Nick over her shoulder and heaved him off the ground. As she ducked under one of the hanging skins to rejoin the rest of the rescue team and hopefully make her escape, she knew something was badly wrong.

All the Elves were in a half circle fighting off twice their number of Orcs and what was worse, the Orcs were coming from the direction they needed to go to get back to the door.

"We'll have to go around them," she told Requis but as she turned to do just that, she saw something that took her breath away. Striding toward her through the smoke and evening mist was a human. Not only was he human, he was wearing jeans and a trench coat but any thought of assistance from him was banished by the skull helm and lacquered breastplate he was wearing and the black scimitar that he held in one hand. Recognizing the threat, Requis charged at him, sword drawn. Astonishingly, the man raised one hand and Requis flew through the air to land on his butt. The man grinned.

"You must be Claire," he said in a gravelly voice as he continued to advance on her. "It's taken you long enough. I was beginning to think you were just going to abandon your brother."

Claire didn't waste time talking to the approaching menace but turned around and tried to run the other direction, knowing she didn't have time to delay. She felt her feet tangle on something and had to toss Nick clear as she stumbled and fell to her knees. She turned in time to see Requis attack again. This time his sword rang against the steel of the man's wicked scimitar and the man frowned in concentration as he fought off the attack and pushed the Elf back. The Elves were falling one by one as overwhelming numbers pushed them back and hacked them down. Claire was close to despair when a horn sounded, clear and bright and loud in the gathering shadows. The Orcs fighting her Elves found themselves attacked from behind as the Elven army led by Alidraal and her Uncle Clark pushed its way into their flank. She knew it was her last hope. There were just too many Orcs for the Elves to defeat. She tried to pick up Nick again who protested that he could run now, so she grabbed him by the hand.

"Fast, this way, Nick. We have to get to the door. Weenie! Here boy!" They started running, Nick slowed somewhat by his lack of shoes. They dodged around Orcs and in between tents, Weenie at their heels and the sound of desperate battle all around. Her side was splitting and she couldn't catch her breath but still they ran. Nick slowed her more and more and soon she was practically dragging him. There were no obvious signs of pursuit, although the sights and sounds of death were all around them as they raced for the magic door and escape. There it was! They had made it!

As her hand grasped the handle to the ramshackle wooden structure that concealed the door to the hallway, she felt triumph surge through her. She had won, Nick was safe! Claire opened the door and pushed Nick through but before she could follow, a heavy gauntlet grasped her by the wrist and the man in the skull helmet laughed a triumphant, hoarse bellow of mirth and menace. Almost as an afterthought, he sent Weenie flying through the air with a twitch of his fingers.

"You stupid child," he chuckled. "This is what I've been waiting for so many years. Escape at last. You have given me all the worlds in the heavens as my playthings!" He threw back his head and laughed with gravelly abandon. She struggled against his iron grip in vain and even kicked his blue jeaned shin. He ignored her and shoved the door wide with his heavy boot. She looked through the door at Nick who was staring at them in horror.

"If you know Bob and Marty, run to them for safety, Nick," she hissed. "I'll be right behind you."

At first Nick looked at her blankly and she thought he didn't know what she was talking about, but then understanding dawned on his face and he scrambled to his feet and sprinted down the hallway. The man watched him go with growing anger.

She looked around and saw Weenie coming back for more. "Weenie! Go find Clark! Go!" she yelled and Weenie obediently turned aside and sped off.

"No matter," her captor snarled as he dragged Claire into the hallway and closed the door on the sounds of battle raging a few feet away. The sounds vanished instantly, leaving them in the unnatural quiet of the carpeted hallway. Her ears rang with the sudden silence. When the man turned his attention in the direction Nick had run, Claire wrenched her hand out of his grasp and snatched Roger's boot knife off her belt and before the man could react used all her weight to strike the only thing within reach of her position on the ground: his boot. The tip found a seam between two pieces of plate on the boot and all her strength and weight drove it down into his foot. His hoarse scream of pain and rage disturbed the silence and echoed energetically down the hallway. Wasting no time, Claire leapt up and ran in the same direction as Nick had gone. The man followed with a pronounced limp, screaming in rage that he was going to kill her slowly. She was careful to not let him get close enough to catch her but not so far that he lost sight of her, either. A couple of times she

223

had to dodge around a corner to keep from being roasted by spells he blasted at her. The walls were scorched and stained by the released energies. Claire fired back with ice missiles and energy bolts but they bounced off his defensive shields and tough armor. She sprinted past the robo cleaner, ignoring it as it blooped at her questioningly. The big man kicked it across the hallway where it clanged against the wall and let out a shower of sparks and a cloud of blue smoke.

Claire was beginning to think she wasn't going to be able to find the door with the alligator skin handle but she spotted it at last. It was cracked open. Nick must have not closed it when he went through. Hoping the man chasing her would follow her through, she shoved the door open and took one running step and leapt onto the bed she knew was waiting inside, shrouded in the nightmare gloom of a boy's bedroom at midnight.

"Oh, hello," said Bob happily. "Nick was just telling me you were on your way. It's like a slumber party!"

Claire collapsed on the bed, panting in exhaustion. Nick huddled in the corner, pulling the covers up to his eyes in fear.

"Is Magnus on his way?" he asked in obvious terror.

"Is that his name?" she asked absently. "Yeah, he's right behind me, limping with my knife in his foot."

"Someone else is coming?" asked Bob with obvious delight. "You didn't say he was bleeding did you?" Claire nodded. "Marty will smell that right off," said Bob. He had no time to finish that thought before Magnus roughly heaved the door open and stepped through into the bedroom.

"Don't tell me you thought you could hide in here?" he asked in amusement as he took another step into the room.

"Please," pleaded Claire, injecting as much fear as she could into her voice so it trembled and wavered. "Don't hurt us, sir. We're just children!"

224

"Dead is what you are!" he yelled at them in uncontrolled rage, spittle flying from his lips.

"Quiet up there! Go to sleep," came an angry woman's voice from downstairs. Bob's mom, presumably.

Magnus looked at the bedroom door in astonishment, then let loose with his laugh that grated on Claire's ears with its coarse merriment. His laugh was cut short as a massive alligator burst from under the bed in an explosion of reptilian fury and knocked him across the room with its mangled tail. With more speed than Claire thought possible, the scimitar flashed through the gloom, deeply scoring the alligator's side. His thick skin turned the blade and kept him from being disemboweled. Angry at the pain, Marty grasped the arm that held the scimitar and violently convulsed back and forth, ripping Magnus's arm clean off.

Magnus sat against the bedroom wall, his shoulder pulsing great gouts of blood and a look of utter disbelief on his face. Marty wasn't done yet. He grasped Magnus in his jaws and made a sound that might have been a gleeful laugh, if alligators could laugh. He spent a few seconds mangling the bleeding body of Magnus, making a deafening racket as he thrashed and armor cracked and split. He stopped abruptly when someone beat on the ceiling downstairs with a broom handle.

"I said quiet up there!" shouted Bob's mother. "Don't make me come up there!" With a comic display of fear, Marty disappeared back under Bob's bed, then crept back out and grasped Magnus by the foot and dragged him under the bed with him. Horrible crunching slurping sounds emanated from under them as Marty broke armor and bones alike with his awful jaws. Claire wept with relief. Nick hugged her and they sagged against each other, both crying and laughing uncontrollably.

They had to wait for Marty to fall asleep before they sneaked across the bedroom floor to the closet. When weird alligator snoring sounded across the floor, they thanked Bob for his hospitality and lied through their teeth as they promised to visit again, then took

225

their leave and gingerly exited back into the hallway, hopefully never to return. Ever. Not for any reason.

Clark saw the huge human follow Claire at a leisurely jog, spells and arrows bouncing off his armor and magical shielding. Too many Orcs were between them for him or Alidraal to follow him. Grimly, Clark tried to hack down all the resistance and get to the man, but there were just too many Orcs and their numbers were growing steadily as all the forces of the camp organized themselves and threw themselves into battle. Soon, the Elven army sounded the retreat and began the difficult and dangerous fighting withdrawal. Few of the squad that had gone with Claire were still alive but the couple that were, including Requis, joined the retreat. They were slowed even more by all their wounded that they refused to abandon to the tender mercies of the Orcish contingent. Clark smiled when Weenie dashed between groups of embattled Orcs and rushed to his side, panting.

The retreat was forced to halt every time the Orcs made an organized attack and the Elves had to set themselves against it. Time after time the Orcs surged like an ocean wave to break themselves against the sharp, armored rocks of the Elven line. It seemed like the retreat took hours but finally, they came to the tree line and as they stepped backwards into the protective embrace of their forest, the Orcs halted, wisely unwilling to follow the deadly Elves into the trees.

Night had fallen and the battered, bloody but victorious Elven army sped up its retreat to the defensive ring around Caras Galadhon amongst the sacred Mallorn trees. Once inside the Deep Fosse, they relaxed a bit and set up camp for the night.

Clark found himself sitting beside a flickering, crackling campfire, weary as he had never been weary before. He fought to keep his eyes open, wishing for a hot shower and a soft bed. Next to him was Alidraal, just as weary and bloody and battle ragged as he was. She leaned her head against his shoulder and clasped his arm with her own. Weenie dozed by their feet. They had all seen Claire and Nick disappear into the door with the armored man. Although proud at their own achievements they were deeply worried about Claire. Their reverie was bitter sweet.

"Can you open the door in the Mallorn tree that you came through?" asked Alidraal, wearily.

"I dunno. I don't think I could even find it, much less open it," he replied.

"I can take you to it, Clark. But not tonight, my brave warrior. We can do no more tonight, I'm afraid."

"We have to try, Ali," Clark urged. "Please, she's my niece. I have to try. Take me there."

"Yes," she agreed with obvious reluctance. "In a minute. I am weary to the bone."

"I hurt in places I didn't even know I had," said Clark with dark humor. Weenie's head came up and his tail wagged.

"Your sentries suck, Alidraal," announced Claire as she sat down opposite them across the fire, her sunglasses glinting in the firelight. Clark and Alidraal stared in shock at the bloody, ragged young woman who grinned at them over the flames. "Think we can get some dinner or something? We're starved. Well, Nick is literally starved, I'm just really hungry."

Clark tried to stand and failed. He sat back down with a thump. Alidraal didn't even try.

"You astonish me, child Claire," she said. "To make it through Elven sentries in their own forest at night. You must be extraordinary in your talents."

"I have my tricks. But it doesn't hurt that they are dead tired and I can see in the dark better than they can with these glasses," she replied modestly. "I had to leave Nick in the hallway. He was so tired he couldn't move. He's sound asleep."

"I should spank you," muttered Clark.

"Kiss me instead," suggested Alidraal. Clark looked at her in surprise as she lifted her head off his shoulder to look him in the eyes. A coquettish smile hovered over her cupid's bow mouth.

"I've never kissed a princess before," Clark mused. But then he did. Claire rolled her eyes in disgust and tried to ignore them. Weenie groaned in sympathy.

Chapter Seventeen: Happily Ever After

"There is no real ending. It's just the place where you stop the story." — *Frank Herbert*

Claire and Nick stood in the hallway outside the open doors of the elevator. Clark and Alidraal stood facing them, their arms around each other's waists. They were obviously an annoyingly happy couple.

"So, you're staying here?" Claire asked Clark, needlessly. The answer was apparent.

"Well, I'll be back in a couple of days to get a lot of my stuff," Clark said abashedly. "And to tell Debbie and Mark that I'll be going away for a while."

"I'm guessing you won't tell them where you're going," remarked Claire with amusement. "Or that your new girlfriend has pointy ears." Alidraal blushed.

"No. Probably not. But I don't know if we can ever really be, uhm, involved romantically," he said sadly.

"Why ever not?" asked Alidraal indignantly.

"There's that whole royalty thing you got going on, Ali," he said resignedly. "Besides, you will live hundreds of years and I won't. You don't want to marry someone who'll die of old age before you're even middle aged."

"You don't get to tell an Elven Princess what she wants, sir," she joked, poking him in the ribs. "And as is said," she added seriously, "'Tis better to have loved and lost than never to have loved at all."

"You know Shakespeare?" asked Claire incredulously.

"Great art transcends the ephemeral boundaries that separate our worlds, child," Alidraal said mysteriously.

"Right. Whatever that means," muttered Claire. "You know, you don't have to grow old, Uncle Clark, right?"

"What?" he asked, surprised out of his thoughts. "What do you mean?"

"Well, if you spend less than one year in a world before coming back through the door, you only age 59 minutes and that's how long goes by in the outside world," she explained. "All you have to do is come back before your year is up, then go back and you will age even more slowly than your girlfriend."

Clark looked at Claire in wonder and then back at Alidraal who smiled beatifically and pulled his head down to kiss him.

"Oh, good grief," said Nick.

"You said it, brother," agreed Claire. She kicked Clark in the shin. He ignored her. "We're leaving," she announced. He waved her away, his attention focused on Ali. They stepped into the elevator and the doors closed, mercifully shutting out the scene of mushy romance.

Back in the library, Claire dug her phone out and found the screen was cracked by who knows what. She wasn't surprised. Even an Otterbox case was no match for the Orc hordes. She wondered if the insurance would cover damage sustained by spells or Orc weapons. At least it powered on with no problems. She dialed her mom's number and she answered on the first ring.

"Claire!" yelled her mom into the phone with excitement and hope.

"Triumphant," Claire said into the phone, grinning.

"What?" asked her mother, confused.

"It's an easy one, mom. Take your time."

"Victorious? Successful, I suppose," said her mom. "Are you saying... you found Nick?"

"Say 'hi,' Nick," she said to her brother and held out the phone.

"Hi," he said dutifully and sniffed loudly.

"Oh, my god, honey. Where are you?"

Claire took the phone back from Nick and shook her head at him. She pressed her forefinger to her lips in a gesture for silence.

"It's a long story, Mom. Can you meet us at the library? We would like to come home. Oh, and bring some clothes for Nick. Shoes at least. His are pretty much destroyed."

Claire walked into the lobby of St. Ignatius Hospital with a balloon bouquet that proclaimed "Get well soon!" There was a card inside that had its cheesy sentimental message crossed out and the words, 'Quit faking, you chancy git!' scrawled in pen underneath. After the past few days dealing with her parents and the cops, Claire was looking forward to seeing Roger. Claire and Nick had been as vague as possible about where they had been but they had to say something and now everyone was on the lookout for a group of violent thugs roaming the neighborhood. And now all the adult parental types were all nervous and paranoid about their kids' safety.

It had taken a lot of convincing to get her suddenly overprotective parents to let her ride the bus alone to the hospital but here she was. Nick had wanted to come with her, but he was still being pampered and made much of by Mom. There was no way she was going to let him ride a bus across town. This would pass with time, but for now Nick lived in a very comfy jail. Likewise, Weenie made it clear that he knew where Claire was headed and he wanted to come with her but Claire was pretty sure Dalmatians weren't welcome in hospitals. It occurred to her briefly that she could pretend to be blind and claim he was a service dog but she discarded the idea as ridiculous. And unethical. So Weenie was waiting at home with Nick.

Claire knew Roger had survived because she had found the story in the newspaper. Roger was apparently claiming amnesia. On a mission, she went to the front desk and asked where Roger Shannon's room was. They had no idea what she was talking about. What about the John Doe that was found shot a few days ago?

"Sorry, no visitors to the ICU," said the large, ugly receptionist in scrubs at the front desk.

"He's in the ICU?" she asked, concerned for his health.

"Standard for GSW," replied the woman. She consulted a clipboard. "Due to be moved to a private room later today, though," she said. "Come back tomorrow and you can see him. You know him?"

"No," she replied quickly. "My church sent me over with this balloon bouquet when they heard he didn't have any family." The nurse looked at her skeptically, then shrugged.

"Whatever," she said. "Bring it back tomorrow."

She abandoned the balloons on a table in the ER and slipped into an exam room that was being used as a storage closet. Marveling at how easy scrubs were to acquire, she pulled some off a shelf and put the drab green uniform on over her street clothes and consulted the hospital directory to find the ICU. Turns out you have to have an ID badge to get the doors to the ICU open. Or a magic wand; those work, too. Once in, nobody paid Claire any attention.

"Wake up, you eejit," she said to Roger who was apparently sound asleep on a complicated looking hospital bed, connected to all manner of things going 'beep' and 'boop.' She was reminded of the cleaning robot in the hallway. Roger opened one eye laconically.

"Oi," he said. "I've been freaking shot. You can be a bit more respectful, can't you?"

"Hey," she replied. "I can leave your Irish butt here to rot or we can make a run for it. Which is it?"

Roger opened both eyes and studied Claire for a moment.

"Find Nick?" he asked.

"Done," she replied. "I did all the heroic stuff while you slept like a lump, you lazy sod," she said mimicking his accent. "Now it's time for you to leg it as you so often say. You stay here much longer and you'll wind up in foster care somewhere. Or deported to Ireland. Besides, we have stuff to take care of. That evil queen isn't going to depose herself. We've got a minotaur to find and a royal family to wake up. Not to mention a psychic alien to track down."

"I've got a bleeding lacerated spleen. Well, literally it was bleeding. Friggin' bullet bounced off my rib and did all manner of mischief to me insides. I'm lucky the powder in that thing must have been wet."

"Want some cheese with that whine?" she asked grinning. "Or maybe some Jell-O?"

"I've had enough Jell-O to last me a lifetime, Claire. Let's blow this pop stand," he said, already pulling leads and wires off his body. They left, and headed into a different story. Weenie tagged along.

www.ingramcontent.com/pod-product-compliance
Lightning Source LLC
Chambersburg PA
CBHW070617130626
46556CB00001B/397